Anxious Girl

By Rosa Silva

Anxious Girl

Copyright © 2024 Rosa Silva

Original title: Uma Rapariga Ansiosa

Translation: Rosa Silva

This book is a work of fiction. The names, characters, places, and incidents are the products of the author's imagination or are used fictitiously. Any resemblance to actual events, business establishments, locales, or persons, living or dead, is entirely coincidental.

All rights reserved. Without limiting the rights under the copyright reserved above, no part of this publication may be reproduced, stored in, or introduced into a retrieval system, or transmitted in any form or by any means (electronic, mechanical, photocopying, recording, or otherwise) without prior written permission of the copyright owner. The only exception is brief quotations in printed reviews. The scanning, uploading, and distribution of this book via the internet or via any other means without the permission of the copyright owner is illegal and punishable by law.

Contents

Chapter 1 ~~~~~~~~~~~~~~~~~~~~~~~~~~~~~~~~~~~~~ 5
Chapter 2 ~~~~~~~~~~~~~~~~~~~~~~~~~~~~~~~~~~~~ 10
Chapter 3 ~~~~~~~~~~~~~~~~~~~~~~~~~~~~~~~~~~~~ 22
Chapter 4 ~~~~~~~~~~~~~~~~~~~~~~~~~~~~~~~~~~~~ 31
Chapter 5 ~~~~~~~~~~~~~~~~~~~~~~~~~~~~~~~~~~~~ 42
Chapter 6 ~~~~~~~~~~~~~~~~~~~~~~~~~~~~~~~~~~~~ 48
Chapter 7 ~~~~~~~~~~~~~~~~~~~~~~~~~~~~~~~~~~~~ 52
Chapter 8 ~~~~~~~~~~~~~~~~~~~~~~~~~~~~~~~~~~~~ 56
Chapter 9 ~~~~~~~~~~~~~~~~~~~~~~~~~~~~~~~~~~~~ 63
Chapter 10 ~~~~~~~~~~~~~~~~~~~~~~~~~~~~~~~~~~~ 76
Chapter 11 ~~~~~~~~~~~~~~~~~~~~~~~~~~~~~~~~~~~ 84
Chapter 12 ~~~~~~~~~~~~~~~~~~~~~~~~~~~~~~~~~~~ 94
Chapter 13 ~~~~~~~~~~~~~~~~~~~~~~~~~~~~~~~~~~ 102
Chapter 14 ~~~~~~~~~~~~~~~~~~~~~~~~~~~~~~~~~~ 113
Chapter 15 ~~~~~~~~~~~~~~~~~~~~~~~~~~~~~~~~~~ 121
Chapter 16 ~~~~~~~~~~~~~~~~~~~~~~~~~~~~~~~~~~ 127
Chapter 17 ~~~~~~~~~~~~~~~~~~~~~~~~~~~~~~~~~~ 132
Chapter 18 ~~~~~~~~~~~~~~~~~~~~~~~~~~~~~~~~~~ 140
Chapter 19 ~~~~~~~~~~~~~~~~~~~~~~~~~~~~~~~~~~ 147
Chapter 20 ~~~~~~~~~~~~~~~~~~~~~~~~~~~~~~~~~~ 153
Chapter 21 ~~~~~~~~~~~~~~~~~~~~~~~~~~~~~~~~~~ 161
Chapter 22 ~~~~~~~~~~~~~~~~~~~~~~~~~~~~~~~~~~ 168
Chapter 23 ~~~~~~~~~~~~~~~~~~~~~~~~~~~~~~~~~~ 173
Chapter 24 ~~~~~~~~~~~~~~~~~~~~~~~~~~~~~~~~~~ 179
Chapter 25 ~~~~~~~~~~~~~~~~~~~~~~~~~~~~~~~~~~ 185
Chapter 26 ~~~~~~~~~~~~~~~~~~~~~~~~~~~~~~~~~~ 192
Chapter 27 ~~~~~~~~~~~~~~~~~~~~~~~~~~~~~~~~~~ 195
Chapter 28 ~~~~~~~~~~~~~~~~~~~~~~~~~~~~~~~~~~ 201

Chapter 29 ~~~~~~~~~~~~~~~~~~~~~~~~~~~~ 207
Chapter 30 ~~~~~~~~~~~~~~~~~~~~~~~~~~~~ 214
Chapter 31 ~~~~~~~~~~~~~~~~~~~~~~~~~~~~ 218
Chapter 32 ~~~~~~~~~~~~~~~~~~~~~~~~~~~~ 223
Chapter 33 ~~~~~~~~~~~~~~~~~~~~~~~~~~~~ 231
Chapter 34 ~~~~~~~~~~~~~~~~~~~~~~~~~~~~ 235

Author's Note ~~~~~~~~~~~~~~~~~~~~~~~~~ 239

Chapter 1

Why am I in such a hurry? And why is everyone else in such a hurry too? I stop and take a look around. It's April 2014, just another Friday afternoon in a big city supermarket, but it feels like a war zone (or a Black Friday). Lisbon might be the biggest Portuguese city, but with just over half a million people, it's more like a cozy town compared to the hustle of London or the craziness of Tokyo (which I totally hated, by the way). I love Lisbon, but lately, I feel like my city is suffocating me.

I'm lost in my thoughts, when a woman in her forties, with platinum blonde hair and a tight red dress that hugs all her curves, almost bulldozes me. Nothing can stand between her and a Dove deodorant. I could get annoyed at the look she gives me, but I decide to show some empathy. Running out of deodorant is a big deal, especially if you've got a date. And dressed like that, I bet she's off on a hot date with some guy she met on the internet, who'll either turn out to be a jerk or, after almost a year of dating, still won't commit.

So, why am I at El Corte Inglés[1] supermarket during the busiest time of the week? I shift my gaze from the fake blonde and head to the feminine hygiene aisle. Scanning the shelves, I finally spot what I need: a box of Tampax. It's a crucial purchase, but it's not my most pressing need right now. Even though I'm on my period and desperately need tampons (because I'm using the last one stashed in my office drawer), there's something else I need even more.

I make my way to the back of the supermarket. Turning the corner from the cookie aisle, I bump into a couple having a heated argument about cookies. Yes, you read it right – cookies. He's all about the decadent Oreos, and she's into those rice cookies that look like Styrofoam. I sidestep them, not catching the end of their dispute but knowing she's likely to win – us ladies tend to triumph in life's small battles. Big battles? That's a different story.

Picking up the pace, I enter the drinks aisle. A middle-aged couple deliberates over red wine for dinner, while two young guys stock up on beer. I try to pass, but the beer-laden cart is blocking the way.

"Excuse me!"

---

1 A fancy supermarket located in Lisbon's upmarket Avenidas Novas district.

One of them, with an eyebrow piercing, shoots me an unfriendly look. Not even my dark gray, austere suit seems to impress him. The other, who looks like he just started shaving, seems embarrassed and gives me a lost puppy look.

"Sorry, it's poker night at our place."

I peek over his shoulder. There they are at the end of the aisle, looking at me. I could spot those clear glass bottles with red labels from miles away.

"All right, I'll wait," I say, though eager to grab a bottle.

While they finish loading their cart, I notice the middle-aged couple, in addition to a bottle of Alentejo red wine, opting for a muscatel. Looks like it's not just the young folks prepping for a party.

"We're done," the freshly shaved guy says as they start moving the cart. "Sorry for the delay."

"No problem, take your time," I say, although I can't wait to get that bottle.

As they move away, I watch them. The one with the eyebrow piercing says something to the other, and they both burst into laughter. I don't hear the joke, but it must be a good one. Suddenly, I feel nostalgic. I reminisce about myself, Maria, Ana, and Ruth back in college, missing those carefree times. Back then our biggest concerns were parties, boyfriends, and 'Sex and the City' episodes.

The guys turn the corner, disappearing from view. Now that there's a clear path, I head directly to the coveted shelf. I grab a bottle of Smirnoff and turn around. With the vodka bottle in one hand and the tampons in the other, I pick up the pace toward the checkout. I've been here for too long, and I'm eager to get home. My brain is racing, and I've had a headache since morning.

I've been in line for almost twenty minutes, growing impatient. I'm tired, and the headache is worsening. I want to crack open the bottle and take a sip right from the neck. I imagine the horrified faces of my fellow shoppers and nearly burst out laughing. I'd give anything for a sip, but I know I can't. The daughter of Judge Lacerda de Brito doesn't drink in public.

The line stubbornly refuses to move. I peek, spotting an old lady who just dumped her purse contents on the counter, seemingly unable to find her debit card.

The fake blonde arrives and joins the checkout line next to me. Alongside the deodorant, she's got a bottle of whiskey. I smile. She's one of my kind. During the week, I'm a well-behaved girl. I get up early for the gym before work, CrossFit five days a week. Then, I work twelve to fourteen hours a day, sometimes more. Except on Fridays. On Fridays, if there are no surprises, I leave around seven in the evening. On Friday and Saturday nights, I like to have a drink to relax. When I don't go out with Rodrigo, when he's in Lisbon, I buy a bottle of vodka to drink at home. I used to go out with Maria, Ana, and Ruth, but Maria got married and moved to Porto two years ago and has a baby now. Ana also got married and moved to Amsterdam about a year ago. Six months ago, Ruth fell head over heels for her Body Combat instructor and decided to follow him to Ibiza. That's how I ended up all alone in Lisbon. So, when I don't have company to go out, on Friday and Saturday nights, I lie on the couch, watching 'Sex and the City' episodes, while I drink myself to sleep. I drink half the bottle on Friday and the other half on Saturday. On Sundays, I have lunch with my parents with a big hangover, but they don't seem to realize it. Sometimes, I think I could vanish, and they wouldn't even notice. And sometimes, that's what I feel like doing – vanishing.

The cookie couple joins my line. She keeps talking non-stop, and he smiles. I see the round Styrofoam-like cookies in their shopping basket, and I feel like laughing. Two packs. He's in for it. He'll spend the weekend picking cookie bits out of his teeth. That stuff is hard to get out. She bends her head down to look at something on her phone, and he sighs and rolls his eyes. I feel like congratulating him. He's as good a pretender as I am.

I spend most of my days faking it, slapping on a smile like it's my favorite accessory. I fake liking my colleagues, fake enjoying my job, even fake enthusiasm during those CrossFit classes. And oh, the masterpiece of my pretense – pretending to agree with my parents. It's a full-time job being a professional faker, but I do it. I fake being happy because faking it's easier than telling people how I truly feel.

We grow up being molded into these perfect daughters, told to chase degrees that promise solid careers, grab jobs with fat paychecks, and then snag a house and a car. But surprise, even with all those accomplishments, you realize there's still a marathon ahead. You need to do more, have more, be more. You need the perfect body to marry the perfect spouse, raise perfect kids, and then be a perfect mother. If you manage all that, congrats! You've got the Perfect Life!

So, here I am, ticking all the boxes – Law degree from the fanciest Law School in the country, a job at a top-notch law firm in the capital, a decent car, and an apartment in the city center courtesy of the grandparents. But guess what? It doesn't mean squat. My efforts feel like tossing pebbles into a never-ending well because, surprise, I was born with a pair of breasts and a vagina. Then one day, it hits you that you're a target of workplace bullying just because you dared to stand up to him. And what do you do when that happens? You shut up and keep showing up at work like it's business as usual. You keep quiet because you're not one to whine. You keep quiet because you're tough. You keep quiet because you're a rock in the middle of a storm, getting hammered by rain and wind. You're a rock, and nothing can crack you, nothing can knock you down. But let's be real, there are days when you don't feel like a rock. There are days when you feel wrecked, shattered, and hollow. Today happens to be one of those days.

The cookie girl tucks away her phone and glances over at her boyfriend. He flashes her a smile, and I can't help but burst out laughing. He's a master at pretending. He deserves a gold medal or something.

Finally, the old lady digs out her wallet and settles the bill. Then she starts packing up the stuff she dumped on the counter at a snail's pace that's driving me crazy. Trapped in this windowless box with a growing crowd, I'm getting anxious. I need to escape.

A guy in a suit and tie hops in line—tall, dark, and handsome. Probably in his thirties. He's got a little girl, maybe five or six, in tow. She's rocking a pink Minnie Mouse sweater and light-up sneakers. The man's glued to his phone, oblivious to his daughter's attempts to catch his attention. I exchange genuine smiles and goofy faces with the kid – a refreshing break from my usual fake grin routine. She giggles and tugs at her father's hand, but he's ignoring her. She tries again, pointing at me, but he brushes her off, engrossed in his call. The kid stops smiling and I stop making faces.

Glancing back at the line, the old lady's is still bagging her groceries. I clutch the Smirnoff bottle tight. She's bagging so slowly, it's like I'm watching a slow-motion movie. Then, out of nowhere, a stabbing pain hits my chest. I grip the vodka bottle harder, trying to suck in a deep breath, but it's no use. The woman keeps bagging. Dizziness sets in. I glance at the cashier, and finally, the woman moves on. The line inches forward, and I manage to load my purchases onto the conveyor belt. My hands are trembling. I lean on the counter, but the shakes won't quit.

The guy next in line takes his sweet time bagging. I'm itching to scream "Hurry up!" but I bite my tongue. The tremors worsen, and my vision blurs. Another jab of pain sears through my chest, stronger this time. What's happening?! I can't faint in the middle of a supermarket! My legs give way, and I slide down the counter, ending up on the floor. People are glued to their phones or lost in their thoughts, and no one seems to notice the crazy lady having a meltdown amidst the groceries. The chest pain intensifies, and I'm struggling to breathe. I'm sitting on the floor, head against one of those chocolate displays by the registers. The girl with the light-up sneakers glances at me, but her smile's vanished.

"Dad!" she shrieks.

The father finally pockets his phone and glares at me. I start breathing loud, trying to force air into my lungs. The chest pain is unbearable. The cookie guy spots me on the floor and comes over. The girl's father looks relieved. He's off the hook.

"Do you need help?"

"Chest pain," I say, gripping his arm.

Ridiculous! Here I am, sitting on this filthy supermarket floor, holding onto a stranger's arm like it's doomsday.

"What's up?" asks the cookie girl, joining her boyfriend.

"Chest pain," he says, trying to pull away.

She eyeballs me, then him, then back at me. After that, she turns to the line and screams:

"Call an ambulance! She's having a heart attack!"

Her voice slices through my brain like a knife. Now I get why the boyfriend's always grinning – with that screechy voice, he'd eat Styrofoam cookies just to stay in her good books.

I close my eyes, hoping it's a nightmare. Heart attack at twenty-nine? Too young, right? But the pain won't let up. I hear quickening footsteps and voices. Opening my eyes, I'm met with a gathering crowd. Some look curious, while others look downright annoyed that I'm ruining their evening.

A supermarket staffer approaches. "Ambulance is on the way! Clear some space, folks, let her breathe!" he commands the onlookers forming a ring around me.

Kneeling beside me, the man places a hand on my shoulder. "Hang in there a bit longer, help's on its way."

His words only ramp up my nerves. Paramedics are soon going to surround me. The thought alone kicks my heart into overdrive. I crane my neck and catch sight of my purchases on the conveyor belt - a bottle of vodka and a box of tampons. What a joke! I can picture the headlines: "Young woman has a heart attack buying vodka and tampons." I wonder if they'll call me a "young woman" in the news? Or maybe "twenty-nine-year-old woman." Because let's face it, I'm almost thirty – not exactly Spring chicken anymore.

The pain intensifies, and I can't help but let out a moan. A woman, sporting purple leggings, kneels down and yells in my ear, "Hold on, the ambulance is coming!" I want to snap back at her, tell her my problem's my heart, not my hearing, but I resist. I shut my eyes once more, attempting a deep breath, but it's impossible. All I can think about is Monday's court hearing. I can't miss it! I can't decide which hurts more - my chest or my head, which feels like it's about to explode.

Out of the blue, the crowd around me scatters, making a path. Two paramedics show up at the supermarket entrance. One, is a tall, muscular mulatto with striking green eyes - a hunk, as Ruth would say. The other is overweight and bald. They approach, and the bald one kneels beside me.

"What's your name?"

Despite the agony, I'm disappointed it's not the mulatto speaking to me. The bald guy continues staring, waiting for a reply. I want to answer, to say my name's Melissa, that friends call me Mel, but the words won't come out.

"What's your name?" he insists, checking my pulse.

My breaths grow louder, and the world begins to blur. I can only think about Monday's court hearing and the vodka and tampon headlines. I shut my eyes, feeling like I'm trapped in an underwater world. The voices fade into the distance.

Vodka and tampons... I'll be the office joke for weeks. I recall Claudio's parting words, and I wonder if he was right.

The alarm clock's at it again, blaring for the third time, and I figure it's time to shut it up. I toss the sheets aside and leap out of bed before I drift back into dreamland. Weekdays, I set that alarm for six, but somehow, I end up snoozing it two or three times. Today's Thursday, and surprise, it's no different. It's six-twenty, so I have to hurry. I throw on clothes in a flash and scarf down a bowl of Greek yogurt with chia, all while skimming the day's news on my tablet. Honestly, what I really wanted was toast slathered in butter, but you know, bread and butter equals extra pounds. So, I settle for the yogurt. As I'm catching up on the news, I stumble upon my father's name in the headlines again. He's playing judge in another high-profile money laundering saga.

After having finished breakfast, I snatch my gym bag and power walk out the door. CrossFit's kicking off at seven-thirty, and I'm not about to be fashionably late. I take the metro and go to the gym. By seven-twenty-five, I'm geared up and prepped for another round of what my trainer likes to call the Beach Body Project. More like a torture session, but hey, I'm here for it.

I'm in the locker room stashing my stuff away when a message pings on my phone. I'm hoping it's Rodrigo. No luck. It's a message from my boss. Should've known Rodrigo wouldn't be texting at this ungodly hour. It's been eighteen long days since I last saw him, and I'm seriously missing him.

I make my way to the CrossFit studio, and there's Leo, the trainer, already in place. Leo's got to be in his thirties, a total hottie - tall, athletic, not overly buff, with this light brown hair and lively green eyes. And apart from being smoking hot, he's one of those people who are always in a good mood. A true *Cappuccino*.

I know it might sound shallow, but my friends and I came up with a system to classify men. Well, it was Ruth's idea. According to her, there are four types of guys. First up, we've got the *Cappuccino*, the kind of guy who just warms your heart and is always there for you. Think of him like a perfect mix of handsome and genuinely good. Leo? Oh, he's like the poster child for *Cappuccino*s. Then there's the *Martini* – dense, strong, and oh-so attractive that you can't resist him. Your brain knows he could spell trouble, but your body couldn't care less. When a *Martini* walks in, all you want to do is ditch your clothes and, well, you know, get busy. Next in line is the *Espresso*, smaller in size but packing a full-bodied, bitter punch. Yeah, he might be the short, ugly guy you might overlook, but surprise, surprise – he's a master in the art of love. He may even have a small dick, but he knows how to use it. And finally, we've got the *Milk Cup*. He's that bland dude who might be a decent guy but doesn't really get your heart racing. Sadly, *Milk Cups* and *Espressos* seem to be everywhere, while *Cappuccino*s and *Martinis* are like endangered species.

Ruth's is convinced the Body Combat instructor is a *Cappuccino*, but trust me, she's off the mark. He's more of an *Espresso*. He's ugly as sin but must be pulling some serious moves in the bedroom because he convinced her to follow him to Ibiza. Ruth might've come up with these categories, but I don't think she gets men or maybe she's fooling herself. And it's not just about the Body Combat instructor; she's also convinced Rodrigo is a *Martini*. Sure, he's a bit vain, but he's no *Martini*. Rodrigo's definitely a *Cappuccino*.

"Hey, Mel! Ready to kick some butt in class?" asks the *Cappuccino* in from of me.

"More than ready," I fib.

Leo leans in, giving me a sly wink. "Got some exclusive news for you."

"News?" I raise an eyebrow.

Colleagues start streaming in, chattering away, but Leo's locked onto me. "Ever heard of Krav Maga?"

"Yeah, but honestly, I'm not sure what it is."

"It's a personal defense technique from Israel."

I chuckle. "So, you think I need to learn how to throw a punch?"

"Sometimes it seems like you want to beat someone up. In Krav Maga, you can do it without getting in trouble for assault."

We both burst into laughter. So, apparently, I give off a "I'm want to punch someone in the face" vibe. No one ever told me that before. I've been called a daddy's girl and even conceited, but this is a first.

"I bet there's someone you'd love to punch in the face. We all got that one person who drives us nuts."

I instantly picture someone and mentally throw a few punches their way. "I may have a person in mind."

"I'm starting Krav Maga classes here at the gym. You should give it a shot. Just think about it!"

"Sure thing. I'll think it over, Leo."

"I bet there's a guy you'd love to teach a lesson." He smirks.

"Why does it have to be a guy?" I ask, twirling a strand of hair.

"Trust me, it's always a guy," he laughs.

He's onto something, but I'm not letting him in on that.

"Enough chit-chat. Let's sweat it out."

As I glance around, I notice the studio is packed. Leo's classes are a hit, especially with the ladies.

"Good morning, you beautiful people!" Leo shouts.

"Morning, Leo!" we all chime in.

"Ready for another class?!"

"Nope," someone from the back shouts.

We burst out laughing.

"Look, I get it. Pain's scary, but trust me, it's your BFF! Pain means you're putting in the work. Come summer, you'll be thanking that pain!"

The music cranks up, Leo's up front and center.

"Alright, time for another round of Beach Body Project!" he shouts over the beats.

We kick things off with jumping jacks, and Leo takes the chance to show off.

"Come on! Just ten more, nine, eight, seven..."

How come everything looks like a breeze when he does it? It's like he's on a whole different level.

After who knows how many rounds (I've totally lost count), we switch to squats.

"Let's go, you beautiful people! Eight, seven, six..."

He spins around to show a newbie how to squat, and this redhead pretends to grab his butt. We all start laughing. Leo turns back, clueless about the mischief.

"You guys are having too much fun. Maybe the workout's too easy. Let's crank it up! I want more, I want to see the pain on your faces!"

My face is probably a pain masterpiece. I'd hate to catch a glimpse of myself in the mirror during these sessions. I must look like I'm auditioning for a horror movie.

After an unknown number of squat sets, we jump into burpees, my sworn enemies. Truth be told, I hate them all – jumping jacks, squats, burpees. But if I had to pick the worst, burpees would take the crown.

"Come on! Pick up the pace! Faster! Faster!!!"

My glutes and arms are in pain. Honestly, my whole body's in pain.

"Nine, eight, seven! Let's get those bodies toned! Six, five..."

Toning?! Who cares about toning?! But why am I even here, pushing through this agony? Why do I keep coming back?

"Keep it going!"

In class, I'm just watching the clock, waiting for this torture to end. But then I hit a store, try on some size 6 jeans, can't squeeze into them, and suddenly I'm convinced I need to train more, lose some pounds. And here I am, bouncing around, trying not to collapse. Legs, arms, abs – everything's screaming. I'm pretty sure every muscle in my body is plotting revenge, but I'm still following the moves. At some point, I tune out Leo and just coast through the rest of the class.

Then, reality hits. I start stressing about work – meetings, demanding clients, a mountain of emails, and prepping for Monday's hearing. It's Thursday, which means I've got two days to get my act together, or the weekend's going to turn into a work marathon. What if I mess up the hearing? Can't let that happen! No way I'm giving my colleagues the satisfaction.

"And that's a wrap for today!"

Leo's voice snaps me back into reality. The class is done, and somehow, I made it through. People start shuffling out, and I hustle to follow them.

"Hey, Mel, don't forget what I told you," Leo calls out as I pass him. "Give it some thought!"

"Sure thing, I'll think it over," I fib. "Catch you tomorrow."

I dash to the locker room, aiming to be among the first for a shower. Time's ticking, and just as I'm getting dressed, my phone starts ringing. Of course, it's from the office. Always is.

"Morning," I greet. "Yeah... okay... sure, set it up for six."

I hang up and notice three missed calls from clients. Seriously, who's on the line before nine? Oh right, my dear clients. I shoot a quick message to Ruth:

Robert Pattinson - Cappuccino or Martini?

It's a little game we play.

I stash my phone, dry my hair in a rush, slap on some makeup, then snatch my gym bag, purse, and bolt out of the gym.

The office is just a couple of metro stops away, which is one of the reasons I opted for this gym. That, and Leo. I took a liking to him right off the bat during my trial class. If it weren't for Rodrigo, I might have actually been interested in Leo.

I hustle as I make my way into the metro station. When I start going down the stairs, I catch the sound of a train whistle and start sprinting down. Out of nowhere, a man appears, and I collide with him, nearly taking a tumble.

"Watch it!" he shouts.

Ignoring his comment, I continue my rush down the stairs. "Stupid!" he hollers after me.

At the foot of the stairs, a cluster of people from the departing train appears, and I maneuver around them, still in a hurry. I accidentally knock into a laptop bag, jolting my leg, but I don't slow down. Reaching the platform, I hear the doors closing. I make one last sprint and fling myself into the carriage. I manage to slide in, but my gym bag and shoulder get caught in the closing door, a sharp pain shooting through my left shoulder. My bag and shoulder are wedged tight, but I yank them both in as the doors reopen.

Glancing around, I realize nobody noticed my struggle with the door. People are absorbed in their phones or lost in a daze. A robbery or a scuffle could break out, and no one would even notice. Welcome to Zombieland!

The train is jam-packed, and I'm squeezed between a towering Moroccan guy, who must be about two meters tall, and a stout woman sporting black and white knee-high socks along with ridiculously short shorts that showcase every curve and bump. Sweat, cheap perfumes, and spices create this funky blend in the air. You got to love the charm of rush hour metro rides.

As I arrive at the office, I offer a nod to Carmen, the receptionist, who's engrossed in a call. I work in one of Lisbon's top law firms, catering to some of the nation's elite businessmen and politicians. The reception area screams serious business—grey, masculine – except for Carmen's nails. She rocks a grey pantsuit and black heels, just like me, but her nails are a vivid contrast. Mine? Subtle French manicure. Hers? Long nails, painted a bright purple. No idea how she gets away with it. Rumor has it she's had or still has an affair with Azevedo, our boss. Whatever it is, she seems to have the green light to flaunt every color on her nails. She waves those purple nails at me, and I dish out a fake smile.

I make my way to my office, turn on the computer, and plunge into my emails. I can't afford to get distracted by Carmen's nail choices. Thirty-two new messages await me, not to mention the one hundred and twenty-two unread ones, summing up to a staggering one hundred and fifty-four emails. Geez! One hundred and fifty-four emails!

The next half-hour flies by, filled with returned calls and replies to emails. By nine twenty-eight, I've managed to tackle three calls and address fourteen emails, leaving a daunting one hundred and forty still unopened. Well, until another one waltzes in. Blast it! Now it's one hundred and forty-one. I swiftly log off before more bombard my inbox. It's meeting time.

I exit my office and stride swiftly towards the meeting room. Sharp at nine-thirty, I step into the conference room. My boss is already settled, accompanied by Claudio, the ass-kisser. I deliberately pick a seat at the furthest end of the table from Claudio. The farther, the better.

Carmen strolls in carrying a hefty box of Portuguese custard tarts, setting it on the table before making a quick exit. I'm the lone woman in the room, the usual scenario since Vera left the firm a year ago. Law's still a man's world. Sadly for my father, instead of a son, he got a daughter in the lottery.

"Good morning, everyone. Let's get started," Azevedo says, after shoveling a tart into his mouth. Azevedo, our boss, is subject to speculation since his partner's death, with bets running high on the next partner.

"Time for the much-loved status update on your cases," Azevedo says after devouring another tart (no wonder he's bulking up). "Jonas, you're up."

Jonas sets down his tart and flashes his best smile at Azevedo. Another ass-kisser. Pastries aren't his thing, yet he eats them just to please Azevedo. He starts droning on about some case involving a politician and money laundering, and I zone out. Those cases? Nah, not for me, at least not while I work at this office. They require a tough man. That's what Azevedo told me when I started working here five years ago. Irony? Jonas? Anything but tough. Dark curly brown hair, round glasses giving off a total nerd vibe. If he wasn't such a jerk, he could pass as a *Cappuccino*. He's the kind of guy who'd step on anyone to shine. In this office, only Claudio can sink lower.

Someone nudges the tart box my way, and I push it right back. Five years in this place, and everyone should know I don't eat cakes. But they conveniently forget, or maybe it's just to rile me up, test if I'll cave. When I shove the box away, I catch Claudio staring at me. I glance away, faking notes. From the corner of my eye, I sense him still watching, and a shiver runs down my spine.

"Melissa, it's your turn," Jonas nudges me.

"Oh, yeah, sure."

"Got distracted?" Claudio butts in.

I act like I didn't hear and launch into my presentation. I spare my boss and colleagues the messy details of my clients' divorces. A quick summary suffices. No need for them to know about the tire tycoon caught in bed with his niece or the socialite with a hefty bust cheating on her husband with her tennis coach, hell-bent on keeping her late mother-in-law's engagement ring. I give a brief overview, and the boss seems content.

Then Claudio takes the stage. I sneak a glance at him. He could pass as a *Cappuccino* if he weren't such a rotten apple. Tall, fit, and good-looking—the typical alpha male. Beyond his looks, he's cunning, excelling at keeping corrupt politicians out of jail. He's got what it takes, and Azevedo knows it: smug, manipulative, and utterly fake. Traits I'll never possess. Hence, I'm doomed to handle the divorces of the rich and famous while I work in this office.

According to statistics, the percentage of divorces per hundred marriages is almost sixty-nine percent. Out of every hundred couples who said I do, deluded by the promise of eternal love, there are sixty-nine who see that dream destroyed. Because that's what divorces do: they turn what was once a dream into a nightmare. With such a high divorce rate, I'll never be short of work.

After Claudio, it's another colleague's turn, and I zone out once more. I have no interest in hearing my colleagues suck up to Azevedo. They've been at it since his partner passed, almost pushing each other to be Azevedo's chosen one for partnership.

I sneak a glance at Claudio and start trying to fit him into one of the categories. But honestly, none of them seem to suit him. He's not the warmhearted *Cappuccino* type at all, and he's even far too shady to be a *Martini*. What category would Ruth make come up with? Maybe *Sour Beer* because he's always so bitter. No, scratch that.

Beer has got its fans, but nobody's rooting for Claudio (though they pretend to). That's out of the question. Wait, *Sour Milk* – yeah, there's something off about him, something spoiled. Bingo! The category fits him like a glove, and I'm itching to share it. Carmen seems like the obvious choice, but she can't keep a secret to save her life. If I told her, she would spill it to Claudio and the whole gang.

"Thanks, everyone," Azevedo says once the last colleague wraps up.

I was so lost in my thoughts that I missed everyone's presentations. I start packing my stuff.

"Hold on, I've got something else to discuss with you."

I settle back down, noticing Claudio eyeballing me once more.

"I've decided we are throwing a VIP weekend retreat for our top clients. We want to show them some love for trusting us."

"What a neat idea!" Jonas, the ass-kisser, pipes up right away.

"Great idea!" the rest chime in, like they're a rehearsed chorus. They're this close to giving each other pats on the back.

"Retreat? What kind of retreat?" I ask.

No response. They don't know either, but sucking up to Azevedo is top priority.

"I need someone to organize it." Azevedo says, ignoring my question.

Crickets. Some lower their eyes and pretend to consult their schedules. Silence rules. Nobody wants to tackle this mysterious retreat.

"Melissa?"

"Yes."

"I'd like you to be in charge of the organization."

"Me?!"

I hear relieved sighs and feel a lump in my throat. The guy must be nuts. I barely have enough time to sleep, let alone organize some fancy event.

"Yes, I'd like you to take care of everything. It's going to be in the Algarve. I'm thinking of a weekend at a luxury hotel."

"I have no experience in organizing gatherings."

"I'm sure you'll do a good job."

Suddenly, I have an idea.

"I think Claudio would be a better fit. I'm sure he'll do a much better job than I would."

A flashy Vegas-style party would probably please most of our clients.

Claudio's expression shifts from smug to furious. I was hoping he'd take charge to suck up to the boss, but it looks like he's not up for it.

"I'd like you to organize it, Melissa," Azevedo declares without sparing Claudio a glance.

"Wouldn't it be wiser to hire an event planner?"

"No, Melissa. It's crucial the office handles this to showcase our unwavering dedication to our clients," he insists.

"I still believe Claudio would excel. He's got great organizational skills!" I say, trying to sound enthusiastic.

Claudio's irritation escalates by the second. A vein on his forehead looks like it's about to pop.

"This needs a woman's touch, Melissa."

My colleagues start giggling. Seriously, they're a bunch of clowns! I should have known that's why Azevedo chose me. How could I have missed it? I see Claudio's smug satisfaction, and I contemplate enrolling in Krav Maga classes with Leo. That guy seriously needs a reality check.

"Well, meeting adjourned. Everyone can leave, except Melissa. I'll brief her to get started on the event right away."

My coworkers start leaving. One of them goes to the boss to ask something, and Claudio takes the chance to come over to me. He grabs my arm. I instinctively step back, but he won't let go. Then he leans in and whispers in my ear:

"Planning parties suits you way better than lawyering."

What a jerk! I bit my lip, suppressing the urge to snap back at him, choosing silence to avoid escalating the situation.

He strolls off, all high and mighty, and has a chat with Azevedo before taking off. Once we're alone, Azevedo hands me a folder.

"Everything you need is in here, Melissa. The guest list, budget details, and the date. I know you'll nail it."

"Rest assured, I'll give it my best," I reply, ready to head out.

"Hold on."

I turn back, putting on my best smile.

"Don't see this as a punishment."

"No, not at all."

"In the office everyone knows who your father is, so I can't show favoritism."

Sure, but did you really have to dump all this extra work on me?

"No worries. I'll do my best."

I leave and, as I walk towards my office, I pass Claudio's spot and can't help but think Krav Maga classes might come in handy. He's on the phone, oblivious to me. I have this urge to scrawl *'Sour Milk'* on his door with a red marker. I'm almost at my office when Carmen shows up.

"I can help with the party. Remember how I organized my sister's wedding last year?"

Pink flamingo balloons and '80s music might not match our boss's vision, but I'm surprised Carmen offered to pitch in.

"I can help you, but you'll need to let Azevedo know I'm lending a hand."

I knew Carmen's offer wouldn't come without a catch. She always has an agenda. I nod and keep moving.

The rest of the morning flies by with back-to-back client meetings. One client, going through a divorce, is willing to stoop to anything to keep her lavish lifestyle, even considering accusing her husband of abusing their kid. Thankfully, I talk her out of that idea. Just when I think I've seen it all, there's always a client who manages to sink even lower.

After lunch, back at the office, I make a pit stop at what I call the "Cemetery of Failed Weddings" (Archive A, officially). It's this huge room, packed with shelves towering up to the ceiling, exclusively housing divorce cases. It's the office's biggest archive. This is where stories like Manuel Botelho Moniz and Beatriz Botelho Moniz end up. They had this fairytale start—met at a dinner party, felt that love-at-first-sight magic, tied the knot at Jerónimos' Monastery[2], had a dreamy honeymoon in the Caribbean, and were blessed with two perfect kids. They seemed destined for a happily-ever-after. But then, reality took a brutal turn. One day, Beatriz returned home early and caught Manuel in the act with the kids' nanny — while the children played Playstation in the living room. That moment shattered everything. Manuel swore he wouldn't stray again, and Maria tried to forgive, but trust was shattered. From then on, every late night at work raised suspicions of flings on the office couch with the secretary. Each bathroom break with his phone triggered thoughts of sneaky texts. Convinced of ongoing cheating, Beatriz sought payback, picking the tennis instructor, a guy young enough to be her son (funnily, tennis instructors seem to be a hit with those seeking revenge in rocky marriages). Five years of betrayals, fights, and ultimatums later, they called it quits. It took Manuel and Beatriz too long to grasp that the worst part of infidelity isn't the act itself—it's losing the ability to trust that person again. When you don't trust the person sleeping next to you, no promises, threats, therapy, or even dabbling in the occult (yes, some couples have even tried that) can salvage the relationship. If my clients' marriage had a tombstone, it'd read:

Here lies the marriage of Manuel and Beatriz. Started in love, ended in hate.

I shove those thoughts aside; it's a downer. I want to hold onto the belief that love stories with happy endings still exist, and that my tale with Rodrigo might just be one of them.

---

2 The Jerónimos Monastery (Mosteiro dos Jerónimos in Portuguese) is a prominent historical monument located in the Belém district of Lisbon, Portugal.

I find the folder I was looking for and head back to my office. In those rare moments between ringing phones, I tackle the tasks on my desk. By late afternoon, I decide to check my flood of new emails. Most scream 'urgent' in big, bold letters. I sigh. I can't deal with another 'life or death' phone call; running out of cash to shop at Avenida da Liberdade[3] isn't a life-threatening crisis, but my last client sure thinks it is.

At 8 p.m., I order a salad from a catering company that feeds the overqualified yet discontented downtown Lisbon workers. As I pick at my meal, I glance across the street at another office building. Many lights are still on, making me feel less alone in this misery. By 10 p.m., I've hit my limit and decide to leave. Most of my colleagues are still glued to their desks, but I'm too worn out to continue.

I hop on the metro and head home. Stepping inside my apartment, I kick off my shoes, take off my blazer, and collapse onto the couch. I'm drained, but sleep isn't beckoning. My mind's caught up in the upcoming event in the Algarve. How on earth will I manage everything in such a tight window? What if things go haywire? What if Claudio finds a way to mess up the party? What if the catered food goes bad and everyone ends up with food poisoning? Or worse, what if the hired band gets caught with illegal substances during a police raid? There are a million ways things can go wrong.

The sound of a message pings, and I grab my phone. It's a new one from the client at Avenida da Liberdade—another set of demands bound to rile up her soon-to-be ex-husband.

I'll handle it tomorrow, I type back.

In response, a heart pierced by an arrow pops up. Nothing from Ruth or Rodrigo—just the wounded-heart message. I shoot a text to Rodrigo.

Missing you! When are you coming to Lisbon?

I turn on the TV, flicking through channels, awaiting his reply. A new message arrives, and in my haste, I drop the remote, making a loud thud (the downstairs neighbors will probably grumble soon). I snatch my phone—it's from Ruth.

Martini! Don't forget, he's a vampire. Sexy, but deadly!

This time, I agree with her. A vampire is definitely not a *Cappuccino*. I stare at the message and decide to call her. The phone rings, one, two, three times... Ruth's not one to answer phone calls often. She says she won't be carrying her phone around all the time. Just when I'm about to give up, a groggy voice answers.

"Do you even know what time it is?!" I can hear the grumpiness in her voice—I've just woken her up.

"Oops! Sorry! I totally forgot what time it is!" Well, I didn't forget, but I assumed she'd be out having a blast at some bar or nightclub. After all, Ibiza is just an hour ahead of Lisbon. Midnight's too early for Ruth to go to bed.

---

3 Avenida da Liberdade is one of the streets with the most expensive shops in Lisbon.

"Can't a woman get some shut-eye in peace?!"

I've just committed a cardinal sin: waking up Ruth, the woman who once dumped a boyfriend for daring to wake her up early on a weekend.

"You messaged me," I say.

"Yeah, then I passed out," Ruth grumbles.

"I figured you were out painting the town red in Ibiza". Ruth's always been the party-loving type—dancing and drinking until she drops. That hasn't changed since college. Ana, Maria, and I became lawyers, while Ruth carried on with her party lifestyle. She picks up odd jobs, saves up, then jet off, sometimes alone, sometimes with someone.

"What's up?" It's odd for her to be asleep so soon. She should be tearing up a nightclub in Ibiza or skinny-dipping in the sea.

"Nothing," she tries to dodge.

"Don't lie, Ruth. Something's up!"

"Mel, give it a rest!" Her sleepy voice morphs into annoyance.

"You can't fool me."

"Alright, fine. I'm broke."

"Broke?! What about the Body Combat instructor? Doesn't he have any cash?"

"He left two weeks ago."

"You guys fight?"

"Mel, so many questions this late!"

"You don't have to tell me if you don't want to."

"No, no fight. He wanted to go to Tenerife; I wanted stay in Ibiza. So, he left; I stayed."

Sometimes I envy her ability to detach from relationships.

"Need money?" We all have lent her money at some point.

"No charity, Mel. I'm teaching Portuguese classes online for cash. Look, I know you'll lecture me about planning things better, but not tonight. Another time. I need sleep!"

She hangs up, leaving me hanging on the phone, unsure how to react. I should've known Ruth can turn into a viper when woken up. I set the phone down, and head to the kitchen for vodka. I don't typically drink during the week, but she's pushed me over. The bottle's almost gone. I pour myself a glass. One sip used to do the trick, but lately, it's not enough. Sitting on the couch, I channel surf while sipping the alcohol.

I wake up fuzzy-headed, still on the couch. It's 2 a.m. I fell asleep holding the phone and remote. No messages. At least, no more wounded hearts from the client. I rise slowly, switch off the TV, tidy the remote, and return to the kitchen to stow the bottle. I must remember to buy another for the weekend; this one's nearly empty, just a finger's worth left. Not worth saving. I drink what's left straight from the bottle.

Finally, it's Friday. I woke up with a killer headache, and barely got any sleep. But today's different—I don't linger in bed. I jump out of bed the second the alarm goes off. Can't afford to laze around, I'm too wound up. I follow my usual routine like a robot: get dressed, gulp down some Greek yogurt with chia, hit up CrossFit, shower, get dressed again, fix my hair, slap on some makeup, then rush out of the gym to the office. Even Leo's usual jokes about the Beach Body Project couldn't lift my spirits today.

When I get to the office, Carmen's beaming, rocking a flashy new nail color—bright yellow. Also flaunting a shiny gold bracelet with a heart-shaped pendant.

"Hey! Two clients called for you. Left their info on your desk."

Can't my clients cut me some slack for once? It's not even nine, and the urgent calls have already started. Husbands running off with their secretaries, women disappearing with their bling, scandals left and right... the list goes on. I wonder if Leo's into flings with married women too. I noticed a bunch at the gym batting their eyelashes at him while wearing wedding rings. I'm hoping he's the real deal, a genuine *Cappuccino* who steers clear of married ladies.

"Are you getting started on the event plans?" Carmen asks, flaunting her yellow nails.

"Not yet."

"Don't forget about me, darling."

I've been upgraded to 'darling.' Carmen's a 'darling'. Part of me wants to fire back with a sarcastic 'don't worry, darling,' but it's not worth the effort. I sneak a peek at the bracelet on her wrist, wondering how her husband manages to put up with her. If he ever wants a divorce, I wouldn't mind handling it for him.

"Eyeing my new bracelet?" she teases.

Darn it, caught red-handed. I try to keep it casual.

"Nah, the nail color caught my eye."

"It was a gift from my husband," she says, tracing the bracelet. "We celebrated ten years yesterday. He took me to that seafood spot in Cascais—the one you usually hit up with your parents on Sundays." Seems like she knows everyone's business. "Isn't it gorgeous?" She waves her hand around.

"Yeah, really nice," I say, hoping she'll change the subject.

"Don't be sad, Melissa."

"Sorry?!"

"One day, you'll have your own ring and kiddos."

I'm caught off guard, not sure how to respond. I flash a fake smile and make my exit. I've got heaps of work waiting, I'm not going to waste time with Carmen's chitchat.

As I walk away, I find myself unable to shake off my curiosity about how Carmen managed to capture such a great guy. She's nosy, self-centered, and has been unfaithful to him for ages. It would make more sense if she settled for someone less respectable, someone nobody else desired. However, her husband appears to be a decent man. I met him when he testified in one of my cases where a client was wrongly accused by her husband of embezzling money from their company. He was the company's accountant, and he risked his job to stand up for what's right. That level of integrity stands out—unlike his wife, who spends every Thursday evening locked in the office with Azevedo after everyone else has left. What bothers me isn't her receiving yet another lavish gift from her husband but her spreading rumors about me, portraying me as some sort of pitiable case. Because I am pretty certain that's what she's doing. And I am not someone to be pitied. Rodrigo has already mentioned he's planning to propose.

I make my way to my office, passing by the pantry where my colleagues are huddled around the coffee machine. They're deep in conversation, and I can't resist pausing in the corridor to eavesdrop. I know I shouldn't, but I can't help myself. They're planning a party for tomorrow night, convinced it's going to be a blast. It's going down in Jonas's backyard with shrimp, soccer, and loads of beer. Ever since Claudio joined the office, I've stopped getting invites to their parties. Not that it bothers me. I've got enough of them during the week. What stings is how things changed since Vera left and Claudio showed up. She and I used to get along with the guys.

"What about the ladies?" Joel asks. "A party without them isn't fun."

"How about inviting Melissa?" Rui suggests.

"She's a rich, pampered girl. Our party isn't her scene," Jonas says.

"Hey, maybe she'll bite," someone chimes in.

"She bites into a lot of things," Claudio says.

"What do you mean?" Joel probes.

"No comment."

I catch a murmur, then Jonas nudges him on:

"You started, now spill."

"Probably best not to."

"You can't leave us hanging!" Jonas pushes.

"Okay, but this stays between us, yeah?"

"Spill it!"

I lean against the wall. My gut says I should leave before things escalate, but I stay put.

"Melissa isn't the saint you all think she is," Claudio says in a hushed tone, though I catch every word. "Shortly after I joined the office, I bumped into her at a bar. She was alone, looking like a lost pup. When she saw me, she lit up, motioning for me to join her. Spent the whole night downing tequila shots and chatting non-stop."

"Tequila shots?"

"Yep, she may look all saintly, but she can knock back shots like a champ. While I sipped a Martini, she polished off like seven or eight tequila shots."

A few colleagues whistle. My stomach feels like it's sinking, anxious about what he'll say next.

"What were you talking about?"

"I barely got a word in. I just stood there, staring at her, clueless, while she kept chattering and drinking."

"What was she chattering about?"

"Beats me, girl talk."

"Keep going!"

"At some point, I head to the bathroom, and when I turn to leave, she's there."

"There? Where?"

"In the bathroom, Rui!" Jonas interjects. "Let him finish!"

"Yeah, in the bathroom."

"And then?"

"Then she locks lips with me and pulls me into one of the stalls."

"Are you serious?!"

"Yep."

"And you?"

"I did zilch."

"Nothing? You didn't hook up with her?" Jonas probes.

"Nah."

"She's pretty hot," Joel says.

"You know who her old man is. Imagine if she started spouting off lies. I'd be in a mess. Plus, she isn't my type."

"Not your type?! You're just upset you missed out."

"Nah, Joel. I'd probably catch something nasty. Given how loose she is, she's probably banged every customer at that joint."

They all crack up, and I slump down the wall until I'm crouched on the floor.

"You know she scored this job because of her old man, right?" Joel says.

"Azevedo told me he had no clue who her father was when he hired her."

"Don't buy that, Rui," someone says.

"Me neither," Claudio agrees.

"Think about it, it's possible. Picture this—Azevedo had no clue about her old man, but in the interview, she pulled a Monica Lewinsky and convinced him to take her on," Jonas adds.

More laughter erupts, and I shrink against the wall. I just want to vanish.

"Picture this: her on her knees, under the desk, showcasing her 'interpersonal skills' to Azevedo," Jonas keeps going.

The laughter gets louder. I can't handle it anymore. I stand up, my legs shaking, and bolt out of there. I barge into my office, slam the door shut, and lock it. I sit at my desk, still trembling, staring into space, clueless about how to handle this. Their laughter, dulled by the walls, has stopped, but it echoes in my head. And it hurts, it hurts a lot.

"Melissa!" Carmen's knocking on the door. "Why's it closed?"

"Just a sec."

"Open up!"

"I'm coming."

"But why did you shut it?"

I take a deep breath, trying to gather myself. I open the door before Carmen kicks up a fuss. She's got a flair for drama. In another life, she'd have been a theater star.

"What's going on?" she asks, scanning the office like she's conducting a search. I feel like asking if she wants to inspect the cabinets too.

"Nothing, must've closed it by accident," I reply, trying to sound as neutral as possible.

She gives me an odd look. I'm sure she didn't buy a word I said, and the whole office will find out I was locked in here.

"What do you need?"

"This letter arrived for you."

She hands me an envelope. It's addressed to me, but there's no sender. The top right corner has a flower illustration. Carmen's lingering at the office entrance. Curiosity's got her, same as me. Is this some dumb prank from the guys?

"Secret admirer, perhaps?"

"Probably publicity."

"Good morning!" Azevedo peeks in, and I instinctively hide the envelope behind my back. Carmen exits.

"Have you started organizing the event?"

"Planning to dive into it this weekend."

"Great!" he says before leaving. Then, he hesitates and doubles back. "Is everything okay, Melissa?"

"Yeah, everything's fine."

The phone rings, and I jolt. Azevedo's still at the door, eyeing me.

"If you need anything, let me know."

"I'm good, just a bit tired."

He seems convinced and leaves. I pick up the phone.

"Has he arrived? Sure, send him in."

I take a deep breath, trying to shake off thoughts from the pantry conversation. I'll figure out how to handle it later. I can't afford to waste my time thinking about it now.

The first meeting is with a big-shot soccer player who strayed. He comes in, all cheery, convinced I'll help him screw his wife over. The meeting turns into a rant, with him listing every fault of his wife's as if that justifies cheating on her with his physiotherapist. Then he spins this theory about her cheating on him too. I can't quite figure out if he's lost touch with reality or just trying to manipulate me. Some clients should seriously consider an acting career—they're that convincing. I force a smile, nodding along, but my attention checks out halfway through.

Sometimes I wonder if this law gig is what I signed up for. But hey, to gain experience and ace those exams for the Judicial Studies Center, I've got to bite the bullet. Truth be told, I'm not even sure if I want to become a judge, but I'm going through the motions. It's the expected path, following in the footsteps of my father and my grandfather.

She bites into a lot of things.

Phone buzzes with a text, probably Rodrigo.

"Are you even listening? I'm telling you she cheated on me too!"

I sneak a peek at my phone and crack a discreet smile.

"Yeah, I hear you. Your wife cheated on you, right? Do you have any solid evidence?"

"I don't have anything concrete, but I know she did."

"You checked for proof?"

He pulls out his phone and starts scrolling, so I sneak a peek at the text. It's from Rodrigo!

Hey there, angel. Thinking about you.

The soccer player is still glued to his phone. I glance at the watch—it's almost eleven. My next client's due soon, so I nudge Mr. Soccer out the door.

"Hey, I have to run. I have another meeting coming up. If you find any proof your wife's been playing around, let me know."

He reluctantly stands up. I walk him to the door, and we exchange a handshake goodbye.

"I'll dig up that proof," he says.

I gently usher him out. Settling back at my desk, I grab my phone. I need to text Rodrigo before my next appointment.

Hey there, missed you tons, Rodrigo.

Missed you too, angel.

Love you!

You know I love you too. Can't wait to see you.

How can I not love this guy?

When are you landing in Lisbon?

Just touched down.

Awesome! Really need to catch up!

We'll have time to catch up.

Having one of those rough days at work.

That guy still giving you grief?

Without Rodrigo's support, I'd be lost.

Yeah, he acted like a jerk again.

What did he do this time?

My boss asked me to organize a retreat for our clients, and he told me event planning suits me better than lawyering. He's a misogynist jerk.

What an asshole! You should totally let your boss know.

I don't want to come off as a whiner.

It's up to you, angel, but I think you should call out that dude. You don't need this hassle.

I just want to be with you and forget about everything else.

Rodrigo is the only good thing in my life right now.

How about hitting up the Estoril Tennis Club tomorrow?

Sounds like a plan!

Meet you there at four?

Absolutely.

Then we can hang out at your place.

Is your place still a construction zone?

Don't even get me started. I'm meeting with the contractor tomorrow morning.

The never-ending renovation of Rodrigo's place is a total nightmare. It was already in progress when we met, and it's dragging on forever.

Okay, we'll stick to my place, as usual.

I can't wait to be with you again. I miss your body.

I'm probably blushing like crazy. Thank goodness I'm alone in the office. While I think of a clever response, another text pops up from him.

I've gotta go. Catch you tomorrow, angel. Love you!

Love you too!

I stash my phone away, feeling a mix of excitement and guilt. I'm psyched to see him tomorrow, but I can't shake this guilt because I haven't come clean about what went down between Claudio and me. I've never had the courage to tell him exactly what happened, fearing how he might react.

I lean back in my chair and feel something against my back. Oh, the envelope! Totally slipped my mind. This time, I take a closer look and spot something written in faded letters. It reads "Invitation." Almost gets lost amid the flowers. But what kind of invitation is this? The hortensias illustration triggers memories of wanting to study Arts instead of Law, but my father shot that idea down. I hold onto the envelope, torn about opening it. What if it's some dumb prank from Claudio and his crew?

She's probably banged every customer at that joint.

The phone rings, and I stash the envelope in my bag. It's Carmen letting me know the next client's here.

The rest of the day whizzes by with meetings, calls, and prepping for Monday's hearing. Before I know it, it's seven in the evening. I have almost everything set, planning to review it all at home on Saturday. I'm not feeling up for anything else today. I'm about to shut down the computer when I spot someone at the office door. Claudio's leaning against the frame, arms crossed.

"What do you want?" I ask, shifting my gaze back to the screen.

"Have you started planning the party yet?"

"It's none of your business."

"It's everyone's business; I work here too, you know."

"Leave me alone, Claudio. I'm not in the mood for your antics."

"Is Daddy's girl throwing a fit?"

I don't bother replying. Not worth it.

"You need a drink. Let's go out tonight."

After everything that went down, he's got some nerve!

"I'm not interested."

"Quit faking it, Mel. I know you like to toss a few back and have a blast."

"Get out!"

Instead of leaving, he steps closer to my desk.

"Stop pretending. I know you."

I lift my gaze from the screen and meet his eyes.

"And you stop spreading lies about me."

"Lies?"

"I heard you in the pantry."

"So what?" He chuckles. "Didn't tell any lies."

I power down the computer and face him again.

"You know that's not what happened."

He leans in, resting his hands on the desk.

"Do you enjoy playing lawyer?"

"I'm not playing. I take my work seriously."

"You still don't get it, do you? A woman's place is in the house, ready to pleasure her man when he arrives."

"Get out!"

"That's what women are meant for: to please the male of the species."

I rise from my seat.

"Get out!"

He smirks.

"No need to be hysterical, I'll leave. We'll continue this talk some other time."

What an absolute jerk!

"We've got nothing to discuss."

"You're mistaken, Mel. We're just starting," he says, circling the desk and coming closer. A shiver runs down my spine. "You'll break," he whispers in my ear, "it might not be today or tomorrow, but you'll break."

His words send chills down my spine.

"Get out!" I say, my voice trembling.

He sneers and exits without another word. I rush to the door, locking it securely. Sitting back down, I attempt slow breaths to calm myself. What a jerk! I shut my eyes, waiting for my heart to steady. When I feel composed, I shut down the computer, gather my things, and cautiously peer into the corridor, dreading running into him. Seeing no one, I quickly grab my bag and make a swift exit. I can't bear another second in the office.

Was that a threat, or am I overreacting? No, it definitely sounded like a threat. Rodrigo's right; I should report Claudio to Azevedo. But what if I report him and Azevedo does nothing? Or worse, what if I report him and Azevedo takes his side? It might be best to keep my mouth shut, pretend nothing happened. Maybe he'll leave me alone. But what if he doesn't? I feel like my head is about to explode. I need to stop thinking about this or I'll drive myself crazy.

I hurry through the reception area, giving Carmen a hasty goodbye. Before heading home, I need to buy a bottle of vodka and tampons. There's a supermarket nearby on the street, but I decide against going in. I'd rather not chance bumping into anyone from the office. Instead, I decide to take the metro to São Sebastião and head over to the El Corte Inglés supermarket.

Chapter 4

I wake up feeling lethargic. I roll over and keep my eyes shut, savoring those extra moments before hauling myself out of bed. I'm still groggy, but something feels off. It's like a whisper nudging me that I'm not in my room. The mattress? Way comfier than mine. I open my eyes and I'm staring at this metal bed, surrounded by blinking monitors. I'm in a hospital room. How did I get here?! I try to shake it off, but I'm stuck in this numb, floating state.

The room's door swings open, and in strides a woman around her forties, decked out in a blue uniform.

"Good morning! I'm Nurse Eva. How are you feeling?"

Nurse Eva is petite with a plump frame and a big pair of boobs, probably a hit with male patients. Not my cup of tea, though; I'm neither a guy nor into women, so her charm's lost on me. Her face is familiar, but I can't pinpoint where I've seen her before. The nurse beams at me, sporting this overly cheerful grin, as if I'm at a luxury spa, not in a hospital. I stay silent, prompting her to step closer. Aha, caught a glimpse of a pimple on her chin that she tried to conceal. Someone needs a crash course in hiding those. I could help. I'm an expert at hiding flaws.

"How're you feeling, Melissa?" she chirps, trying to get cozy with the personal touch, using my name like it's the golden ticket to connection. Nice try, but I'm still floating, lady.

"I feel numb," I say, my voice sounding weirdly slurred.

"That's normal, it's just the meds," she explains, focusing on the monitors like they hold the world's secrets.

Thank goodness for meds, beats a bottle of Smirnoff any day. The supermarket scene pops into my head. A bottle of Smirnoff, a box of tampons, sirens blaring, ambulance ride, and then darkness. Feels like eons ago.

"What day is it?"

"Saturday."

Huh, I didn't sleep as much I thought.

"Did I really have a heart attack?"

"The Doctor will fill you in," she deflects, her eyes glued to those screens.

I decide not to press further. My chest isn't screaming, and my breathing's okay. Better than my dramatic floor display at the supermarket. Maybe they put a pacemaker in there or, God forbid, a pig's heart! Nasty thought. Even on this mystery drug, my mind's running wild. This is why I love my sleep. When insomnia isn't crashing the party, my brain gives me a rest.

"I need to measure your blood pressure and check your pulse."

I try to focus on Nurse Eva to get my mind off things. There's this nagging feeling like I've seen her before. As she checks my blood pressure, I notice a tiny nose piercing. I always thought nurses couldn't wear piercings. Me? I'd never wear one. My colleagues would tease me, and heck, some judges might even stop me from entering the courtroom. I can't have that since I've got a hearing on Monday. Nurse Eva leans down to check my blood pressure, I can't help but notice her, uh, figure, and that's when it hits me where I've seen her.

"Your blood pressure looks good, and your pulse too," she says.

"I know you," I blurt out.

"I've been at this hospital for years, so you might've seen me around."

"No, not from the hospital."

"Then I'm stumped."

"You were shopping at El Corte Inglés supermarket yesterday evening, right?"

"Yeah, but how'd you know that?"

"I remember you. You were wearing a tight red dress."

"Yep, that was me," she says, then she squints, like she's trying to recall. "After I left, I was waiting for my ride when I saw an ambulance pull up. Was it for you?"

I nod.

"Was your boyfriend coming to pick you up?" I know it's prying, but I can't help myself.

"No boyfriend."

"From the way you were dressed, it looked like you were heading out for a date."

"Yeah, but he's not my boyfriend. We had fun, but it's a one-night thing for me. I rarely do repeats."

I probably look intrigued or something because she starts laughing.

"At thirty-five, I decided I was done with being used, so I figured I'd play the field. Have a blast, but no attachments."

"That's an option," I mutter, not sure what else to say.

"You know how it is with guys, right? They always seem to want just one thing from us women: sex. After being let down too many times, I figured I'd play the same game. I go out, have a blast, but when it's bedtime, it's just me in my bed."

Hearing her talk makes me realize I want the complete opposite. I want Rodrigo in my bed every night. I want to build a life with him. I want to start a family with him. Because he's the one. I knew he was the one from the moment I first saw him.

Nurse Eva gets a message and steps away with her phone in hand. Suddenly, I remember I had plans with Rodrigo, but I can't remember what they were.

"What time is it?"

She doesn't answer, engrossed in her phone.

"What time is it?"

It's like I'm talking to a wall. The allure of the virtual world seems to overshadow everything here in the room. And if we think about it, how can the real world compete with the virtual world? The virtual world is where influencers flaunt perfect lives and flawless bodies—a far cry from our real world. Here, in the real world, we deal with pre-date pimples, arguments with friends, toxic colleagues, or the embarrassing supermarket fainting episode that lands us in the hospital. In the real world, you're stuck with who you are—no magical filters to change it.

"Nurse Eva, do you know what time it is?" I insist.

"It's three p.m.," she replies, eyes still glued to her phone. She must be setting up her next date or something.

It clicks. I was supposed to meet Rodrigo at the Estoril Tennis Club. I'm not a fan of tennis—it bores me to death—but Rodrigo loves it, and I do anything to make him happy. Three p.m., hmm, what time did the tournament start? I try to remember, but my head just throbs. Whatever. The main thing is not to leave him hanging. Sometimes he has to bail on our plans, but I get it. I'm bummed, but I get it. Rodrigo's got a high-flying job as a pilot at Emirates. I decide to shoot him a text. My voice is in no condition for a call.

"Hey, where's my phone?"

The nurse is still fixated on her screen.

"I hate to bother you, but I really need to reach my fiancé," I push. Rodrigo isn't officially my fiancé, but Nurse Eva doesn't need that detail. He says as long as he's flying those long hauls at Emirates, proposing isn't on the cards. But he's mentioned that once he shifts to shorter European flights, we'll get engaged. If I spilled this to Nurse Eva, she'd probably sermonize about men, and I'm not in the mood for lectures. I'm floating here and her theories aren't on my radar, especially when she's not exactly on point. Not all men fit the same mold.

She finally glances at me and chuckles. I brace for some sarcastic quip about men, but instead, she says, "We put your stuff on that bedside table," and then exits the room.

I pop open the bedside table drawer, and there's my bag. It feels like an eternity to fish out my phone. I'm moving at a snail's pace. I pull up the messages, tap on 'new message', and then hesitate before typing.

Sorry, can't make it today.

I hit send and clutch the phone, waiting for his response. Leaning back against the pillows, I await the doctor's visit.

Hey, angel. Everything okay?

For a moment, I consider texting back all's good, but then I give up.

I'm in the hospital.

What happened? Are you alright?

What should I tell him when I'm still clueless about what happened myself?

I was feeling ill, but now I'm doing better. Still waiting for the doctor to swing by.

I'm on my way. Which hospital are you in?

I suddenly realize I don't even know where I am. I glance around for a hint and notice the hospital's name printed on the sheets.

I'm at Santa Maria Hospital, I reply.

I'm coming right away.

You don't need to, I type.

Of course I do, angel.

His answer makes me smile.

"You're awfully smiley," Nurse Eva remarks as she returns to grab some stuff.

"My fiancé's coming to see me," I relish the sound of the word 'fiancé'.

Nurse Eva offers a smirk and heads out. I can't help but feel a pang of pity for her. There must be a lot behind her deep dislike for men.

I lay there, staring at the ceiling, recalling the day I met Rodrigo. I haven't forgotten it; it was eleven months ago in Dubai. Ruth figured I needed a break after what went down with Claudio and convinced me to join her for a week's getaway. On the flight to Dubai, she hit it off with a plastic surgeon attending a conference. That day, while the surgeon had free time in the afternoon, Ruth went out with him. I returned to the hotel loaded with shopping bags. With the scorching heat in that dry land, shopping centers were my escape. As I entered the hotel lobby, I noticed an elevator had just arrived and hurried toward it. As the doors started closing, I hastily lunged forward, forgetting about my bags. In my rush, some of them got caught, and as I tugged to pull them inside, I ended up tripping and falling. There I sat surrounded by a heap of bags when someone reached out to help. Glancing sideways, I first saw a pair of black shoes and dark blue pants. I grabbed the hand extended to me, surprised by how easily he lifted me up. And when I looked up at his face, I was captivated. Blond hair and striking looks. Our eyes locked, sending a shiver down my spine. His blue eyes stood out against the dark blue suit.

"Did you get hurt?" he asked.

I couldn't muster an immediate response. I was too stunned to form a single word, let alone a sentence.

"Are you alright?" he insisted.

I stepped back a few inches, letting go of his hand. His touch sent shivers down my spine. Taking a deep breath, I tried to focus. The last thing I wanted was for him to think I was awkward. My throat felt dry; I worried I wouldn't be able to speak.

"Yeah. Thanks for your help," I managed to say.

He flashed a smile and bent down to collect the scattered bags. It was then I noticed the gold-striped cuff on his suit – a pilot's uniform. As he handed me the bags, our fingers brushed, and that jolt of electricity zapped between us again. He seemed disinterested, swiftly grabbing his phone after passing me the bags. I must look awful, I thought. I stole a glance at the elevator mirror. My hair was a bit disheveled, and I was blushing. I quickly fixed my hair and smoothed out my dress. After making a fool of myself, the least I could do was regain composure.

The elevator stopped at the twentieth floor. He prepared to leave, and I felt a pang of disappointment. As I reached for the shopping bags, I sensed his gaze fixed on my back. Turning around, I caught him still standing at the elevator door, looking at me.

"See you around," he said.

I must have looked completely stunned because he chuckled and winked. When the elevator door closed, I mentally scolded myself for the embarrassing display I'd put on.

When I returned to my room, I received a message from Ruth, saying she'd be dining with the surgeon. Once again, I'd be dining alone. I showered, slipped into a snug black dress, and applied makeup. I spent a good half-hour scrutinizing myself in the mirror, making sure I looked impeccable in case I bumped into the pilot again. Then, I headed out and called for the elevator.

Arriving at the ground floor, I headed for the bar. A drink before dinner was in order. As I entered the bar, I suddenly halted. A Chinese couple behind me stumbled, nearly causing another embarrassing scene. They passed by muttering something, but I paid no mind. My attention was fixated on someone else – the stranger from the elevator, now seated at the bar sans pilot's uniform. Surrounding him were two young, stunning women who looked like flight attendants —one redhead, the other brunette. The redhead whispered in his ear, making him laugh.

I took a seat at the opposite end of the bar and ordered a Martini. From the corner of my eye, I noticed the women still hovering around him. He sat at the counter, elbows resting, sipping a Martini too. The redhead took a sip from his glass, and he leaned in to whisper something to her. That's when his gaze met mine, and my heart skipped a beat. Despite the redhead's proximity, he couldn't seem to take his eyes off me. Downing his Martini in one go, he stood up, flashing me a smile. When he sat down beside me, and I almost forgot to breathe.

"Hi, I'm Rodrigo. What's your name?"

I took another sip of my Martini.

"Melissa, but call me Mel."

"Mel..." he repeated, savoring my name. "Nice to meet you, Mel."

He ordered another drink, and we silently sipped our Martinis. When he suggested showing me the view from his room, I chuckled.

"Does that line usually work?"

He grinned.

"Yes."

"I don't know..." I toyed with my glass. "We've just met. You're still a stranger."

"I can stop being one."

"Alright, but let's stick to seeing the view."

He smiled.

"I'll get the bill."

When he unlocked his room, he pushed me against the wall, his body pressed close to mine. I shut my eyes. No talk. Just kissing, nibbling, sighing, and moaning. I've enjoyed sex before with other boyfriends who had experience, but nothing compared to what I experienced with Rodrigo. I spent that night in his room, then the next, and the one after. When I came back from Dubai, I was completely in love.

I'm lost in these memories when the door to the room swings open, and an elderly man in a white coat steps in. He could pass for my grandfather. My parents trail behind him. I must look perplexed because I certainly wasn't expecting them there. My mother approaches the bedside and plants a kiss on my cheek.

"Are you okay, Mel? We were so worried about you!" she frets.

I nod. My father, on the other hand, stands near the door, barely casting a glance my way. He seems annoyed. Unexpected situations are his kryptonite, and his daughter landing in the hospital definitely qualifies.

The doctor draws near, and my mother takes a seat at the edge of my bed.

"Good afternoon, Melissa. I'm Doctor António Silva. How are you feeling?"

Why does everyone keep asking the same thing? Should I spill that I feel like I'm floating? Probably not.

"Fine," I fib. Well, it's not an outright lie. I'm far better than I was sprawled on the supermarket floor. Besides, I've learned long ago that when people ask how you are, they don't really want the truth. No one wants to hear you spend your weekends drowning your loneliness on the couch with vodka until you pass out.

"Great. That's good to hear."

I almost blurt out my urge to escape, but I bite my tongue. Lately, I feel a constant itch to flee wherever I am.

"Can you tell me what happened? Did I actually have a heart attack?"

The doctor settles on the bed's edge, adopting that solemn expression doctors wear when delivering grave news. Despite feeling numb, anxiety starts creeping in.

"No, Melissa. Your heart's fine."

Fine heart? Well, that's a relief! But if it wasn't a heart attack, then what was it? The doctor keeps that serious face, and now I'm thinking it might be worse than a heart attack.

"If it wasn't a heart attack, then what was it?"

My parents' stern expressions trigger thoughts that I might have something serious, perhaps more severe than a heart attack. A flood of diseases floods my mind, each one seemingly more alarming than the last. Maybe ignorance is bliss. I steal a glance at the doctor, who maintains the same stoic expression.

"You experienced a panic attack, Melissa," he says slowly.

A panic attack?! I arch an eyebrow, trying to process his words. The man must be mistaken. I must look perplexed (and I genuinely am), as he leans in closer and places a hand on my shoulder.

"A panic attack is a sudden burst of intense fear triggering extreme physical reactions..."

"I didn't have a panic attack."

"Melissa, listen..."

"I've already told you I didn't have a panic attack."

"Melissa, I've discussed this with your parents and explained everything. What you experienced in the supermarket was indeed a panic attack, not a heart attack."

"No, it wasn't."

"Yes, it was, Melissa."

The doctor is unyielding.

"We conducted several tests, and your heart is healthy. The results showed no abnormalities."

"I didn't have a panic attack because I've had two before, and they're not like this."

The first one happened before my trip to Dubai with Ruth. I was wrapping up arguments in a heated divorce case when I started feeling lightheaded, my heart racing, and hands sweating. I asked for a break, grabbed a bite, and returned to finish. Back then, I dismissed it as a drop in blood pressure. The second one happened right after I returned from Dubai, at a nightclub in Porto. Ruth got together with the doctor she'd met in Dubai, and I was supposed to meet Rodrigo, but he canceled due to being stranded at an Australian airport.

I see my mother trying not to gasp too loudly, her hand shooting up to cover her mouth. And bam! It hits me—I just blurted that out in front of my parents. I glance at the door and see my father's face, unchanged, stoic. Sometimes I wonder if he's secretly a robot pretending to be a human. Meanwhile, my mother's wearing this look of sheer horror. She's probably freaking out about how she's going to explain this to her friends. Mental health stuff is seriously tricky to explain. When I opened up to Ruth about it, she brushed it off, suggesting that a night out with drinks and fun would fix me up. Like, seriously? As if it were that simple. As if there were a panic switch I could easily flip off.

My father's face is still impassive, except for this raised eyebrow that screams disappointment, even though he doesn't say a word. No matter what I do, I can't seem to make him proud of me. Witnessing that disappointment during Sunday meals shatters me. But today, under the influence of this mysterious drug, I couldn't care less.

"How long have these panic attacks been going on?" the doctor inquires.

Now that I've started, might as well lay it all out there.

"I had the first one almost a year ago, then another. After the second, I went to see a doctor." I went to a doctor outside Lisbon because my mother knows all the doctors in the capital. "That's why I'm sure what happened in the supermarket wasn't a panic attack. It was completely different."

"Panic attacks vary. What you experienced, Melissa, was a severe panic attack. Your brain signaled danger to your body, and your body reacted to protect you."

"Are you sure? I felt a sharp pain on the left side of my chest."

"Yes, Melissa, I'm certain. Your heart's in good shape. It was a panic attack."

I glance at him, trying to understand, but the meds have clouded my thoughts. I nod and maybe manage a smile. I don't feel up for a debate.

"Who's the therapist you're seeing?" my mother asks.

For a second, I consider lying, then give up. She's a doctor herself (a gynecologist, but she knows nearly every doc in Lisbon and would uncover the truth in no time).

"No one."

"No one?!"

"That's right. The doctor I saw prescribed emergency pills, and that was it."

My father steps closer, and I can still spot the disappointment in his eyes.

"Doctor, I want my daughter transferred to the Arcos Clinic, as we discussed."

My mother nods along.

"Yes, of course. We'll arrange the transfer immediately."

My father faces me finally.

"It's all arranged. I've spoken to Azevedo. You'll take a few weeks off and get admitted to the clinic."

Cláudio won't let this slide once he finds out. I'll be the office joke.

"I have a hearing on Monday."

"Don't worry, everything's sorted with Azevedo."

"But I've got everything set for the hearing."

"It's all taken care of," he insists. "You've got to take care of yourself, Melissa. In three months, you've got the aptitude exam for the Judicial Studies Center, and you need to be prepared."

Of course, it's the exams. That's why my father's so worked up. His worrywart side is showing. His daughter needs to be calm and well-behaved, not on edge if she's aiming to be a judge. Nobody wants a frazzled judge.

My phone buzzes with a new message. I hope it's Rodrigo. I need him to get me out of here, pronto.

Sorry, angel, but I can't make it. Colleague's sick, and I've got to cover for him. Got a flight to Dubai in half an hour.

Sometimes, I hate his job.

It's okay.

Sorry.

Don't worry, I'm good now.

Love you, angel.

Love you too. Safe flight.

"You can set up the transfer," I hear my father saying.

My father always has everything under control. Just like when he decided to pay a visit to Azevedo after I started at the office. Even after five years there, I still get an earful from my colleagues. They all believe he pressured Azevedo into hiring me, but truth be told, he didn't even know who my father was when I was hired. I used my mother's maiden name.

"No," I say.

"Excuse me?" The doctor's taken aback.

I'm still floating, feeling like I can do anything. So, for the first time ever, I challenge my father.

"I don't want to go to the Clinic."

"Quit being silly, Mel. My daughter isn't in any position to make decisions."

"I'm not crazy, Dad. I might have had a panic attack, but I can make decisions just fine."

"Mel, you need help."

"I'm not going to that place where rich, drugged-up kids go."

My father's eyes widen, and I can tell he's furious, but he doesn't say a word. I think he's shocked I'm going against him.

"Maybe a clinic in Porto or Madrid would be better," my mother suggests.

"For heaven's sake, Madalena, our daughter's unwell, and all you care about is what others will say."

"I don't want to go to any clinic. I'm good."

The doctor places a hand on my shoulder and offers the most sympathetic expression he can summon (the same one he probably adopts with schizophrenics facing violent commands from their inner voices):

"You should take some time off," he suggests.

"Mel, you're not fit for work," my father insists.

"Fine, I'll take a few days off, but I'm not going to that Clinic." The meds they gave me are working wonders. "Dad, thanks for talking to Azevedo. I know you're trying to help, but I don't want to go there." I pause, expecting him to lecture me about doing as I'm told, but he doesn't say anything.

"Mel, please," my mother urges.

"Mom, it's okay. I'm fine. It was just a hectic day, and I felt sick. That's all. I'm good." I try to persuade myself and her that it's true. "I'll take a few days off, and I'll be okay."

Realizing they can't change my mind, my parents leave with the doctor, and I wait for Nurse Eva to remove the catheter so I can get dressed and leave. In a few minutes, she arrives.

"Your boyfriend didn't show up?"

"He had an emergency at work."

"An emergency? Is he a doctor or a firefighter?"

"No, he's an airline pilot."

"Pilot? I didn't know pilots had emergencies."

"One of his colleagues fell ill, and he had to cover for him."

"Don't be naive, Melissa."

"What do you mean?"

"Men handle illness terribly. He's probably out having drinks with his buddies or another woman. Men always have a couple of female 'friends' to turn to."

"Rodrigo isn't like that."

"Are you sure?"

"Yes, absolutely!"

"You're done. You can get dressed."

She doesn't understand Rodrigo. If she knew him like I do, she'd know he's not like that. He truly loves me.

Chapter 5

I wake up, feeling like I'm stuck underwater. I'm conscious, but this heavy numbness holds me down, like there's a weight on my chest. The bed seems familiar, yet somehow it doesn't feel like mine. Slowly opening my eyes, it takes a while to focus on the ceiling. Finally, I realize where I am—a wave of relief hits me. I'm not in the hospital anymore. I'm at my parents' place, in my old teenage room with that somewhat tacky pink lamp. I remember how I insisted on redoing the room in shades of pink and baby blue, even swapped my grandma's lamp for this bubblegum pink thing. Looking at it now, I can't believe I ever thought it was a good idea.

Memories start coming back, piecing together how I ended up here. After leaving the hospital, heavily medicated, I wound up at my parents'. I tried to head back to my own place, but they insisted I stay put. The trip from Lisbon to Cascais, where my parents live, was painfully silent, almost like attending a funeral. Once home, I just went straight to my room and crashed. I can't remember anything beyond that.

I drag myself to the bathroom and attend to the basics: splashing water on my face, stealing a quick glance at my reflection in the mirror. Then there's this weird disconnect. The person in the mirror isn't me. Same hair, eyes, nose, and mouth, but something feels off. Stepping back, I can't shake the feeling that I'm looking at a stranger. What on earth is happening to me?!

"Mel?" my mother's voice pulls me back to reality.

"I'm in the bathroom, Mom."

"Everything okay, dear?"

"Yes, I'm going to shower."

I get into the shower. Standing under the water, it's almost as if I'm trying to wash away the memories of the past few days. But those memories won't go away.

After I'm done, reality sinks in—I'll have to make do with my old teenage clothes stuffed in the closet. I settle on a pair of jeans and a pink tee with an illustration of Louboutin shoes—thanks to my mother for trying to grant my wish. I remember how my friends' parents also shot down the idea of Louboutin's, despite our thinking that happiness hinged on owning a pair just like Carrie's (we were naive, but happy). I slip on the tee and decide to skip the mirror this time. I don't want to look at the girl in the mirror again.

"Mel, time for your medication."

My mother walks in, holding pills in one hand and a glass of water in the other. Seems she's turned into my nurse.

"I'm okay," I say, pushing away the pills.

"You need to take these."

"Mom, seriously, I'm fine. I don't need meds."

She shakes her head.

"Please, Mel, don't make this harder. Just take them."

I reluctantly take the pills and pop them in my mouth. She hands me the water and stands there until I swallow.

"Do you want to come to the living room, or do you want to rest a little longer? We're having lunch at home today."

We never do lunch at home on Sundays. It's always our spot in Cascais (same place where Carmen's husband took her to dinner). My parents must feel mortified by what went down. By now, word about Judge Lacerda de Brito's daughter having a breakdown in a supermarket might be all over Lisbon. Or worse, they might think I OD'd, considering my parents wanted to ship me to the Arcos Clinic, the place where Lisbon's elite sends their troubled kids. I'm beat, and the last thing I want is to deal with my parents and their awkward silences.

"I'll just rest a bit more."

"Okay. I'll call you when lunch is ready."

"What's for lunch?" I ask. Today's the housekeeper's day off, and I can't picture my parents' ordering takeout.

"Spaghetti Bolognese, your favorite," she says, trying to crack a smile.

"Wait, are you cooking?!" I'm genuinely surprised. I can't remember the last time I saw her cook.

"Definitely not, Mel. You know I'm terrible in the kitchen. Your father's the chef today."

I'm floored. Ages ago My father used to cook amazingly well, but ever since he got involved with the Supreme Court, cooking (or spending time with me) became a rarity.

She leaves, and I fish out my phone from my purse. There's a new text from Rodrigo.

Feeling better, angel? Out of the hospital yet?

Yeah, feeling heaps better. Are you still in Dubai?

I put my phone down and spot an envelope in my purse. Grabbing it, I turn it over, trying to remember what's it about. Carmen gave it to me on Friday, just before the chaos at the supermarket. Friday feels like ages ago, the office seems a world away, and Claudio, even further. Thinking about all that starts to make me anxious, so I shake my head, trying to push those thoughts away. I stare at the envelope, imagining countless possibilities until I gather the nerve to open it. I need to know what's inside this mysterious envelope. It holds a card with the same flower illustration and the following text:

Congratulations! You won a week's vacation at the Hortensias Garden - Rural Tourism unit.

Wow, what a surprise! A whole week's vacation at the Hortensias Garden. But wait, did I even enter any contests? And where on earth is this Hortensias Garden? Flipping the card over, it reads:

Hortensias Garden. São Miguel. Azores[4].

Well, that clarifies it. Spending a few days in the Azores might not be a bad idea. I check the card, but there's no extra info, nothing about the room type, amenities, or even if breakfast's included. What kind of contest is this anyway? I seriously don't recall entering one. Maybe it's an office prank, but it doesn't seem like something Claudio would do. It's too innocent for that jerk. I slide the card back into the envelope, and as I do, I realize there's something else inside. A handwritten note.

Dear Mel,
I'd love for you to visit my rural tourism spot in the Azores.
Love,
Aunt Gabriela

And below, her phone number.

Why on earth would Aunt Gabriela send me an invite? And why now, after all this time?! I'm feeling more and more confused.

I grab my notebook and start sketching Nurse Eva, with her piercing. Drawing is my escape. When I'm drawing, it's like I'm in a trance, and all my problems vanish. I once got scolded by a judge for sketching people in the courtroom. Today, I decide Nurse Eva's getting a huge pair of boobs. I doubt she'd mind, and her male friends wouldn't either.

I can't shake off thoughts about my aunt's invite. Why now, after all these years? The door opens again, and my mother strolls in.

---

4 The Azores is an archipelago of Portugal composed of nine volcanic islands located in the Atlantic Ocean. São Miguel Island is the largest and most populous island in the Azores, and its capital is Ponta Delgada. Ponta Delgada is the largest municipality and executive capital of the Azores, and it is the economic and administrative capital of the region.

"Lunch is ready," she announces. As she's leaving, she spots the envelope on the bed. "What's that?"

"An invitation to a college alumni party," I fib.

"Going to parties and drinking alcohol isn't a good idea, Mel. You need to rest."

What I really need is to be left alone.

"Yeah, I know, Mom." I stash the envelope back in my purse to dodge more questions.

We eat in silence, seated at the grand dining table in the dining room that my mother insisted on setting up with all the grandeur. We could've easily eaten in the kitchen, but my parents don't even do breakfast there. That's what having a housekeeper does. They're spoiled. I was too, until I moved out on my own. Then I had to fend for myself. When I moved out, I didn't even know how to cook rice, never used an iron, and had never paid my own bills. But I got the hang of being independent, and I'm proud of it. Actually, life was going smoothly; college graduation, a job without relying on my father's help, living in the apartment my grandparents left me, and hanging out with Maria, Ana, and Ruth. Sure, work hours were long, but I still had the energy to go out with them on weekends. But everything changed when they moved away. Now, here I am, all alone, stuck in a job I hate, just waiting for Rodrigo to propose.

Another message pops in.

Yes, still in Dubai.

When are you heading back to Lisbon?

Not sure. Got a ton of flights lined up in the next few days. My colleague is still out sick.

That's a shame. Wish I could be with you.

Same here, angel. Miss you loads.

"Mel, can you give your phone a break?"

I've got to run. My mother's on my case, as usual.

Love you, angel!

Love you too!

I drop my phone and pick up the fork, but my appetite's vanished.

"You're not eating?" my mother asks.

My father stays quiet, hardly making eye contact.

"Having a bite." I shove pasta into my mouth, hoping she'll leave me alone.

We return to silence. I poke at the pasta, lost in thoughts about tomorrow - back to the office and the court hearing at ten. Luckily, I've prepped everything already. My parents seem to have lost their appetites too. They're picking at their food like me. My mother's back on some diet, this time Paleo, so forcing down the pasta must be a real effort for her.

"You don't like the pasta?" my father finally acknowledges my existence.

"The pasta's good, Dad. I'm just not hungry."

"For a sec I thought my cooking had tanked," he smiles, a sad smile. "Are you okay, Mel?"

"Yeah, just a bit queasy. Must be the meds."

"Those pills have side effects, but you need them."

"Yeah, Mom, I know."

We lapse into silence again. I keep shoveling pasta, trying to please them. The rest of lunch feels like a gloomy affair. After finishing, she brings out homemade chocolate mousse, my father's handy work no doubt. Seems he had a productive morning.

"I don't feel like having desert."

Ignoring me, he fills a bowl.

"You have to eat, Mel. Can't take meds on an empty stomach."

While eating the mousse, I tally how many CrossFit sessions it'll take to burn these calories. Leo and the Beach Body Project come to mind, and guilt creeps in. Shouldn't be eating this mousse.

"We need to sort out the clinic matter."

"We'll discuss it later," my father says. "Let your daughter finish her lunch."

"I'm back to work tomorrow."

My father raises an eyebrow. I already know what he's about to say.

"Mel, I've spoken to Azevedo. You're not going in tomorrow," his voice, as calm as ever. Come to think of it, I've never seen him excited or laughing out loud. Well, at least not recently. I mean, there was that time at the zoo when we found a chimpanzee named Fernando, just like my father. "Hi, I'm Fernando," the sign read. We laughed like crazy. I think that was the last time I saw him laughing out loud. That memory feels like a lifetime ago, like it belongs to someone else's life, not mine.

"I have a hearing at ten."

"Everything's taken care of. Azevedo handed the case to one of your colleagues."

"Dad..."

"If you don't want to go to the Arcos Clinic, that's okay, Mel. We can find another clinic or another solution."

"Maybe a clinic in Porto or Madrid," my mother insists. "We don't want the press finding out about this. A clinic outside Lisbon might be better."

I can tell from my father's expression that he disagrees with her. He seems angry. The last thing I need now is for them to argue because of me.

"You're not fit to go to work, Mel. You need to take care of your health."

"I'm fine, dad. I'm going to work tomorrow."

I don't know where this courage came from, but I decide I'm not going to let my father make all the decisions as if I were a child.

"I've already spoken to Azevedo. You're taking a month off. You still have plenty of vacation days from last year. You need to rest and..."

And stop being a nervous wreck, is that what you mean, dad? That I need to fix my head because I had a meltdown, lost my mind, went crazy? That's what I feel like saying, but instead I say:

"I'm going to work tomorrow, it's decided." I get up from the table. "Now I'm heading to my place to rest."

I leave the dining room without looking back.

Chapter 6

My father wanted to drive me home, but I said no. I don't need him to babysit me. I'm at the Cascais station, waiting for the train to Lisbon. Sundays are supposed to be chill, but this one isn't. The sun comes out and suddenly everyone from Lisbon and nearby areas flocks to the beach. I take a deep breath, soaking in the sun's warmth on my skin. It feels good—just the right temperature, not too hot, not too cold. Perfect. It's mid-afternoon, and there's still a bunch of people at the beach, so the station isn't too packed. The train arrives, I hop on, and take a seat. A few more people get in, and the train starts moving. I rest my head against the train window and shut my eyes. The sun keeps shining on my face, and I let myself drift off. I figure when I get home, I'll have to lie down again. We stop at Paço de Arcos station, and I glance out the window to see a crowd outside. I can't figure out where all these people came from. The doors open, and a flood of people rushes in. They're shoving, pushing, arguing. A pregnant woman tries to find a seat, but a tall, strong guy is hogging the only priority seat.

"Excuse me, that seat's for priority passengers."

The man gives her a nasty look and stays put.

"Excuse me, that's for pregnant women or disabled people."

"Then maybe you shouldn't have gotten pregnant," the man snaps rudely.

"The lady's right," an elderly woman starts to say, but the man shoots her an angry glare, and she falls silent. Nobody else says a word. The man must be six feet tall, looking like a bouncer at a club or something. Muscular, shaved head, tattoos on his arms and neck. Nobody dares to confront him.

I stand up and signal to the pregnant woman.

"You can take my seat."

She looks relieved and makes her way through the crowd.

"Thank you!"

I take her spot amidst the chaos, and before I know it, I'm surrounded by people—tons of them. My throat tightens. People are everywhere, no way out. I glance around, looking for an escape, but I'm trapped in that sea of bodies. A woman accidentally elbows me and gives an apologetic look. We stop at the next station, and nobody gets off. Instead, more people pile in, pushing us further into the carriage. As the train starts moving again, I notice many passengers still waiting at the station for the next train. I'm stuck between a couple and a guy who seems to be friends with the other. He's tall, built, tattoos all over. My throat feels even tighter, and I start feeling dizzy. I clutch onto the nearest seat tightly. Two more stations until my stop. I start counting the seconds in my head, trying to ignore the crowd, but the suffocating feeling doesn't fade. The couple decides to start kissing right there, practically on top of me. Seriously, what's wrong with these people? I turn away from them, trying to shift, but it's hard to move.

"Where do you want to go?" the huge, tattooed guy in front of me asks. I'm surprised by the high-pitched voice coming from that massive body, and for a second, I feel like I might burst out laughing in his face. I lift my chin, trying to hold it in, but I can't say a word. He leans down a bit, eye level with me, and asks:

"Everything okay?"

I nod, but he doesn't seem convinced. I notice a snake tattoo starting from his elbow and ending at his neck, as if it's coiling around him. There are more tattoos on his other arm, but I can't make them out.

We're approaching the next station, and I decide to get off, even though it's not my stop. I need to get out. I try to push through the crowd, but it's no use.

"Do you want to get off here?" the giant asks.

"Yes."

He grabs me around the waist with one arm and lifts me off the ground.

"What are you doing?!"

Then, he starts maneuvering through the crowd, carrying me under his arm like a sports bag. I try to kick, but he holds onto me. Is he taking me to his place or worse, some dingy basement filled with more tattooed giants? I'm about to scream for help when he says:

"Relax, I'm not going to hurt you. I just want to help you get out."

With his other arm, he pushes people aside, clearing a path toward the exit door. I hear the doors whistle to close, thinking I won't make it, but he keeps the door open with one hand. Then, he tosses me toward the door, and I leap out of the carriage, as if jumping onto a lifebuoy. As the doors close, I glance back, and the giant's smiling at me behind the train windows. I smile back, waving at him, feeling both foolish and grateful. He waves back, and I stand there, watching the train pull away, only realizing I'm crying when I feel a tear running down my neck.

When I finally get home and shut the door, I can finally breathe. After getting off the train, I decided to call an Uber. I just wasn't up for getting on another train.

I head to the bathroom and take out the pills I pretended to swallow from my pocket. They're disintegrating. I toss them into the toilet and flush. Then I glance at myself in the mirror. This time, I recognize myself, but what I see is a faded version of who I am. Messy hair, swollen eyes, dull skin. I dig into my bag, taking out the prescribed pills. I pop one white and one yellow pill as per the doctor's instructions and wash them down with water. This time, they go down.

Next, I head to the bedroom, getting everything ready for the next morning. I sit on the bed, going through my notes. The hearing kicks off at ten. When I'm done, I sit there, staring at the folder, starting to feel anxious. I take a deep breath.

You'll break. It might not be today or tomorrow, but you'll break.

I close the folder and step out of the room. Collapsing onto the couch, I check my phone. No new messages.

Are you awake? I text Rodrigo.

I decide to text Ruth too.

Hey! Can I give you a call?

Flipping on the TV, there's a show about the Azores playing. The host is in São Miguel's hot springs, savoring a stew cooked in a hole in the ground. Two men pull out a giant pot from the earth, and the presenter's excitement resembles that of a child discovering a treasure. "Come and try this exclusive Azorean delicacy," he says.

I dig into my bag and pull out the envelope. While the host devours the stew, I stare at the envelope for what feels like an eternity.

Glancing at my phone again, hoping for a new message alert, but there's nothing. Neither of them has replied. I consider texting Ana or Maria, but they're caught up with their husbands and kids. Well, Ana's still trying to get pregnant. As much as I love them, a pang of envy hits me. They seem to have their lives sorted while I feel more lost every day.

I glance back at the TV. Not even the smell of sulfur from the steam holes deters the host from his meal. The show's wrapping up, and the man, after gulping down the stew, shows a panoramic view of lake and ends with, "It's for this natural beauty and these delights that you must visit the Azores!"

THE #1 SUSTAINABILITY ARCHIPELAGUE IS WAITING FOR YOU I can read on a sign behind him.

I grab the envelope again, staring at the letter from my aunt. What if I gave her a call? No, that's a silly idea. But what if I did? I take a deep breath. I have a court hearing tomorrow; I can't just jet off to the Azores. But what if I gave her a call? No. I'm heading to work tomorrow. Everyone at the office probably knows what happened. Carmen, that gossip, always knows everything. I bet Azevedo told her, and she's already spread the word. I can picture the looks on my colleagues' faces when I walk in. Not pity, just smug grins.

You'll break. It may not be today or tomorrow, but you'll break.

I curl up on the sofa, trembling. His words won't leave my mind. I lie there for what feels like ages, trying to calm myself. If only I had a bottle of Smirnoff at home. I could use a drink so badly. I don't think the pills are working. Vodka would definitely hit faster.

When I finally manage to calm down, I grab my notepad and start sketching the giant who helped me. I draw the snake tattoo, but in my drawing, it's not constricting him, it's more like a hug, a protective one. I spend the next half-hour drawing him, putting a smile on his face because that's how I remember him, smiling behind the train window. I decide he's a *Cappuccino*. Behind that muscular frame lies a kind man, a true gentleman. Yes, he's *Cappuccino*, no doubt. I think he and Nurse Eva would make a great pair, if only she'd stop fearing falling in love.

Drawing helps me relax, and with a clearer head, I realize I'm not in any shape to head to work. I need to get out of Lisbon for a bit, sort myself out, and straighten up my life. Then I'll come back, and everything will be okay. Yes, everything will be okay. That's the plan. I grab my phone, dial the number I've got memorized, and take a deep breath. The phone on the other end rings once, twice, three times, and I consider hanging up.

"Yes?" says a voice on the other end.

Suddenly, I don't know what to say.

"Who is this?"

What should I say?

"Who is this?"

"Aunt Gabriela?"

"Mel?! Mel, darling, it's so good to hear your voice!"

Chapter 7

The plane starts its descent toward the island, getting ready to land. It's kind of ironic—I've been to Dubai, Tokyo, London, Madrid, even Ibiza, but never to the Azores. It's weird for a Portuguese person not to know their own country, right? My aunt lives in a small village on the island of São Miguel. Supposedly, it's the perfect place to chill and recharge, but I'm feeling jittery, even with my meds. I haven't told Rodrigo I came here. I'm scared he'll leave me if he knows my parents wanted to check me into a clinic. I'll just tell him I needed a vacation. Yes, that's it, I needed a vacation.

We're descending, and I glance out the window. The whole island's a vibrant green, surrounded by the bluest sea. It could've been a beautiful moment from a romantic movie if I wasn't feeling nauseous from the meds. And instead of Rodrigo beside me, there's this huge man who's taking up his seat and almost half of mine. I've been crammed between his bulk and the window for three hours. Not to mention the smell—the guy's been sweating buckets and wiping his forehead constantly.

When the plane lands, it bounces a bit. I'm so queasy that I don't know if I can hold back from throwing up. Back at the hospital, I asked the doctor to prescribe me the same mystery drug, but he chuckled and said it's only for emergencies. The pills he gave me are awful—they make me feel queasy and drowsy. I try to focus on my breathing: inhale, exhale, inhale, exhale... I don't want to vomit on myself.

Flashback to one wild night in the Algarve with Ruth. Summer break after the second year of college, she "borrowed" her father's Mercedes, and off we went to Albufeira. We hit a club at like three or four in the morning and boozed ourselves silly. I met this hot German guy and ended up spending the night with him on the beach. It was going great until I puked on him. He stormed off, not even a backward glance. It wasn't one of my best moments.

My seatmate keeps mopping his forehead with the handkerchief, and I can feel the moisture of his sweat when he rests his arm next to mine. I'm squished against the window. After a few more bumps, the plane finally lands, and I'm relieved I survived without vomiting or getting squashed by my neighbor. People start standing and grabbing their bags, but my neighbor stays put. With his broad shoulders, it's not even worth trying to get up. Honestly, I'm not in that big of a rush myself. I needed to leave Lisbon ASAP, before my parents stopped me from coming here and checked me into a clinic (or before I chickened out and checked myself in). I called my boss early in the morning, packed a few things, and dashed to the airport to catch the first flight to São Miguel, feeling like some fugitive on the run.

Azevedo didn't ask any questions. I don't know what my father told him, but he was cool about it. He said it was no problem, that my cases would go to my coworkers. Today's hearing got shifted to Jonas, who's probably cursed my name a bunch by now. He hates dealing with divorces.

The plane door opens, and people begin to disembark. Eventually, my neighbor decides to rise, treating me to a view of his massive butt crack, nearly brushing against my forehead. Seriously, why don't people buy clothes that fit?

Stepping off the plane, it's a gray, sterile scenario. All I see is concrete and planes. It's nothing like the green island I glimpsed from the window. We're walking to the airport on foot since there's no bus—it's just a few hundred meters from the runway to the terminal. I'm dragging my carry-on behind me, putting in a real effort. These pills make me feel weak. I start wondering how the heck I'll find my aunt. I've got no clue what she looks like. I only saw her when I was little, and her face's a total blur.

When we step into the terminal, I realize there's no need to worry. The airport is small and empty. It seems our plane was the only one that arrived at this time. Finding my aunt shouldn't be difficult. I follow the other passengers outside. Some take the bus, some take a taxi, and a few of us wait. By now, the hearing must have ended. I wonder how it went, so I take out my phone and call Jonas. I'm not in the mood to talk to him, but I need to know what happened.

"Good morning, Jonas."

"Well, well, well, look who it is, daddy's little girl."

"Cut the jokes. I just want to know how the hearing went."

"I can't tell you."

"You can't tell me?!"

"Orders from Azevedo."

"What does that mean?"

"You've got some nerve, Melissa. You decide to take a month off, just like that, and Azevedo says we can't bother you. So don't act smart. Where are you?"

"That's none of your business."

"I bet you're off in the Caribbean or Dubai."

I realize that Jonas probably doesn't know what happened yet.

"I'm not in the Caribbean or Dubai."

"I don't care where you are. I just know you're having fun, while we're stuck here with your cases."

"That's not it, Jonas."

"Of course it is, Melissa. I know why you took a vacation."

I take a deep breath. What rumor did Cláudio make up this time? I interrupt Jonas before he can say anything else.

"If you're not going to tell me how the hearing went, then we have nothing else to talk about. Goodbye." And I hang up.

I'm tired of Jonas, and I'm tired of Cláudio. I don't want to hear what he said about me. Just thinking about him gives me chills. Suddenly, I smell the cologne he was wearing that night. A citrusy touch with incense. I look around and realize that the perfume comes from a tall, muscular passenger with a crew cut. Another *Sour Milk* guy, I bet. That must be their official scent. I take a deep breath and look away. I need to stop thinking about Cláudio.

A small, red car arrives and stops in front of my hefty neighbor. A very short and skinny woman gets out. The man drops his suitcase and rushes to the woman. For a moment, I'm afraid he'll knock her over, but what happens next surprises me. She runs to him, and he lifts her until her face is at his level, and then he kisses her. They stand there, kissing, as if the rest of the world doesn't exist. Some passengers smile, others look away. The scene, which should make me want to laugh, makes me sad because I've never had anyone so happy to see me.

My neighbor and the short girl drive away, and when I realize it, I'm alone in front of the airport. Or rather, it's just me and a gray-haired woman with a long-flowered tunic, hippie style. The woman smiles at me, and I pretend not to notice. Then she starts to approach me. If she wants information, I'm not the right person. She looks like one of those vegan fanatics who want to save the planet and came to São Miguel to be in touch with nature.

"Hey there!"

"I'm waiting for someone."

"I know."

Well, that shouldn't be too hard to figure out. She's probably waiting for someone too. We're the only ones here at the airport entrance. Maybe she needs a ride or something.

"You must be Mel."

I raise an eyebrow. The last thing I need is this middle-aged hippie turning out to be some kind of psychic fortune-teller.

"How do you know?"

She bursts into laughter, making me even more skeptical.

"Because you're waiting for me."

Then, before I can react, she pulls me into a hug. I freeze, but she doesn't let go. Next, she showers my cheek with multiple kisses, treating me like I'm a kid. She smells like lavender and basil.

"Mel, darling, I'm thrilled you came."

"Hello, Aunt Gabriela," I manage to say.

I'm stunned. I can't wrap my head around how this middle-aged hippie could be my father's sister.

"Call me Gabi, Aunt Gabi. The only person who calls me Gabriela is your father."

Chapter 8

Aunt Gabi is at the wheel, talking non-stop. Seriously, non-stop. While we're on the road, she's listing off all these places I should check out, but I'm barely paying attention. The airport's right at the entrance of Ponta Delgada, yet we're not heading into the city. Instead, we're going the opposite way, and after a few miles, we're on a road flanked by lush green fields. I've seen plenty of photos of the island, but the sheer greenery catches me off guard. I'm not used to this much green. As we leave the city behind, I notice that the green landscape is dotted with black and white grazing cows.

I'm still feeling queasy, but Aunt Gabi's driving at a snail's pace, so I'm managing. She keeps chatting away, and I'm putting on this big smile, pretending I'm all ears. I'm half expecting her to pop The Question any minute now. But she just keeps chatting, like it's completely normal for her long-lost niece to drop by out of the blue after over twenty years. I mean, I'm also not exactly sure why she decided to invite me now, so I guess we're on the same page.

We roll up a hill, and once we reach the top, she parks next to some cabins. There's a wooden sign that reads 'Hortensias Garden.'

"This is my rustic retreat—mine and Jasmine's, my business partner."

Six cabins dot the landscape, with one resembling a reception area, its sign clearly reading 'Check-in.' Emerging from this particular cabin is a striking figure—a tall, slender woman with fair, porcelain-like skin and a mane of voluminous, curly red hair. She appears to be around Aunt Gabi's age, radiating an undeniable presence that captivates attention. There's something unique about her, an air of vibrancy that's hard to miss.

As Aunt Gabi steps out of the van, she signals for me to follow suit.

"You won't believe what the Germans who are staying at the Flower Cabin did! I'm furious!"

Aunt Gabi clears her throat to attract the woman's attention, as it seems I've gone unnoticed. When our eyes meet, the redhead falls silent, her gaze fixed on me. Freckles speckle her face abundantly, giving her the appearance of a red-haired girl trapped in a grown woman's body.

"Mel, meet my business partner, Jasmine."

"Nice to meet you!" I offer my hand in greeting."

There I am, arm outstretched for a handshake, but Jasmine? Not moving an inch, just staring at me. I start thinking, 'Is there spinach stuck in my teeth and Aunt Gabi forgot to give me the heads up?' Then, Aunt Gabi shoots her this look, and finally, she snaps out of it. But instead of a handshake, she dives in for this bear hug. Seriously, what's up with these people and hugs?! And the redhead also smells like lavender and basil. Must be the go-to perfume for nature-loving types. Even after the hug, she's still staring at me like I'm some mystery she's trying to crack.

"Jasmine, darling, what did the Germans do?" Turns out Aunt Gabi calls everyone "darling."

Finally, her partner looks away, and I can let out a sigh of relief. I hate being watched.

"They chucked makeup wipes in the toilet, and of course, it ended up clogging it! Can you believe it!?"

"Call Mr. Zé, he'll sort it out."

"It's already sorted, but I'm fuming! When I called them out, they had the nerve to argue back."

"You shouldn't let it get to you. It's not good for you."

I bet my aunt handles public relations. Her business partner doesn't seem like the friendliest PR person to me. They keep on chatting about clients, but I zone out. Looking around, I realize I can see the sea in front of me. At the top of this hill, it's just a blanket of green until it meets the sea, spotted with white and black from the grazing cows. While they're going on about clients, I decide to hike up to the highest point. Surprisingly, I can see the sea on both sides of the island from up there. I knew the island was narrow and long, but I never figured I'd get a view of both seas from a hilltop. The sun's starting to set, casting a magnificent light over the fields, giving them a magical touch. If I wasn't feeling so queasy, I might've twirled down the hill like Julie Andrews singing 'The Sound of Music' (except I don't know the lyrics, I just remember it starts with 'the hills are alive with the sound of music').

"It's beautiful, isn't it?" Aunt Gabi shows up behind me.

I nod.

"Now you understand why I left Lisbon and moved to the Azores?"

No, I don't, I'm still clueless about what happened, but I keep quiet and smile. I mean, surely, she didn't relocate for the view. Enjoying green fields and sea views doesn't seem like a good enough reason to get kicked out of the family."

"Mel, I'm really sorry, but it seems you'll have to stay at my place. I didn't think you'd take me up on my offer this fast, and I didn't manage to reserve any of the cabins. Plus, we're in the middle of working on a few of them."

"I'm sorry, I shouldn't have just shown up like this."

"You did the right thing by coming, darling. It means we'll get to spend more time together! Now, come on, I want to show you around."

I follow along as she guides me around the cabins. Several are already occupied by guests. Externally, they all share a coat of white paint accented with dark wooden shutters, yet inside, each boasts a distinct decorative style. Aunt Gabi enlightens me, mentioning that every house embraces its unique theme. One exudes a coastal feel, decked out in shades of blue, evoking a nautical ambiance. Another flaunts vibrant greens adorned with floral patterns, while a third resonates with warm tones reminiscent of Africa. Despite their snug dimensions, these cabins radiate an undeniable coziness. Shame I won't be crashing there. I know my aunt is family, but we're still kind of strangers.

When we return to the van about two hours later, Jasmine's waiting. I climb in, waving goodbye. She gives me a strange smile and chats with my aunt for a few minutes. I sit in the van, waiting for my aunt to join me, watching the sun set. The view's great, but honestly, I just want to get to my aunt's house and rest. I'm beat. I close my eyes, feeling drowsiness creeping in.

"She looks just like your brother."

"I said so," my aunt replies. "See you tomorrow."

I open my eyes, but Jasmine has already walked away. I wonder where she recognizes my father from—probably from TV or the newspapers. Sometimes I forget that his face is in the news almost every week. I've never heard anyone say I look like him. It's something I've never really considered, but perhaps she's right. We're both tall, with green eyes, and that bronzed skin. However, that's where the similarities end. I'm not as cold and ruthless as Judge Terminator. If he ever found out about Ruth's nickname for him, he'd be furious. Truth is, it fits him like a glove. He may be a kind of superhero, locking up the bad guys, but he's also like a robot, devoid of any emotions.

We leave Hortensias Garden and head downhill. After about five or six kilometers, we hit this tiny village. It's got a main street lined with maybe two or three dozen white, single-story houses. I catch sight of a grocery store along the way. We cruise to the end of the street, take a left onto another road with only a handful of houses. Aunt Gabi pulls up at the very last one, a simple single-story home. There's a cute wind chime swaying on the porch and a cozy wicker couch with yellow cushions. As we hop out of the van, it starts to drizzle a bit.

"You'll get used to it," she says, grabbing my suitcase from the van. "Here in the Azores, you get all four seasons in a day."

A pickup truck, resembling Aunt Gabi's, arrives and parks in front of the adjacent house. An old man, approximately seventy years old, gets out of the truck.

"Hey there, neighbor!"

The man glances at us and mumbles something.

"This is my niece, Mel."

"So, this is the city girl..." he mumbles, then studies me.

"Mel, meet Mr. Manuel. If you need anything and I'm not around, feel free to ask him."

"Hi, nice to meet you," I say, trying to be friendly.

The old man just stays quiet, giving me this unfriendly look. I don't think he's the one I'd go to if I need anything.

We step inside, and the interior's just as simple as the exterior. It's one big open area, doing double duty as both the kitchen and the living space. Right there in the kitchen, you've got this wood-burning stove. The rest of the house is sectioned off by a door. There's a small bathroom with a shower, Aunt Gabi's room, and the tiny bedroom that's going to be mine for a bit. It's got a single bed, a nightstand, and a teeny closet. Above the bed, there's this huge yellow ceramic sun with rays in orange. Oh, and the bed's got one of those old patchwork quilts—totally retro.

Aunt Gabi tosses my suitcase on the bed and then leads me straight into the kitchen.

"I've already prepared dinner; I just need to warm it up."

I wonder what's for dinner. Probably some kind of unique vegan dish. I often enjoy vegetarian meals, but I can't stand fanatics who try to push their beliefs on others. And Aunt Gabi looks like one of those. She fires up the oven and starts setting the table. I should offer to lend a hand, but I'm so exhausted that I opt to plop down on the sofa.

"So, have you figured out what you're going to do while you're here?" she asks, smoothing out a tablecloth decorated with sunflowers.

Yellow pillows, suns, sunflowers – there's a solar theme running through this entire house. If Carmen were here, she'd probably adore it. She'd even paint her nails yellow to match the decor. As for me, I'm starting to feel like I'm drowning in yellow. I shift my attention away from the large sunflowers on the tablecloth and concentrate on the question she's asked me. What am I going to do? I'll try to convince Rodrigo to come spend a few days with me, and maybe even propose. That's the plan, but I'm definitely not telling her that. I don't want to hear a lecture about how women don't need men, they just need to quit eating meat, wear hippie dresses, and decorate their homes in shades of yellow (maybe I'm being harsh, but I still can't fathom how this woman in front of me is related to my father). While I wait for Rodrigo's visit, I'll work on some cases on my laptop and chill on the wicker sofa, lounging against those yellow cushions, soaking in some sun, and sipping on vodka.

"Haven't really thought about it," I say. I don't think it's wise to share my plan of lounging on the porch sipping vodka. "Is the internet decent around here?"

"Sorry, dear, but I don't have internet at home. I'm not much of a fan of new technology."

There goes my plan to work on cases. Looks like I'll be spending my afternoons lounging around, sipping vodka, and sunbathing.

Aunt Gabi retrieves a dish from the oven, and a delightful aroma spreads throughout the room. Surprisingly, it's a beef and potato dish. While she's not paying attention, I pour myself a glass of water and quickly swallow the pills. As I reach for a plate to serve myself, she swiftly snatches it away.

"You're too thin, you need to eat," she insists, heaping food onto my plate. "As for keeping yourself occupied, don't worry, dear, I've got plans for you."

Surprised, I choke a bit and start coughing. She thumps my back, but I signal for her to ease up before she breaks one of my ribs. She's quite strong.

"I'm fine now," I say, still a bit hoarse. "What do you mean when you say you've got plans for me?"

"Forget about that for now, darling. Eat!"

I'm not sure how I feel about Aunt Gabi calling me 'darling,' but when she says it, it's way less annoying than when Carmen does. Despite feeling a bit queasy, I'm famished. I haven't had anything to eat since morning. So, I dig in and save my questions until dinner's done. She chatters on about the island's marvels, the rural tourism, and shares amusing stories about the guests. Once we've washed the dishes and tidied up the kitchen, I gather my courage to ask again.

"So, what do you have planned for me?"

"It's a surprise."

"Want me to lend a hand at Hortensias Garden?"

"No need for that. It's the off-season, not much happening besides a few eccentric German and British couples. Unfortunately, I can't spend my days with you. I've got construction to oversee and need to keep an eye on Jasmine's temper," she says, flashing a smile.

"If you don't want me to assist with the retreat, then what are your plans for me?"

I toy with adding, "You probably don't want me to spend my days lounging on the porch, soaking up the sun, and getting drunk," but I keep it to myself.

"Hey, it's already eleven p.m. I lost track of time! I'll show you to your room so you can get some rest," she says, guiding me to where I'll be staying.

Once again, I'm caught off guard with a bear hug and more cheek kisses. How old does she think I am?!

"See you tomorrow, darling!"

I bid her goodbye and step into the room. Despite the affectionate gestures, I'm relieved she didn't ask The Question. I bet she also relieved I didn't ask her why she was banished from the family. I'm really curious, but I don't want to intrude.

I glance around. The room is tiny. I've stayed in hostels with larger rooms. I unpack and organize my things quickly; I didn't bring much. That's what happens when you travel without planning. Usually, I always plan trips weeks in advance.

This is the first time I've traveled on short notice. I close my suitcase and stash it on top of the wardrobe. Then, I kick off my shoes and flop onto the bed. The mattress is one of those soft ones, and I sink into the patchwork quilt. I'm not sure if I'll be able to sleep on this mattress.

I grab my phone. There's a new message from Ruth. It's a photo of her at a nightclub in Ibiza with a drink in her hand and some guy hanging onto her. He must be the replacement for the Body Combat instructor. I consider sending a witty reply but draw a blank. I want to chat with her, but she seems occupied, and I'm not up for dealing with her mood swings again. Besides, listening to other people's problems isn't Ruth's forte. Instead of calling her, I send a photo I took of the island from the plane window with a caption: *On my way to the Azores*. I decide to change into my PJs and go to bed. There's nothing else to do. Despite the medication, I'm restless. I check my phone several times, but no new messages. I bet Ruth's wrapped up with the guy from the photo.

I wonder how the hearing went. I could message Azevedo, but he'd probably tell me to forget work—I'm on vacation. My father most likely instructed him to do so. And nobody dares to defy Judge Terminator.

I send Rodrigo a text.

What are you doing?

Luckily, he texts back right away.

Hey, angel! How are you feeling?

Much better. I decided to take a few days off and visit my aunt in the Azores.

Didn't know you had family there.

I didn't know she lived in the Azores. It's been ages since I last laid eyes on her. She was banned from the family.

Banned?! What went down?

No clue. It's a big family secret. My parents never revealed the secret. All I know is that my grandfather booted her out.

And how're things going with her?

Pretty good so far. She seems nice.

Glad you're hitting it off.

I wish you could be here with me.

I'd wish that too.

I start writing a message, asking him to swing by São Miguel for a few days, but then another message pops up.

Gotta rush. Catch you later!

I'm feeling down. I'll have to hold off on inviting him to visit me. Placing my phone on the nightstand, I shut my eyes. I lie there for what seems like ages but sleep just won't come. I can't shake off thoughts about whatever Aunt Gabi has planned for me. What if it involves a boat? Boats make me queasy. Or maybe diving? I'm scared stiff of diving. If only I had a bottle of vodka. A sip would ease my mind. Aunt Gabi doesn't really know me. I hate surprises.

Chapter 9

"Good morning, darling."

I struggled through a night of restless sleep, constantly interrupted by moments of wakefulness. Just as I hoped to finally doze off, Aunt Gabi barged in, enthusiastically pulling open the curtains as if it were a grand theatrical performance. The sudden flood of sunlight makes me squint, prompting me to swiftly cover my face with the sheets.

"Come on, it's a lovely day!" she says, gently tugging the sheets away.

Blinking against the unexpected brightness, all I can see is her vibrant flowery dress—seriously, it's as wide as a tent.

"Time to rise and shine! You have plans at nine-thirty."

I stay put, but she settles in beside me, treating me with an affectionate pat on the head.

"You'll love the surprise, darling," she assures, planting a kiss on my forehead.

Why does she treat me like a kid? And that 'darling' bit? Instant flashback to Carmen and her flashy nails.

"Hurry up!"

I don't feel like getting up, but I'm pretty sure she won't leave until I do. So, I drag myself to the bathroom. The shower's a sardine can—I bump into the walls a few times while washing up. I quietly curse to myself; I don't want to seem rude to Aunt Gabi. Once finished, I stare at my clothes. I have no clue what to wear to... wherever we're going. But I figure I'd better dress decent, so I swap out leggings and tees for white pants and a dark blue silk blouse.

In the kitchen, it's like a hotel spread—bread, jams, pineapple, cheese. A real buffet. I drink some water and swallow my pills. Staring at the table, I debate. No Greek yogurt or chia. What should I eat? I settle on whole wheat bread with cheese—seems healthier. The first bite surprises me. The cheese is different from what I'm used to. Can't quite put my finger on it. Thicker and creamier, maybe.

"This cheese's amazing!"

"I'm glad you like it. It's one hundred percent organic—straight from Azorean cows, only grazing on grass," Aunt Gabi says. It reminds me of that Azores documentary I watched, 'The #1 Archipelago in Sustainability.' She could do ads with that voice.

"Yeah, it's really good," I say between bites.

After indulging in that slice of bread with cheese, I decide to go for another with passion fruit jam. And then finish off with a slice of fresh pineapple. I'm famished. I can't believe I still have this much appetite. Could it be a side effect of the pills? That's the last thing I need. If I keep eating like this all month, I'll head back to Lisbon with three or four more pounds. Leo will freak out. He'll make me do two CrossFit classes a day. And start attending Krav Maga classes.

"How are your parents?"

"Fine."

"Fine?"

"Yeah, fine."

What should I tell her? My parents are distant and absorbed in their careers, as always, so I guess they're fine.

"My father is judging another high-profile case. You must've seen it on TV."

"Ah, yes. Money laundering, right?"

"Yep."

"And your job, how's it going?"

My job? What can I say? That it's going well, quite well, actually? So well that my boss suggested I should switch from being a lawyer to becoming an event planner because, as per a coworker, my organizing skills for parties surpass those for law.

"It's going well."

"Do you deal with money laundering cases like your father?"

The question almost makes me laugh. My aunt's clueless about the legal world. If she knew, she'd realize I lack two things to lead a case like that: a pair of balls and a penis. At least in my office. Though sometimes I doubt some of my colleagues have balls. I can't tell her that, so I say:

"Those cases are for the more experienced lawyers in the office. I mostly handle divorce cases." And organize parties, I feel like adding. Before she can ask anything else, I jump in, "My boyfriend might come to the island to see me."

"That's great! I'd love to meet him."

I'm not sure if Rodrigo will feel the same. Rodrigo isn't a fan of hippies.

"He's a pilot."

"Really? That must be an exciting job."

"Very exciting." I gulp down another piece of pineapple. At least pineapple's supposed to have a cleansing effect, but I doubt it'll cleanse my body from the two slices of bread I stuffed myself with.

"Sorry for sending the letter to your office, I didn't have your address."

"It's okay." Although you scared me half to death; thought the envelope had Anthrax or something. "How did you know which office I work in?"

"A friend in Lisbon told me. You must know her, Maria Luisa, who's also a lawyer."

"Oh, yeah, I know her. She and her husband are friends with my parents."

"You must have been surprised by my letter."

"A little," well, more like a lot—a tremendous amount, actually. It was an enormous surprise. I had almost forgotten I had an aunt. She hadn't crossed my mind in years. Until yesterday, my aunt existed solely as a black and white photograph tucked away in my grandma's sewing kit—a photograph worn by time. But now, she's a living, breathing person. A real person, though completely different from what I anticipated. I'm not exactly sure what I expected, but it certainly wasn't this hippie woman with short gray hair and flowery dresses.

"Mel, it's been countless years, but you've never left my thoughts. I'm truly thrilled that you've accepted my invitation."

That's all very nice, but what I'd like to know is why she was banished from the family. What I'd like to know is what sin she committed for my grandfather to forbid the whole family from even mentioning her name. I'm dying to know what happened. I have The Question on the tip of my tongue, but she hasn't asked me yet why I decided to come to the Azores overnight, so I keep my mouth shut.

When we finish, I help her with the dishes. Besides not having internet, she also doesn't have a dishwasher. I'm finishing washing the dishes when someone knocks on the door.

"It must be Carlos, coming to pick you up."

Carlos?! Who the hell is Carlos and why is he coming to pick me up?! What is my aunt up to? For a moment, I imagine that she hired an escort to be my tour guide. Maybe that's why she was banished from the family. The rustic retreat is a facade. Her real business is a luxury escort agency. I almost burst out laughing just thinking about Aunt Gabi surrounded by tall and muscular men, dressed in tiny thongs that leave their butts exposed.

She gets up and heads to the door. I'm half-expecting a tall, muscle-bound guy to swagger in, grooving to 'You Can Leave Your Hat On,' all dressed up as a cop or a firefighter. Why is it that women go weak for a uniform? It's a universal mystery that needs a scientific investigation. I'm dying to know the scientific explanation behind it because, truth be told, I can't resist a man in uniform either. When Rodrigo shows up rocking his pilot attire, all I want to do is tear that uniform off and dive right into bed with him!

The door swings open and in comes a guy who must be about my age but is dressed like a teenager. He's wearing a Snoopy t-shirt, and his hair is a little messy. He's only slightly taller than me and needs to lose a few pounds. I have no idea who he is, but from his appearance, he's definitely not an escort. I don't know if I should be disappointed or relieved.

"Hi, I'm Carlos. Nice to meet you!"

I stare at him, trying to figure out what's going on.

"This is my niece, Mel."

"Sorry, I'm not fully awake yet," I say, while holding out my hand. "I'm Mel."

He gives it a light shake, wearing this goofy smile, and I'm still clueless about who this Milk Cup is and why he's here to pick me up.

"Carlos is a photographer. He's been photographing the island's flora and fauna," Aunt Gabi explains, shooting me a knowing look. But I'm still lost. What's the surprise here, anyway?

"When you were little, you loved to draw," she says. I'm surprised she remembers that. "I figured you might enjoy joining Carlos while he photographs the island. You can get to know the place and sketch some landscapes." She pulls out a drawer from the sideboard. "I even got you a drawing set from the island's art store."

This isn't exactly what I had in mind.

"I also got you a waterproof backpack," she adds, pulling out a flowery one from another drawer. "Rain's a daily thing here in the Azores, thought you'd need something to keep your things dry."

"Thank you," is all I can muster. I'm left speechless.

My aunt's beaming at me, looking mighty pleased with herself. I grab the backpack (which is dead ugly), stuff my things inside—my purse included because the backpack's massive—then sling it on my back. She plants a kiss on my cheek.

"I'm sure you'll have a great time."

As I scrutinize her face a bit closer, I notice her smile is authentic. There's genuine pride in her eyes for her plan. It's evident she's genuinely happy to have me here. Even though I'm not enthusiastic about following this Milk Cup guy, I realize I can't disappoint my eccentric aunt. It's been forever since someone has been this genuinely thrilled to have me around.

Carlos is still there, grinning away by the door.

"Ready?" he asks.

We say goodbye to my aunt and walk out onto the street. I notice a red motorcycle parked next to her pickup truck.

"We're taking this?"

"Yeah, any issues with that?"

My heart begins to race, feeling the onset of anxiety.

"Are you afraid of riding a motorcycle?" he asks, that unyielding smile still on his face. So, I resort to what I do best: flash a smile and pretend everything's perfectly fine.

"No, not at all."

He hands me the helmet, and I swiftly put it on before he notices my panic. Then he hops on the bike, motioning for me to join. I settle in behind him, lightly resting my hands on his waist. My palms are sweating, and my head's spinning. What am I doing? Why don't I just tell him the truth?

"Hold onto me tight, so you don't slip off."

I cling to him tightly, taking a deep breath. It's going to be a very, very long ride.

※ ※ ※

After navigating numerous winding roads, Carlos finally brings the motorcycle to a stop, and a wave of relief washes over me. My hands and legs are still trembling. I made it through the ride, but the anxiety hasn't subsided. I'm hoping he doesn't catch onto my trembling. Thankfully, it seems I'm in the clear as he doesn't spare me a glance. He's preoccupied with retrieving a backpack from one of the motorcycle's compartments. Perfect. No need for him to realize I'm a ticking time bomb, ready to explode at any moment.

I look around and notice we've arrived at the entrance of Terra Nostra Park. There's no line at the ticket office, only an Asian couple in raincoats, equipped with umbrellas and cameras (as expected). If this were one of those tourist-packed destinations, it'd be bustling. Yet, here in the Azores, hailed as the top sustainable archipelago, the island is home to more cows than people.

Thump! Thump!

I jerk my head, startled. Carlos just tapped my helmet, as though knocking on a door. I watch him mouthing words, but I can't decipher a thing. Now he's gesturing, yet I'm still clueless about what he wants. I take off the helmet.

"What?"

"I was saying that the view is better without the helmet," he chuckles.

"Oh, got it."

"Welcome to Terra Nostra Park."

I force a smile.

"Let me take your helmet."

I hand it to him, observing as he retrieves a substantial bag from another compartment on the motorcycle and stows the helmet inside.

"It's my photography gear."

I force another smile. I'm not in the mood for conversation. Since I stay silent, he signals for me to follow him. The Asian couple has already entered, and there's no one at the ticket office now. I unhook the backpack from my back, ready to grab my wallet.

"No need. I'm working, and you're entering as my assistant."

I return the backpack to its place. He moves ahead and chats with the woman at the ticket office, who seems to know him well. They exchange words, giving me a chance to glance around. There's a sign with a map of the park, revealing a thermal water tank for bathing and several areas featuring different species of trees and flowers. God, this is going to be so boring. Carlos bids farewell to the ticket office woman, and we step into the park.

We spend the morning among flower beds. Carlos keeps talking about the flowers, and I nod along, lost in my thoughts. There are numerous white flowers whose name I missed, and plenty of hortensias. No need for him to mention their name; they're practically iconic in Azores tourist photos. Everything's stunning, but it doesn't captivate me. I feel detached, numb. It must be the pills.

While he keeps on taking thousands of photos of the flowers from every angle, I sit on a bench because my legs are starting to ache. I seize the opportunity to examine the *Milk Cup* in front of me. Carlos must be in his early thirties. He seems pleasant enough, but that's about it. If he shed a few pounds and ditched the Snoopy t-shirt for a shirt, he might just edge closer to Cappuccino territory. Maybe.

Rodrigo should be here with me instead of him, even though parks like this aren't really his thing. When he comes to visit, I'm eager to introduce him to the island's best bars. Rodrigo adores spending evenings at a bar, sipping gin and catching up with friends. I'll need to scout out the finest bars scattered across the island. Surely, in Ponta Delgada, there are some fantastic spots for a few drinks. Then, I'm going to urge him to propose. I'm tired of waiting for him to wait for the perfect job conditions.

"Don't you feel like sketching?" Carlos interrupts my thoughts.

"Sketching?"

"Yes. Your aunt said you're quite talented at drawing."

My aunt hasn't seen me for twenty years.

"Not really."

"Maybe you'll feel more inspired by the Bromeliads."

"Brome... what?"

"Bromeliads. They're vibrant flowers," he explains, signaling for me to follow.

I get up, annoyed, and trail after him. We pass through an area with bushes resembling a jungle, that keep hitting me in the face. When we finally pass that area,

I'm stunned by an explosion of yellows, oranges, and reds. The flowers' vivid colors against the greenery of trees and bushes are striking. I have to admit he was right.

"They're beautiful."

"I told you so."

I stand there, admiring the vibrant flowers, contemplating buying some red lingerie. I don't own anything red. Yes, I must buy some red lace lingerie. I bet Rodrigo will love it.

"Well?" he prompts.

"Well, what?"

"Aren't these flowers worth sketching?"

"Maybe."

I pull out my sketchpad and a pencil from my backpack, settling on a bench. Drawing flowers isn't exactly my strong suit. Since I entered the workforce, my sketches have revolved around lawyers, judges, and fractured relationships. I figure the last time I sketched flowers, I was probably sixteen or seventeen. Back then, I was idealistic, imagining I could sustain myself through my art. I envisioned heading to Paris for art studies, spending my days in Montmartre, painting alongside fellow artists. Little did I anticipate that my days would be consumed by handling divorce cases. It's ironic how life has a way of shattering our dreams.

Carlos starts photographing the bromeliads, and I fixate on the paper. I clutch my pencil and begin sketching. One stroke at a time, the drawing takes shape. It's slow-going because I want to savor the process. I'm surprised to realize that I'm doing it, I'm capturing the delicacy of the flowers on paper. I don't know how long I've been at it but, before I know it, I've crafted an entire garden on the sheet.

"Your aunt was right." Carlos's voice startles me from behind.

"What are you talking about?"

"Your drawing. It's really beautiful."

"Do you think so?"

"Yeah, you've got talent."

"Thank you."

"Want to grab some lunch? I'm starving."

Glancing at the clock, I notice it's nearly one o'clock. Turns out time slipped by faster than I anticipated.

"I'm not very hungry," I admit, still feeling a tad queasy.

"You'll love Azorean cuisine."

"I really don't have an appetite."

"What will your aunt say if I don't take you to lunch? Come on!" He gestures for me to follow.

I stare at the vibrant flowers and let out a sigh. The medication has made me feel so numb. I gaze at the colorful flowers and sigh. The pills have left me feeling numb. I hate feeling like this. I wish I could feel as vibrant as those flowers.

"Wait a sec!" I've had a brilliant idea. "Can you take my picture?"

"Sure!" He grabs his camera.

"With my phone."

He chuckles. "Your phone might be decent, but a camera has better quality."

"It's for my boyfriend."

"Your boyfriend?"

"Yeah."

He looks hesitant. Men and their gadgets. He probably thinks my phone's a piece of junk. I hold my phone in my hand, waiting to see if he'll change his mind.

"Okay, hand it over."

I strike a few poses near the flower bed and discover that this *Milk Cup* guy is really good at giving directions. And, while guiding me, he doesn't say anything about the quality of my phone's camera. When he hands my phone back, I'm shocked by the photos. I mean, my phone may not be a fancy camera, but the pictures he took look amazing. As we're heading towards the park exit, he stops to chat with someone he knows, and I take the chance to take a better look at the photos. I'm thinking of choosing one to send to Rodrigo. He'd probably want something a bit more explicit, but for now, he'll have to settle for the one I'm about to send him.

"Ready to go?" Carlos asks. "There's a quaint restaurant nearby. We can walk there."

If walking's an option, I'm totally on board. I'm absolutely petrified of hopping back on that motorcycle. I trail behind him, completely engrossed in scrolling through the photos. I know I should make some small talk, but right now, picking the perfect picture to send to Rodrigo feels way more pressing than trying to strike up a conversation with this poor guy my aunt roped in to babysit me. We make it to the restaurant in, like, under five minutes. My phone's practically glued to my hand, and as I head towards the entrance, I stumble. Luckily, he's quick and grabs my arm before I totally faceplant. I figure I better pocket my phone before I cause any more embarrassing accidents.

Taking a quick scan around, it's a pretty straightforward place with those classic red and white plastic tablecloths. Yet, the handwritten menu posted at the entrance promises the finest delights in the Azores.

"You should try the barnacles," he suggests.

"I would prefer a salad."

He chuckles, and I wonder if he's mocking me or genuinely amused by my request. We take a seat at one of the plastic tables. The place is nearly empty, except for the Asian couple from Terra Nostra Park, seated at the far end.

"Good afternoon. Looks like you're in good company, Carlos," a woman, probably in her fifties or sixties, approaches. She's petite, slender, and sports a bun atop her head—the kind I haven't seen in ages.

"Good afternoon, Mrs. Maria. This is Mel. It's her first time in the Azores."

"First time? Then you must try the barnacles," she says, stern and unwavering.

"I'd prefer a salad…"

"Nonsense. No arguments here, miss. You're having the barnacles." Then she turns to him. "You're starving your friend, Carlos; she's as thin as a toothpick."

He flashes a smile.

"And for drinks?"

"I thought you might try Kima. It's an Azorean soft drink made from passion fruit," he suggests.

"I don't usually drink sodas."

"Nonsense. Visiting the Azores and not drinking Kima is like going to Rome and not seeing the Pope! Two barnacle shots and two Kimas." The woman hollers inside before heading toward the Asian couple's table.

"If you don't want Kima, I'll order a bottle of water later. Sorry, but Mrs. Maria can be a bit forceful."

A bit? The woman's a real dictator.

"No need, I'll have the soda."

"Are you enjoying the park?"

"Yes, it's quite nice."

The park is stunning, but what I truly wish for is Rodrigo to be here with me. He should be the one joining me for lunch. Even though he'd never step into a restaurant with plastic tables and chairs. This place isn't his style.

"Have you been to the Azores before?"

"No, it's my first time."

"Did you decide it was time to take a vacation?"

Suddenly, I'm tempted to spill everything. About Cláudio, the panic attack, my parents plotting to commit me to the Arcos Clinic, and my escape to the Azores. Is that what I'm doing—running away from problems? Maybe I should have stayed in Lisbon. At this time of the day, I'd usually be at the office answering calls and emails. I open my mouth, but only one word escapes:

"Yes."

"I think it was a good call. São Miguel is the most beautiful island in the world."

I chuckle.

"Yes, I might sound biased since I was born here, but I truly believe it. This is the most beautiful island in the world."

He probably hasn't ventured beyond the Azores. There are places much more breathtaking than this one.

Mrs. Maria returns with the soft drinks, almost slamming them on the table.

"Here are the Kimas!"

"Thanks," he says, pouring himself another glass. "So, what do you do in Lisbon? Are you an artist?"

I chuckle.

"What's funny?" he asks.

"I'm not an artist. Living costs in Lisbon are through the roof; if I were an artist, I'd be in trouble. I'm actually a lawyer."

"A lawyer? Seriously? I thought you were an artist."

"Why's that?"

"I don't know. It's the way your aunt spoke about you."

"But I'm not. Actually, I quit drawing years ago. I mean, occasionally I doodle during boring court hearings, but that's pretty much it."

"Don't you miss drawing?"

That's quite a question, hanging there in the air as I twirl the Kima bottle in my hands, trying to figure out what to say. He's waiting for my response, eyes locked on me, but I'm not sure where to start. Honestly, I rarely think about it. It's just easier not to get lost in thoughts about what life might've been if I'd taken a different path.

"I do miss it," I confess, feeling an odd pang—I haven't been aware of how much I've missed drawing anything other than scenes from the courtroom. Being a lawyer has never filled me with the same joy as drawing did.

"Perhaps it's time to rediscover your artistic streak," he suggests, taking a sip of Kima. I keep fidgeting with the bottle. "Give it a shot," he points to the bottle, "you might find it enjoyable. If not, we can always get a bottle of water or another drink."

I pop the bottle open and pour a bit into the glass. Raising it slowly to my lips, I take a sip of the yellow liquid. Surprisingly tasty, even though I can't shake off the thought of all the sugar and calories in it.

He excuses himself for a bathroom break, giving me the chance to shoot Rodrigo a photo. I choose a flattering one and scribble a caption:

The island's breathtaking! Come and join me! and hit send.

"Here come the barnacles!" Mrs. Maria plops a massive platter on the table. "Dig in! You need to put on some weight!"

What a character! I look up to see her still scowling. No wonder the place is almost empty; her manners probably scare off customers. Meanwhile Carlos returns.

"Don't mind Mrs. Maria. She's got a strong personality, but she's good-hearted."

We start eating, and once again, I'm pleasantly surprised by the flavor; it's like a taste straight from the sea.

"So, enjoying it?" Mrs. Maria yells from the counter.

I nod, and she seems happy with that.

"You could sketch Mrs. Maria," He suggests, winking at me.

I chuckle.

"Yeah, she'd make for an excellent muse to reignite my artistic vibe."

We both crack up laughing.

Meanwhile, the restaurant fills up with Portuguese groups and tourists, and soon, every table's taken.

"The place is buzzing."

"People even come from Lisbon just to dine here."

"Is Mrs. Maria the cook here?"

"Nah, she handles the tables, and her husband does the cooking."

As I indulge in the barnacles, I start to understand why folks travel from far and wide just to eat here. The service might be terrible, but the food is simply divine.

He starts talking about island spots I should check out. Sneakily, I glance at my phone, hoping for a message from Rodrigo, but nothing yet. I'm eagerly waiting for his response. Lunch goes on with him still talking about spots I should visit while we savor barnacles and sip Kima. Even though I'm not entirely tuned in, I keep up the charade of being engrossed with nods and smiles.

We head back to the park after lunch, surrounded by all these leafy trees and shrubs, like we're lost in a sea of greenery. But, strangely enough, instead of feeling all calm and relaxed, I'm getting this kind of uneasy feeling. I mean, this place is supposed to be peaceful, right? But there's this restlessness creeping in, and I can't quite shake it. Maybe it's the pills wearing off or just feeling weird in all this quiet. And Rodrigo being so quiet himself—it's adding to this weird, eerie feeling. Then, the drizzle starts.

"You know, in the Azores, we get a taste of all four seasons in a single day," he notes, packing up his gear.

"Yeah, I've heard about that."

When the rain starts pouring harder, he nudges me under a group of trees, hoping they'll shield us. But soon enough, the downpour finds its way through the leaves, hitting us both. He fishes out a raincoat from his backpack.

"Here, put this on!"

"What about you?"

"I'm used to this," he shrugs, handing me the raincoat. "Go on, put it on!"

I put on the raincoat he offered. "It's got a hood," he mentions, pulling it over my head. "At least it covers you down to your knees."

We stand there, surrounded by the drumming rain, a blanket of quietness enveloping us. The wind picks up, and I start to shiver. My face, hands, and ankles are completely drenched. Doubts start creeping in—perhaps coming to the Azores was a bad idea. I should've stayed back in Lisbon or chosen somewhere warmer, like Dubai. Yeah, Dubai's warmth sounds perfect right now. I long for that scorching heat, for Rodrigo's skin on my skin. His absence feels too real. Should I have taken a quick trip to Dubai instead? Rodrigo has stopovers there. Probably I should've. Instead, here I am, stranded on an island in the middle of the Atlantic, seeking refuge from the rain while a *Milk Cup* babysits me.

I can't even fathom how long this rain has been pouring down, but it feels like an eternity. A whirlwind of thoughts swirls in my head—the argument with Cláudio at the office, that scene in the supermarket, waking up in the hospital, my parents' scheming, and now being stuck here in the Azores. It's been a chaotic storm; everything happened so fast, I couldn't catch my breath. Right now, I should be seated at my desk, sorting out clients' cases, but instead, here I am, drenched in the Azorean rain. What was I thinking by coming here? Maybe I should just grab a flight straight back to Lisbon, or maybe I should give in to my parents' advice and check into that clinic. What on earth am I doing here?

"Hey, rain's stopped," he says, snapping me out of it. I stand there, a bit zoned out, until he taps my arm. I dry my hands, pull out my cell from my backpack. With all the rain noise, I might have missed Rodrigo's reply. Zilch. Rodrigo's still hasn't texted back.

"Ready to head out?"

I glance at him, totally drenched but in high spirits, like it's no big deal. He seems so laid back.

We head towards the exit and pass this Thermal Water Tank, all murky brown. Despite the rain, there are people in the water, including that Asian couple from the restaurant.

"Do you want to take a dip?"

I raise an eyebrow. He's he kidding me?!

"We're already soaked," he says.

Seriously, the water looks muddy as heck. It doesn't scream 'trustworthy' to me.

"I didn't pack swimwear."

He catches on to my suspicions. "The water's brown because it's full of minerals and heated to nearly forty degrees."

Might be, but I won't be taking a dip in it.

"You might want to bring a swimsuit along. I usually have my swimming shorts with me, just in case."

"But that water seems like it would ruin my swimsuits."

He laughs. "Just bring an old one. Sometimes it's fun to give new things a shot, even if you're not too excited about it."

Sure, he talks a big game about being adventurous, but he doesn't strike me as that type. I feel like poking fun at him, but I hold back.

"Can we go, please? I'm freezing," I say, baffled how he's not shivering.

"Sure thing. Let's go."

Following him, I dread having to ride on that risky two-wheeler again. I just want to get to my aunt's place, have a hot shower, change clothes, and book a ticket back to Lisbon.

Chapter 10

He pulls up the motorcycle in front of my aunt's place, and I let out this big sigh of relief. I take off my helmet and hand it to him. While he's tucking the helmet away, I check him out. His hair's totally soaked, dripping water like crazy. Those drops land right on Snoopy on his T-shirt, and now Snoopy's looking like a wet mess. I feel kind of bad for both him and Snoopy—this rain messed them up, but I managed to stay dry from the ankles up, thanks to the raincoat. I should've remembered to pack one. Everybody knows in the Azores you can't skip the raincoat.

"I feel bad you got all soaked."

He flips up the visor of his helmet and grins. "I couldn't let you get drenched," he says, acting like it's no big deal. But I'm still feeling guilty, worried he might catch a cold.

"Even Snoopy took a hit," I point out, eyeing the crumpled illustration on his shirt.

He chuckles. "Snoopy's used to it. That's the price you have to pay for living on the most beautiful island in the world."

His easygoing attitude surprises me. If it were Rodrigo, he'd be in a sour mood right away. I remember once in a restaurant, a waitress spilled wine on his favorite Calvin Klein shirt, and he was fuming. The restaurant had to pay the dry-cleaning bill. I glance at the Snoopy tee and can't imagine Rodrigo in something like that—and, besides, it'd probably look too loose on him.

"I should have brought a raincoat."

"Don't sweat it, I'm good."

I hand him back the raincoat.

"You can keep it."

"You'll need it."

"You keep it," he insists. "I've got another. Consider it a gift." Then, he flips down his helmet visor, revs up the motorcycle, and adds, "Catch you tomorrow! Ten o'clock, I'll be here!"

Wait, did I hear that right? He's coming to pick me up again tomorrow? What did my aunt set up with him?! I fish out the key from my bag and struggle to open the door (I'm not the best with keys). All the while, I'm racking my brain for an excuse to bail on sightseeing with him again. He seems like a nice guy (and a total gentleman, I have to give him that), but the idea of getting back on a motorcycle makes me anxious. I'm picturing us driving up those twisty, steep roads again. I don't want to get back on that motorcycle. Plus, I'm seriously contemplating heading back to Lisbon.

I step inside the house, not even bothering to change out of my clothes, and immediately check my phone. Still no reply from Rodrigo. He's probably in the air by now.

I decide to shoot Ruth a message.

Who's the hottie in yesterday's pic?

She responds with another photo; this time she's hugging him. He's tall, ripped, and inked up. Definitely a lot more eye-catching than the Body Combat instructor. In her caption, she writes:

His name's Frank. American. 31. Knows how to pleasure a woman.

I grin. At least someone's having a good time.

Cappuccino or Martini?

Martini, without a doubt!

Ruth switches between *Espressos* and *Martinis*. She thinks *Cappuccinos* are too sweet. Me? I find *Martinis* too intense for my taste.

Chat later. Off to hang with Frank.

Ruth handles the revolving door of men in her life like a champ. She's not looking for anything serious, so she doesn't seem to mind when her relationships fizzle out. And then there's me, hoping for something steady, drawn to guys who run from commitment like it's their kryptonite. Before Rodrigo, there were others—mostly younger, flings that were doomed from the start due to their immaturity. But with Rodrigo, it's going to be different. He's promised me a ring.

Then, out of the blue, a new message pops up. It's from Rodrigo! It's like he read my mind. We're on the same wavelength.

Hey there, angel!

You've been on my mind!

You're always on my mind, angel.

Quit teasing.

Nah, I mean it. I can't get you out of my head.

Did you enjoy the photo?

I loved it, but I'd rather see one in lingerie.

I grin.

I'll consider it.

Oh, come on, Mel. Miss your body.

I find a bikini pic from Dubai and send it.

That's more like it.

How do you like it?

Yep, but I'd rather see you in person.

Then come visit me in the Azores.

I'll try to make it happen.

You won't be disappointed.

I know, I've never regretted spending time with you.

When do you think you'll come?

Not certain yet, I'm trying to switch my shifts around.

But are you seriously planning to come?

Absolutely. Can't wait to see you.

Love you.

Love you too, angel. Gotta run, got a flight.

Suddenly, a rush of determination floods through me, and I'm all fired up, ready to conquer the world. Right now, choosing to come to the Azores feels like the greatest decision ever made. This island might not be the most stunning, but it seems like the ideal place for me to pop the question. Rodrigo will get it. I'll make sure he does!

I swiftly hop into the shower, change into fresh clothes, and plop down in the living room. Aunt Gabi hasn't shown up yet, and I'm battling sheer boredom. If only there were internet here, I could catch up on studying for my exams at the Center for Judicial Studies. Instead, I find myself at a loss with nothing engaging to do. Life in Lisbon is an endless whirlwind—barely a moment to catch a breath. By the time I crash into bed at night, I'm completely spent. I usually unwind on the couch, and before I know it, it's the wee hours of the morning. Then, it's the same routine all over again the next day. It's like being a mouse on a wheel. But now that I'm off that wheel, I feel adrift and purposeless.

As I sit there on the couch, gazing at the yellow-themed decor, inspiration strikes. I need to do some shopping, better prepare for tomorrow since Carlos is coming to pick me up. The anticipation of Rodrigo's visit gives me a thrill. I want to explore the island, scope out the perfect spots for Rodrigo's stay. Time to head to the village store for a bit of shopping.

Just as I'm about to step out, my phone starts buzzing persistently. I glance at the screen and let it ring a few times... I'm really not in the mood for a chat with my mother. We haven't spoken since Sunday. Surprisingly, neither she nor my father called earlier; it seems they've moved on. I should have realized by now that I'm on my own. Actually, I've always been on my own. I let it continue ringing, hoping she'll give up, but nope, she's persistent.

"Hello, Mom," I answer, resigned.

"Mel, where are you? I'm at your place."

"How did you get in?"

"With the key you gave us," she responds, and I hadn't even remembered giving them one. They'd never used it before. "We thought you were resting. Dad spoke to Azevedo, and you didn't go to work. Where are you?"

"In the Azores."

"In the Azores?! Why are you there? You need to come back. I spoke to a therapist and set up an appointment for tomorrow."

"I'm not going back, Mom."

"What do you mean?"

"I'm spending a few weeks in the Azores."

"Who are you with? Ruth or Rodrigo, those troublesome ones?"

"I'm not with either of them."

"You just went alone?"

"I'm staying at Aunt Gabi's place."

I hear her gasp.

"Aunt Gabriela's?"

"Aunt Gabi. She prefers that."

She takes a deep breath. I anticipate her urging me to leave immediately, expecting her to express concerns about Aunt Gabi being involved in dubious things, but her response is different.

"If you're with Aunt Gabi, then I can relax."

I didn't see that coming.

"But I still think you should make it to the appointment."

"We'll talk about it when I'm back in Lisbon. I need to run now. I need to grab some stuff at the village store before it shuts. Everything closes early here."

"Maybe it'll do you good to spend some time in the Azores surrounded by nature."

"Yeah, I'm already feeling better. I need to go. Love you."

"Love you too, Mel. Call if you need anything."

That went better than I expected.

I hang up, sling my bag over my shoulder, and head outside. The sky is so clear; you'd never guess it had just rained. However, it's getting chilly, and I'm regretting not grabbing a jacket. Glancing around, aside from a dozen scattered houses, all I see is an endless expanse of green. I'm still amazed by the sheer amount of greenery.

As I step into the grocery store, I realize it doubles as a café. On the right side at the entrance, a pair of round plastic tables hosts a handful of elderly men sipping wine and engaged in a card game. I wander through the three small aisles, on the lookout for something handy for tomorrow. I spot what I need – a raincoat and a sun hat. Also, I'm after a reusable water bottle. Making my way to the adjacent aisle, I stumble upon the reusable bottles. As I snatch a metal one, I realize this aisle has an alcoholic drinks section.

I glance across the shelves and spot them. There they are, those transparent bottles adorned with vibrant red labels, calling out to me. Maybe I could take one, just to unwind. A little nightcap might lull me to sleep better than those darn pills. I reach for a bottle of Smirnoff, but then I stop. What if my aunt sees it? She'll think her niece is a drunk and a fool. I backtrack and return the bottle to its place on the shelf. I head to the counter to pay, yet there's no one there. Come to think of it, I haven't seen any staff at the counter at all. I should probably grab that bottle. What harm could a glass or two do? I retreat to the drinks section and snatch the bottle again. I'll keep it in my room. No need for my aunt to know. Decision made. The bottle comes along. I return to the counter and bump into the last person I expected to see – my aunt's less-than-friendly neighbor.

"Afternoon," he grumbles between his teeth.

"Good afternoon," I reply, unloading my purchases onto the counter.

"A hat, a reusable water bottle, a raincoat, an umbrella," the man announces each item as he bags them up. Great, now the whole store knows my shopping list.

"And that's it."

The bottle of vodka remains in the same spot on the counter.

"I'm taking the bottle too."

He gives me an odd look.

"Vodka isn't a drink for girls."

"Pardon me?!"

"I won't sell you vodka."

"Why not?"

"Come on, Manuel, ease up," one of the men playing cards interjects.

"Stay out of it, Chico!" Then he redirects his glare at me. "You heard me. No vodka for you."

"Why not?" Is it because he thinks I'm underage? People sometimes think I'm younger. "I'm twenty-nine."

"So what?"

"So what?!"

"Yeah, so what? I don't care how old you are. I'm not selling you the bottle. Period!" He crosses his arms, firm in his stance.

I shake my head, unsure of what to say.

"There's no point arguing with him, miss!" says one of the other men. "When Manuel puts his mind to something, no one can change his mind."

I briefly consider continuing the discussion with the man, but I decide against it. I don't want him to tell my aunt that I wanted to buy vodka. So, I swallow my pride and ask in the most neutral tone I can manage, "How much is it?"

"Fifteen euros."

I give him a twenty, and he stares at me. I look away to avoid saying anything I might regret. After all, the man is my aunt's neighbor. I'm waiting to hear a lecture, but he opens the cash register and gives me five euros in change without saying a word. Then hands me the shopping bag. I grab it and leave. I'm furious.

When I get to my aunt's house, I go straight to the bedroom. As I start to take things out of the bag, I see that inside is a pack of Smarties.

"What the hell is this?!" I ask, out loud. I must be going mad. Or else the old man is completely crazy. I'm sure I didn't put the Smarties in the bag. Is this a silly prank by the old man? Then, I hear a knock on the door. I hope it's not him accusing me of stealing the Smarties! No way! He wouldn't have such nerve.

"Mel, it's me! I forgot my keys."

I recognize my aunt's voice, and for a second, I'm picturing the old man wearing a wig and mimicking her. But hey, my imagination tends to go a bit wild. I open the door and breathe a sigh of relief when I see it's just her, without any disguise or funny business.

"Hello, Aunt Gabi."

"Hello, darling! How was your day?"

"It went well." I decide it's best not to tell her that I got Carlos completely soaked.

"What's that in your hand?"

That's when I realize I'm still holding the pack.

"These?"

"Oh, it's Smarties! I didn't know you still liked eating Smarties."

"How did you know I liked Smarties?"

"The last time I saw you, you were with your grandma in the Suiça Pastry Shop[5] and I remember you were eating Smarties."

---

5 The Pastelaria Suíça in Lisbon was a historic and iconic café-restaurant

She must think I'm a spoiled child. A spoiled twenty-nine-year-old. So, I hasten to clear up the misunderstanding.

"I went to the grocery store to buy some things and when I got home, I found a pack of Smarties in the shopping bag. I don't know how they got there."

My aunt starts laughing.

"Hey Mel, there's absolutely nothing wrong with enjoying Smarties! No matter how much we age, that kid in us never really goes away."

"I'm telling you the truth."

She clasps my arm and plants a kiss on my cheek.

"I'm fifty-six years old and still have a thing for M&M's."

I give up trying to persuade her and opt to assist her with dinner instead. We grill some burgers made from beef that she bought at the local butcher's. I manage to convince her to whip up some veggies to complement the meal. I've got to get a grip on my diet; otherwise, when I return to Lisbon, Leo will make me suffer in those CrossFit classes.

We spend the evening chatting about my trip to the park with Carlos, and my aunt shares tales about their rural tourism guests. Her and Jasmine's experiences range from delightful encounters, like a Japanese couple who gifted them a silk-screen print of Tokyo, to downright bizarre guests, such as a French couple who brought a pet tarantula along, intending to show the spider the wonders of the Azores. I can't even fathom the potential spider-related drama if they ever split up.

After dinner, I catch sight of the Smarties pack lying on the kitchen counter, and it's as if my aunt can read my mind. She grabs the packet and places it in front of me on the table without saying a word.

"I'll handle the dishes tonight."

"No need, darling. I'll take care of it. You must be exhausted."

I sit there, eyeing the pack and realizing I'm actually craving it. I reach for a piece and savor the chocolate slowly, finding comfort in that familiar taste. I grab another one, letting it melt in my mouth. As I sit there, munching on Smarties, in the home of an aunt I haven't seen in over two decades, it hits me - I miss those days—miss being a child.

In our childhood days, life was wonderfully simple—just eat, sleep, play. We eagerly raced toward adulthood, only to realize later that life was much simpler back then. The truth is, nobody truly preps you for the intricate dance of adult life. The moment you're officially an adult, it's like diving into a whirlwind of complexities—bills, taxes, rent, and the whole shebang. Suddenly, your to-do list feels like an

---

that held a significant place in the city's cultural and social scene. Located in the heart of Lisbon at Rossio Square, it was renowned for its elegant and charming ambiance.

insurmountable mountain, while everyone expects you to slap on a smile the whole time as if everything's just fine.

I notice my aunt gazing at me.

"I've missed you so much, Mel."

I want to reciprocate, but I hesitate.

"You don't have to say you missed me, Mel. You were a child. It's normal that you barely remember me."

And for the first time in forever, I don't feel the urge to pretend.

"I really miss those times when I was a child."

My aunt walks over and gives me a hug. This time, I don't pull away. This time, I hug her back. I hug her back because I'm starting to like this hippie aunt who dresses in flowery tunics, and showers affection with hugs and kisses. I can't fathom why she's been banned from the family as if she were a criminal.

Chapter 11

I dragged myself out of bed at six to force myself into a run. Not that I wanted to, but if I keep eating like this without moving, I'll start resembling a balloon. Curiosity about the office is eating me alive, but I know those guys won't spill a word. Carmen is the only person I can expect to spill all the rumors, but I don't feel like talking to her because I can predict her third-degree interrogation. She's likely cooked up a million tales about me by now - from an overdose to a booze-induced coma or even eloping with a CrossFit guru to Ibiza. Carmen has a wild imagination.

Just as I'm finishing breakfast with my aunt, a knock echoes at the door.

"It must be Carlos," my aunt says.

Even though I want to explore the island, my gut wrenches at the thought of hopping back on that motorcycle again. Why can't I just tell him the truth?

"Morning!" Carlos strides in, all smiles, seemingly forgetting yesterday's drenching episode.

Today, he's wearing a Homer Simpson tee, arms up, shouting "Woo Hoo". Between that and the Snoopy one, I can't decide which is uglier. Doesn't he realize he's outgrown his teenage years? I can't pinpoint his exact age, but he's old enough to step away from the teen look and dress more like an adult.

"Have a seat and drink a cup of coffee!" my aunt offers.

"If it's not too much trouble, I'll take it."

He settles in, and my aunt pours him coffee – he puts two spoons of sugar in it. I should nudge him about that sugar intake. It's not doing any favors for his health or waistline. But what if he takes offense? Better zip it about the sugar.

"How're your parents and sisters doing?"

"They're good. Joana's diving into the swimming championship next week."

"Joana's the youngest, right?"

"Yeah, she's twelve."

"How many sisters do you have?" I ask.

"I've got three. I'm the oldest. Inês is twenty-seven, Rosa is twenty-five, and Joana's the baby. What about you?"

"I'm an only child."

I envy him a bit. Having siblings must be a blessing. Being an only child means I have to put up with my parents on my own. There's no one to share that load with.

"Back when we all lived under one roof, my dad and I were outnumbered. Four women versus two men."

"It must be nice having a big family."

"Depends. Sometimes it wasn't easy, but now that I live alone, I miss all that chaos. Then again, having my own space is pretty great. My sisters used to grill my girlfriends, and if they didn't approve, they'd find ways to scare them off."

"Really? My dad was the one who scared off my boyfriends. Once they knew he was a judge, they'd vanish."

"We're both tragic cases. Nosy relatives ruined our love lives," he says. We both start laughing.

I get up to tackle the dishes.

"Is the cramp gone?" My aunt asks.

"Yep." When I got back from the run, I had this awful cramp. Maybe I shouldn't have pushed myself that hard.

"That might be due to low magnesium. Let me grab a banana from the pantry."

"No need, Aunt Gabi. I think I probably overdid it on the morning run. Pretty sure that's what it was." She brushes me off and heads to the pantry.

"So, you're into running?"

"Not really. Truth is, I hate it."

"Then why do you do it?"

"To stay in shape."

"There are easier ways to keep fit, you know."

"They're not as effective."

"I think people shouldn't do what they hate."

"You don't run?" Silly question. He doesn't strike me as the running type. Or the exercise type at all.

"Nope. I prefer diving. Way more interesting than running. You should give it a shot."

I half expected him to be into chess, checkers, or some kind of board game. Anything but diving. He must rock an XL suit; that little belly definitely won't squeeze into a smaller size.

"Here are two bananas." My aunt comes out from the pantry, a bunch of bananas in hand. She hands me two and tosses the rest into the fruit bowl.

Carlos stands up, about to wash his cup, but my aunt stops him.

"Forget it, sweetie. I'll take care of it."

"Are you sure? I can wash it."

"Yes, carry on."

"Thanks, Gabi. Ready?" He beams at me. Why's he always in such a good mood?

"I just need to grab my backpack."

"How was your tour yesterday?" I hear my aunt ask as I head to the bedroom.

"Everything was great until we got soaked at Terra Nostra Park."

"You got soaked?! Mel, why didn't you tell me?" My aunt asks when I return to the living room, backpack in hand.

"You got the worst of it, Carlos. I only got wet from the ankles down. I didn't have a raincoat, and Carlos lent me his. But this time, I'm prepared—I've got an umbrella and a raincoat."

He chuckles, and for the first time, I notice his dimples when he laughs.

"Here's your raincoat."

"I told you it's a gift. You can keep it."

"Carlos is such a sweetheart," my aunt giggles. "That's why I asked him to show you around the island. I wouldn't trust just anyone with my favorite niece."

"I'm your only niece."

"But you're still my favorite." She pulls me into a tight hug, and I hug her back.

"Shall we head out?" Carlos asks.

I nod and sling the backpack over my shoulders.

"Wait. I've baked Portuguese muffins. I'll pack two in a lunchbox for you to take along."

"No need, Aunt Gabi. If I keep eating like this, I'll balloon up."

"Nonsense, Mel. You're slim, you need to eat."

And she hands me the lunchbox. I don't want to be rude, so I unzip my backpack and slip the box in. Maybe Carlos fancies a bite. He seems like a cake person.

We say goodbye to my aunt and step out. Instead of the motorcycle, there's a pickup truck parked—it's almost a replica of my aunt's. Seems like the island's official ride, everyone's got the same one.

"What happened to the motorcycle?"

Carlos chuckles, those dimples back in action.

"Today, we're rolling with the van."

I spy the motorcycle parked in front of the neighbor's house. I bet the old man's about to step out and give Carlos a lecture for parking in front of his place.

"Yesterday, I had the feeling you're not a big fan of motorcycles."

Looks like I didn't hide it as well as I thought.

"Yeah..." I'm lost for words.

"No problem, Mel."

I glance at him, meeting his gaze. He's smiling, not in a teasing or judgmental way. It's weird, but it feels like he can see past the mask I wear every day, like he can see the real me. I look away, embarrassed.

"I'm not used to riding a motorcycle," I admit. There's no sense pretending anymore.

"That's okay. Today we're going with the van."

We climb in, and he revs the engine, which sputters to life with a bang. The truck needs some serious maintenance. I hope it doesn't break down in the middle of the road.

"Is this truck yours?"

"Nope, I borrowed it from my grandpa."

We turn onto the main street of the village, passing by the grocery store. Mr. Manuel is outside chatting with other old-timers. Carlos gives them a wave, and Mr. Manuel surprisingly waves back, even cracks a smile.

"Mr. Manuel seems unusually chipper today."

"Why'd you say that?"

"He's usually not so friendly. I went to the store yesterday, and I didn't leave with the best impression."

"I know my grandpa can be a bit grouchy, but he's a good guy."

"He's your grandfather?" Oh boy, is Carlos going to be mad at me now? That's the last thing I need.

"Yep."

"So, this is his truck?"

"Sure is."

Should've recognized the pickup, but they all look alike to me.

"Sorry about what I've said. I had no clue he was your grandfather."

"It's all good, Mel. I love him, but I know he can be a handful." Carlos chuckles.

He looks unruffled. Suddenly, I'm envious of him. Always so chill. I wish I could pull that off. Even with the pills, I never truly unwind. My mind keeps running through a million ways things could go wrong. Rodrigo hasn't texted back yet, and I've been stewing, imagining he's had enough of me or found someone else. Worse yet, I'm picturing something awful happened. Every news bit about an air accident triggers thoughts of his flight. I take a deep breath, and glance at my phone. He still hasn't texted me back.

As we drive up the hills, the road becomes narrower and curvier, but the view is stunning, all green with spots of colorful hortensias.

"You picked the right time to come to São Miguel. Everything's blooming in spring."

"It's beautiful."

We keep going up and I start feeling queasy. Darn pills.

"Carlos, can you pull over?"

"Yeah, sure. Let me find a spot with a verge so we're not stuck in the middle of the road."

A few hundred meters ahead there's a side road, and he steers the van onto it, bringing it to a stop. I step out and lean against the trunk.

"Are you alright?"

I nod.

"Sorry, maybe I was driving too fast."

I think about making an excuse, but then I decide to come clean. I don't want him thinking it's on him.

"No, it's not your fault. It's this medication I'm taking."

He heads to the truck and returns with a water bottle.

"Drink up! It might help."

I take a sip and focus on breathing. He doesn't ask about the meds, and I don't talk about it either. There's a fallen tree log nearby. Carlos motions for me, and we both sit in the shade. I'm not in the mood to talk, and he seems to get that, so we sit in silence for a while.

A bird lands on a nearby tree branch, and I notice butterflies fluttering around. Carlos grabs his camera and starts snapping shots of the butterflies. One of them, with turquoise wings, lands on my shoulder, and he starts taking pictures of me.

"Cut it out, Carlos! I probably look terrible."

"No, you don't."

"I'm probably as pale as a ghost."

"Not at all. These shots will turn out great."

He keeps snapping, and I muster a smile. I don't want to look like a moody ghost in the pictures.

"You'd make a great fashion photographer."

"I hate being cooped up in studios. I prefer the outdoors."

"You could probably make more money in fashion."

"Maybe, but it wouldn't make me happy."

"And you're all about doing what you love, right?"

He grins and winks at me.

"That's it! You're starting to get me. I'd rather make less money but do what I love and be close to my family. These photos I'm taking are for a website run by the Azores Tourist Office."

"I hope none of my photos make it onto that site."

"No way. These are for my personal stash." Then he seems to get flustered. "I mean, if that's cool with you."

"As long as I don't look like a ghost, we're good. But if I do, you must promise to delete them."

"Deal."

"You better promise!"

"I promise."

"Thanks for bringing the truck. That was nice of you."

"I'm a nice guy."

"If you weren't, my aunt wouldn't have entrusted you with her favorite niece."

We both crack up.

"How are you feeling?"

"Better now. The fresh air did wonders."

"Ready to hit the road again?"

"Yeah, let's go."

We drive the rest of the way in silence, but it's not awkward; it's more like two people soaking in the scenery. The road's adorned with hortensias on both sides, adding a pop of color. The are lots of curves, but I'm feeling better. I'm hoping I can make it without puking in his grandfather's truck. I can't fathom what the man would do if I threw up in there.

When we arrive, Carlos parks by a viewpoint, and I hop out of the van behind him.

"Hey, come check this out."

I stroll up to the viewpoint's edge, taken aback by the unexpected beauty. I'd scrolled through numerous photos and knew this place was stunning, but being here in the flesh magnifies its allure. Down below lie the two lagoons of Seven Cities

Lake, embraced by the vibrant greenery of the volcano. The lagoons interconnect, yet one gleams blue while the other radiates a deep green hue.

"Pretty impressive, huh?"

I nod, at a loss for words to capture the emotions swirling within. Those images in magazines or online always seemed too perfect, like they'd been retouched with Photoshop or something. But now I realize those photos barely scratch the surface of this place's true beauty.

"Why's one blue and the other green?"

"There's this legend," Carlos grins, his eyes brimming with excitement, "so, the story goes that the island's kings had a daughter who'd wander into the fields daily. One day, she bumped into a shepherd on his way home with his flock. They hit it off and started meeting daily, exchanging vows of love. Trouble was, the princess was betrothed to a prince from a neighboring kingdom, set by her parents. When her father got wind of her rendezvous with the shepherd, he put a stop to it, granting them one last meeting to bid farewell."

"Her dad sounds like a real tyrant!"

"When they met for the final time, they cried so much that two ponds formed at their feet. One pond, with its blue waters, emerged from the tears shed by the princess's blue eyes. The other, tinted green, sprung from the shepherd's weeping green eyes. They couldn't be together, but the ponds born from their tears remained forever linked."

I'm itching to tell him that it's probably just a tale, that there has to be some scientific reason behind those lagoons rocking different hues despite being linked. But I bite my tongue. It might be a sad tale, but it's a beautiful love story. And I'm a sucker for a good love story. So, I stand there, soaking in that beauty, marveling at how nature can whip up something so breathtaking, so flawless. I inhale deeply, relishing the pure air filling my lungs.

"Isn't this most breathtaking island on the planet?" he taunts.

"Yes, it is. It's a magical place."

He grabs his gear and starts snapping pictures.

"I need to capture it before the fog rolls in."

"Fog?"

"Yep, we're lucky. Fog's a regular here. Lots of folks miss out on seeing these lagoons when they're here on vacation."

"I'm lucky, then."

"Very lucky."

And that's exactly how I feel, despite everything that's gone down these past few days. Despite Cláudio, the stint in the hospital, my parents being cold as ice. I'm fortunate to be here. The view of the lagoons, embraced by vibrant hortensias, is stunning. I'm in the ideal setup for a fairy tale, just missing the Prince Charming who never bothers to reply to my texts.

"Can you snap a photo of me?"

Carlos tears his gaze away from the lens and faces me.

"With your phone?" I catch the amusement in his eyes.

"Don't mock me!"

"I'm not."

I notice he's trying hard not to laugh. He sets down the gear, and I hand him my phone. After a few pointers, I strike a pose amidst the hortensias. When he hands back my phone, I'm taken aback yet again by the photo quality and how good I look. Most times, I cringe at seeing myself in pictures. I always think I look awful, like I've gained weight or lost my neck.

"They came out really nice."

"The model was a big help."

I glance up from the screen and meet his gaze.

"You're beautiful."

A warmth spreads across my cheeks, and I realize I'm blushing. Carlos is smiling at me, those dimples carving his cheeks, and I suddenly feel shy, without a clue why. He seems a bit awkward too, shifting his focus away. He goes back to his photos, and I take the chance to pick a picture, sending it to Rodrigo with a caption:

Missing out on this—wish you were here to see for yourself.

We linger at the viewpoint, Carlos capturing shots while I sketch the lagoons hugged by hortensias. By the time the fog shrouds the two lagoons, it's lunchtime. We head down and grab a meal at a quaint restaurant in a village right by the lagoons. Despite its charm, it's missing that touch of authenticity without a Mrs. Maria. We munch on fried mackerel and, of course, sip on Kima. Tomorrow, I need to lace up my running shoes again.

After lunch, it seems like the fog has lifted, so we return to the lagoons. Carlos occupies himself photographing some ducks nearby. I dip my hands into the chilly waters of the blue lagoon, relishing the pleasant sensation despite my freezing fingers. I wonder if there's any truth to the legend. I want to believe there is.

Carlos wanders off behind a duckling, and I perch on the low wall encircling the lagoon. The phone rings, and I feel a surge of nerves for no apparent reason. I hope it's Rodrigo. I fish my phone out of my bag, but as soon as I glimpse the number on the display, disappointment washes over me. It's a call from the office. Suddenly, the office feels distant, my life in Lisbon even more so. I let out a sigh but decide to answer. It might be something important.

"Hello?"

"Hello, princess."

I recognize Claudio's voice instantly and a chill runs down my spine.

"Good afternoon."

"How are you doing?"

"What do you want?"

"So cold, Mel."

"What do you want?"

"I can't find the football player's file."

"It's in my office cabinet. Bottom shelf."

I hear the cabinet door open and the shuffle of folders.

"Heard you had a breakdown and ran off to the Azores."

I swallow hard. By now, everyone at the office must know what happened.

"Do you need anything else?" I ask, trying to keep my cool.

"I do."

"Then spit it out."

"I mean, you need it. You need someone to straighten you out."

"If that's all, I'm hanging up."

"Wait, I need to tell you something."

"What?"

He goes quiet for a moment and then whispers:

"It sucks, doesn't it? The moment you realize you're just a scared little bitch."

His words hit me hard, and my first instinct is to fire back. But then I decide it's not worth taking the bait because I know that's exactly what he wants, and I won't give him the satisfaction. I hang up on him. What a jerk! Leo was right; I should enroll in Krav Maga classes. Nothing would feel better than giving this guy a good beating, but it's just a pipe dream because he's bigger and stronger than me. Plus, when I'm around him, I lose my cool and get really nervous. Just like now. I'm fifteen hundred kilometers away from him, and he still managed to push me to the brink of a breakdown. I stash the phone in my backpack, worried he might call again, but minutes go by, and it stays silent.

Carlos returns, and I try to hide my nerves.

"Everything alright?"

"I got a call from work. Same old drama, you know."

"Nah, clue me in."

"Yeah, you're lucky without a boss or annoying colleagues."

"Which can have its downsides too."

"Downsides?"

"Yeah, sometimes it can get a bit lonesome."

"I hadn't thought of that."

"That's why I appreciate you keeping me company."

"I thought you only brought me because you couldn't say no to my aunt."

"Of course not, Mel! If I didn't want to bring you, I wouldn't."

"Because you only do what you want."

He chuckles.

"Exactly!"

I want to smile. I really want to smile, but I can't. Claudio's words are stuck in my head.

"I think that's enough for today," Carlos says.

"Yeah, the sun is starting to set."

As he packs up the equipment, I gaze at the lagoons and sigh. I can't stop thinking about Claudio. That jerk managed to ruin my day.

"Is everything okay, Mel?"

It seems I can't hide anything from Carlos.

"Yeah, everything's great. I'm just a little queasy."

"Do you want me to head to the café and grab you some sparkling water?"

"No, it'll pass. Can you drop me off in Ponta Delgada? I need to do some shopping." I need a bottle of vodka. This time without tampons.

Chapter 12

Carlos drops me off near the City Gates. The sun begins its descent, casting a warm orange glow that breaks through the clouds, painting the streets with an enchanting hue. Stepping out of the van, I venture until I spot a supermarket. Determined to grab a bottle of vodka and leave swiftly, I stride through the entrance, only to collide with a throng of tourists. They all have that Northern European appearance, seeming as though they were dumped here by a tourist bus. The sight of so many people crammed into this confined space steals my breath away.

"Excuse me," I say, but no one pays me any mind. "Hey, excuse me!" I insist, but they keep ignoring me. Two big guys block my way, chattering away in a language with a ton of consonants and hardly any vowels that I can't even place. I backtrack and try to find another aisle to pass through because these guys won't budge. Eventually, I squeeze through another aisle and aim for the drinks section.

"This feels like a Viking invasion!" I overhear a girl say to her friend. Besides me, they seem to be the only Portuguese customers. They're both short, like really short, especially next to these towering Vikings.

"Let's hurry up! I need to get out of here! I feel like I can't even breathe with all these people!" the other woman says. "Just pick out your chocolate!"

I get shoved by a red-haired guy and find myself caught between two groups engaged in a loud conversation. My anxiety spikes, and I realize I've got to get out of there, pronto. I weave through the crowd, elbowing my way until I finally spot the drinks aisle. I grab a bottle of Smirnoff and head to the cashier. But it's chaos over there. Everyone who was leisurely shopping is now at the only two counters open. Suddenly, I'm squished between a tall blonde, probably six feet tall, and an even taller bald guy. Breathing becomes hard, my chest tightens, and I feel another panic attack creeping up. I need to get out before things get worse.

I abandon the line, leaving the bottle on a random shelf, and rush towards the exit. There are fewer people there now because they're all crowded at the counters. My legs shake and my head spins. Not again! I can't let this happen again! I spot the exit and muster every bit of strength to bolt out.

I step through the door, and the sunlight blinds me. Trying to take a deep breath feels like a struggle with a weight on my chest. The wind, though, cuts through, a refreshing sensation on my skin. An empty bus stop catches my eye, so I make my way over there. The place seems deserted. I collapse onto the bench, attempting to calm myself down, yet my body continues to tremble uncontrollably. Leaning against the bus stop's glass, I can't shake this feeling. Will I ever manage to go to the supermarket again? And how on earth am I going to get back to Aunt Gabi's place? Maybe asking Carlos to drop me off here in Ponta Delgada was a mistake. This vodka errand wasn't worth it!

Standing up, I try to look at the bus schedule posted at the stop, but it's all names of other destinations—none heading towards my aunt's village. What if I call for a cab? I reach for my phone in my bag, but my mind's in chaos. How do you even find a cab number? Okay, calm down, take a breath! The thought of calling Rodrigo crosses my mind, but he's thousands of miles away. Then it dawns on me—I have my aunt's number. I dial frantically, and just when I'm on the verge of giving up hope, she finally picks up.

"Hi darling."

"Could you come pick me up?" Urgency laces my voice.

Without hesitation, my aunt responds, "Tell me where you are, and I'll be there in a flash."

I glance around, but there are no street signs in sight.

"I'm not sure."

"Calm down, darling. Look around, see if there's something you can spot."

The supermarket.

"I'm at a bus stop right across from this downtown supermarket, near the City Gates."

"I know the place. I'll be there in fifteen minutes."

I hang up the phone and rest my head against the bus stop's glass. Closing my eyes, I ponder what to tell my aunt. I don't want her thinking I'm losing it. Maybe I could say I had a sudden drop in blood pressure. Yeah, that's it. Everyone's had a blood pressure drop at some point.

"Do you need help?"

I open my eyes and spot an old lady holding a shopping bag.

"I'm okay, thank you. Just feeling a bit dizzy."

"Would you like me to go to the café over there and grab you a glass of sugared water?"

In Portugal, sugared water is the cure-all, but it's not going to help in this case. What if I asked her to fetch me a bottle of vodka from the supermarket? A sip might help me unwind. Stupid idea, Mel!

"No, thanks. My aunt's on her way."

"Are you sure you don't need assistance?"

"I'm sure. It'll pass, and like I said, my aunt's coming."

The old lady studies me but she doesn't seem convinced. She sets down her shopping bag and takes a seat beside me.

"I'll keep you company until your aunt gets here."

"It's really not necessary."

"You know, I have a granddaughter around your age."

I muster a smile. While I appreciate her good intentions, I'm not in the mood for stories about her granddaughter. Unfortunately, she doesn't seem to pick up on that. She rummages through her bag and retrieves a water bottle.

"Here, take it. Have a sip; it'll help."

"Thanks, but I'm not thirsty."

"You should have a little water, dear." She hands me the bottle, and I take it because I don't want to offend her. There's something about her that reminds me of my grandma. Maybe it's those pearl earrings or the gray hair, but there's a sense of familiarity, something comforting.

Listening to her chat, it brings back memories of my grandma. I really miss her. Those moments we spent together—savoring tea and scones, exploring bookstores in Lisbon, and our talks at Suíça Bakery in the evenings—I long for those. Grandma embodied what my grandfather saw as a 'good woman'—you know, dutiful and obedient. He never explicitly stated it, but I could sense his beliefs. Thinking back, I can hardly recall having many conversations with him. He remained reserved, even after retiring, preferring the company of his old work buddies over spending time with his granddaughter, who was just a kid and a girl.

"My granddaughter, who's around your age, studied in Lisbon. She's an architect. Right now, she's in Japan doing an internship at a big architecture firm."

I take a sip of water and inhale deeply. My hands are still trembling slightly, but at least the shortness of breath is gone.

"She was home for Christmas, but I already miss her. The good thing is, with these computers, I can see her on my son's computer. It's not quite the same, but it beats just writing letters. Back in the day, it was all about letters. My husband worked in France for a while, and I'd write him a letter, then wait weeks for a reply."

I take another sip of water and flash a smile.

"But you know, despite all these modern gadgets that make life easier," she leans in, her voice dropping, "I feel like the world is declining. In the past, we knew everyone in the neighborhood, had these huge family gatherings, and kids played freely in the streets. When we were together, we were truly connected. Now, I see a couple in the park, each on their separate phones, engrossed. They don't communicate, don't engage, just absorbed by their screens, as if they were strangers."

"Technology has alienated us. We are increasingly connected to the network, but more disconnected from our humanity."

"That's it! That's exactly what I meant. Sure, chatting with my granddaughter on the computer's nice, but it's not the same. I can't hug her, or kiss her, or even smell her."

"You're right, it's not quite the same." And I find myself thinking of Rodrigo and the countless messages we've exchanged over the past year. I miss kissing him, holding him close. I miss his smell, the taste of his lips.

"I'm so relieved you get it."

"Mel, are you alright?!"

"Aunt Gabi, I'm so glad you're here!"

"How are you feeling?"

"I got a bit lightheaded, but I'm better now. Must've been a sudden drop in blood pressure."

The old lady grabs her bag and gets up. "Now that your aunt's here, I'll go."

I get up too. "Thank you."

"I didn't do much, just stayed for a bit to keep you company."

"You did a lot. Thank you!"

"Thank you for looking out for my niece."

The old lady smiles and walks off with her shopping bag. My aunt comes over and wraps me in a tight hug.

"Are you really feeling okay?" I feel safe and sheltered in that hug. "Should I take you to the hospital?"

The thought of it sends shivers down my spine. No way, I absolutely don't want to set foot in any hospital.

"No need, I'm good now."

She eyes me suspiciously but eventually drops the hospital idea.

"Let's get going, you need to rest."

What I truly need is a drink, but I have to push that thought away. If it wasn't for that vodka run, I wouldn't have even been at the supermarket, wouldn't have had another panic attack. Maybe it's a sign to lay off the drinking.

I follow my aunt and hop into the van. She drives toward the city exit. Glancing at her, for the first time, I see a hint of my grandma in her: the eyes, the nose. How did I never notice that before? My grandma was a kind soul, and I know she never stopped loving her daughter, even after my grandfather kicked her out. I found that out during a tea session at Suíça Bakery, just before my grandma passed away. I asked about my aunt. I remember Grandma smiling, but it was tinged with sadness.

"Your aunt defied your grandpa." That's all she said, tears welling up. Then she quickly reached for her handkerchief, dabbing her eyes.

"Do you think grandpa will ever forgive her?"

"Disobedience is something your grandpa takes very seriously."

And she stashed the handkerchief away. Not another word, as if even discussing it was an act of defiance. Then she ordered two custard tarts and chamomile tea because chamomile was her solution to everything—as if chamomile tea could solve any problem.

"Mel, you don't have talk if you're not ready, but I'm here if you need me," my aunt says, "I sense something's up, but I won't push."

I lean back, silent for a moment. I want to open up, spill everything, but it's like I'm gagged. I want to trust her, but fear grips me. What if she reacts like Ruth did when I first mentioned the panic attack? What if she ships me back to Lisbon? What if...

Her hand finds mine, and I clutch it hard. Thoughts whirl, my head feels ready to burst.

"I had a panic attack," I blurt out, before I can reconsider.

My aunt doesn't respond, but she tightens her grip. We veer off the main road, winding upward. I notice that isn't the way home. But where is she taking me? We keep ascending until we hit a spot that looks like a viewpoint, offering a stunning sight of the island. She parks the van and hugs me.

And I try to hold back the tears. I try to hold back the tears because I'm a rock in the middle of a storm, battered by rain and wind. I'm a rock and nothing can break me, nothing can knock me down. But there are days when I don't feel like a rock. There are days when I feel defeated. Today is one of those days.

The tears start flowing, unstoppable. She holds onto me even tighter.

"You're getting your clothes all damp."

"It doesn't matter, darling. I'm here."

"That's why I came to the Azores," I manage between sobs.

"Because of the panic attacks?"

"Yeah, I had a major one at a Lisbon supermarket. Ended up in the hospital; they thought it was a heart attack."

"Oh, dear. When was this?"

"Last Friday."

"Then you decided to take a break here in the Azores to recover?"

"Then my parents wanted me in a clinic."

"In a clinic?"

"Yeah, but I refused. It sounds nuts, but your invite came, and I figured some time in the Azores might do me good."

My aunt cups my face, planting a kiss on my forehead.

"Best idea, Mel! Even though it's been years, I've never stopped thinking about you. You're my only niece, and I love you."

I've got The Question itching at the tip of my tongue. But now's not the time to ask it.

"I love you too," I say, and it hits me that I really mean it. My aunt stands out from the rest of the family, and I've grown to like her.

"Those pills you've been taking, are they for anxiety?"

"Yeah, the doctor at the hospital prescribed them, but they don't seem to do much. They just make me feel sick and dead tired."

"You had another panic attack at the supermarket?"

"Yeah. Not as intense as the one I had in Lisbon, but yeah, it was a panic attack. I walked into the store, and it felt like an alarm bell ringing in my head."

"Are you seeing a therapist?"

"Nah, I believe this will fade away on its own. I know it will."

"Mel, darling, you really should get some help. When I started with panic attacks over thirty years ago, things were way different. Lots of doctors didn't know much about it. But now, there are good professionals who can help you."

"You had panic attacks too?!"

"Yes. It was when..." I hear my aunt gulp, "it was when I decided to quit my job as a college professor. It was tough. Your grandfather didn't approve."

"I didn't know you taught at the University."

"Yeah, at the Faculty of Arts and Humanities. After I left your grandparents' place, I had a rough patch. Saw several doctors, but when I described the symptoms—heart flutters, hard time breathing, dizziness—they sent me for heart and lung tests, even a brain CT scan. Nobody knew what was up, and I felt worse and worse. I started having attacks nearly every day, I freaked out, I thought I was going to die anytime. Your grandma would sneak me to the best doctors in the country, but none of them could really help me out."

"Grandpa didn't help you?"

"Your grandfather was a tough, demanding man. I was a letdown to him, a disappointment who walked away from a career as a university professor for love."

"For love?"

"Someday, Mel, I'll tell you the whole story."

"And then what happened?"

"I was so desperate that someone mentioned a doctor in London. I booked a ticket and flew there. When he told me what I had, I couldn't believe him. I was convinced I had some fatal disease, that I was about to drop dead any minute. He explained I wasn't going to die; my lungs and heart were fine. It was my brain playing tricks, making me think I was on the edge."

"I thought I was going to die when I was on the floor of the supermarket in Lisbon."

She holds my hands tightly.

"You're not going to die, Mel! I mean, we'll all go someday because no one's eternal, but panic attacks won't kill us."

"And how did you get better?"

"There's no magic fix. Eventually, I got better with therapy and meds, had years without an attack, but I know it can come back. Anxiety is like a monster you keep hidden in the closet. You try to hide it from everyone, even from yourself. But you can't hide the monster forever. One day you have to face it. One day you have to open the door and look it in the eye. The day you face it is the day you start controlling it. And sometimes it remains meek and obedient for years, but then one day it comes back at you when you least expect it. But by then, you're already prepared, and you get it under control again."

"And does it get any easier?"

"It's not a walk in the park, I won't sugarcoat it. But it does get easier because you know it's doable, you know you can stand strong against it. When you rang me last week, I felt like I was on the edge of a crisis, but then Jasmine helped me calm down."

"Why were you anxious when I called?"

"I started imagining that you wouldn't like me, that I'd be a letdown to you."

"That's silly, Aunt Gabi."

"So, does that mean I'm not a letdown?" She asks, grinning.

"Of course not. I..." I pause, "I'm not great at sharing my feelings..."

"I get it, Mel. Our family's not big on expressing emotions openly."

"No, we're not. And we hardly ever hug or kiss."

"You're not a fan of my hugs?" She teases.

"I'm getting there."

"Well, better get there soon because I'm not stopping with the hugs and kisses," she says, giving me a tight hug and a kiss.

We both crack up laughing. When we stop laughing, she looks me in the eye and says:

"Darling, you need help."

"It's just a phase, Aunt Gabi. It's just that things haven't been easy lately. I've been having some trouble at work."

"Trouble?"

"Yeah, with a coworker, but I don't feel like getting into it right now," I can't even bring myself to say his name aloud. "The worst part is the office probably thinks I've had a total meltdown or something. When I return, I'll have to put up with their jokes for months."

"People often fear what they don't understand. That's why many people still keep their mental health issues to themselves. But we're not crazy, or helpless, or faking sickness to skip work."

"Yeah, but that's what worries me. I don't want my coworkers to jump to conclusions."

And most importantly, I don't want Claudio to think he's got the best of me. I won't give him that satisfaction.

"We're dealing with an illness, just like any other. We shouldn't have to hide or feel ashamed."

"I know, but sometimes I just want to escape. Start fresh somewhere new."

"Promise me you'll seek help, Mel."

"When I get back to Lisbon, I'll figure things out, Aunt Gabi. I promise."

"Alright, darling. Let's head home."

She turns the key in the ignition.

"Why did you reach out to me now, after all these years?"

I sense a brief pause in her response, as if she's carefully weighing her words.

"I've realized life's too short, and I wanted to get closer to my niece. And having you here with me brings me joy."

"I just came here to give you a hard time."

"You're no trouble at all, darling. Tonight, I'm making your old favorite dinner. Do you still like spaghetti Bolognese?"

She remembers. My aunt remembers my favorite meal.

"I love it," I say, feeling a smile stretch across my face. I'm smiling because I feel less isolated. I'm smiling because I know I can count on this bohemian aunt wrapped in flowery tunics, living in a yellow-themed house.

Chapter 13

This morning kicked off with an early call from my mother while I was wrapping up my run. She's still adamant about me heading back to Lisbon to see her therapist friend. At least, this time she didn't bring up the Clinic. After convincing her that everything's fine and I'm genuinely enjoying my time at Aunt Gabi's, I head to the kitchen. There's a delightful aroma wafting in the air. Did my aunt bake a cake?

"I made pancakes for breakfast," she announces.

Ah, so that explains the tempting scent. I'm about to devour countless calories, but at the moment, I couldn't care less. I'm ravenous. I grab my pills and spread some of Aunt Gabi's homemade pineapple jam onto a pancake.

"These pancakes and jam are fantastic."

"I'm glad you enjoy them. Was that your mother on the phone?" Aunt Gabi inquires.

"Yeah, she was curious about when I'd be returning to Lisbon."

"And what about your dad? Have you talked to him?"

"Nah, he's probably buried in work. No time for me."

"I'm sure he's worried about you, Mel."

My aunt mentions this, not having seen him at the hospital. To him, I'm just a nuisance. His career takes precedence over everything.

She slides another pancake onto my plate.

"Thanks, aunt. These pancakes are really good." This time, I add a dollop of butter. "You know, when I was little, my father used to cook."

I don't know why that memory resurfaced.

"Your grandma taught us both how to cook when we were kids. Your grandpa didn't approve of your father in the kitchen. He believed that cooking was for women. But your grandma kept teaching your father in secret. He adored cooking and was way better than me. Doesn't he cook anymore?"

"Rarely," I reply, recalling the post-panic-attack lunch. "He stopped cooking when he became a Supreme Court Judge. He doesn't have the time anymore."

"That's a shame. He had a real passion for it. There was a time when he even considered studying Gastronomy in France, but your grandpa wouldn't allow it."

I nearly choke on my pancake. "Gastronomy?!"

"Yes, didn't he tell you?"

"No, I always assumed my father wanted to be a judge since he was a kid."

"No, darling, it was your grandfather who determined that he would pursue a career in law."

"I'm in shock. My father wanted to study cooking. COOKING! Can you believe it?" I spread some more jam on another pancake and start to imagine what life might have been like if my father had become a chef instead of a judge. "Would he have let me study Arts? I don't know what might've happened, but perhaps my father would've been happier. Because when I look at him, I don't see a happy man. I see a competent, respected professional, but not a happy one. It's crazy how we lose ourselves trying to meet others' expectations.

I'm still processing this bombshell when my phone rings. Could it be Rodrigo? He hasn't reached out in a while, and that's starting to worry me. My aunt goes outside to water the porch plants, and I pick up the call. It's Ruth. What does she want at this ungodly hour?

"Hey, Ruth."

"Hi, Mel. How are you?"

Her voice sounds sweet, but I know her well enough to know that sweetness usually comes with a favor.

"I'm good. What's up with you?"

"I'm fine too. It's scorching here in Ibiza."

"That's nice. You can hit the beach every day."

"Yeah."

"So, what's on your mind?"

"I don't want to bother you..."

"You're not a bother. What do you need?" I act oblivious, even though I can sense where this is heading.

"I need you to lend me some money. I'll pay you back soon."

Predictable. So predictable.

"Weren't you teaching online classes?"

"I was, but, and please spare me the lecture, the American guy bailed and took all my money."

"You mean he stole your money, right?"

"He left."

"He stole your money."

"Yeah, fine, he stole my money." Her tone gets pushy, as always. "So, will you lend me some or not?"

"Isn't it time to head back home?"

I can almost hear her sigh on the other end of the line.

"What home, Mel, what home?!"

"The house of your parents," I remind her, considering her father's status as one of the wealthiest businessmen in the country.

"If they didn't want me home as a child, do you really think they'd want me now?"

"Don't think that way, as if they don't care."

"You weren't the one sent to a boarding school at six, only home during holidays. I felt like a burden, an unwanted accident. I don't even know why my mother didn't choose to abort."

"Please don't say that, Ruth."

"What else can you say? That deep down, they love me? They only have eyes for my brother, the perfect son." Her brother, a decade older, works in their father's company.

"Your father wanted you to join the family business after college. It could've been a way to connect."

"Because that's going great for you, right? Embracing a career chosen by your father?! Spare me."

I swallow hard, opting for silence. I don't want to argue with her.

"Sorry, Mel. I shouldn't have said that, but I'm furious with Frank."

"And your parents..."

"And my parents. You're not the only one having parental issues. Did that lead you to the Azores? Did you have a row with your parents?"

I contemplate lying, saying I came to explore the island, spend time with my aunt. But I'm tired of the facade, of pretending everything's alright.

"No. I fell ill and ended up in the hospital."

"And you didn't tell me?!"

"You had your hands full."

"Mel, I'm sorry. I had no clue. You should have told me! How are you?"

"I'm doing better now. I'm in São Miguel, at my aunt's."

"The one who was cast out of the family?"

"Yep, that's the one."

"That's surprising. How did you end up there?"

"She sent me an invitation in a letter to visit the Azores."

"Just like that?"

"Yep. Figured I'd swing by."

"Did you find out why your grandpa booted her?"

"No, I didn't have the guts to ask. She didn't ask me anything either when I called her on Sunday, asking if I could jet to the Azores the next day. I needed to get out of Lisbon."

"What went down in Lisbon?"

"I was in no shape to hit the office."

"Is that jerk colleague of yours at it again?"

"How'd you know it was him?"

"I didn't, just guessed. What did he do?"

"He spread stories about me at work."

"What kind of stories?"

"Said I hit on him at the bar that night, followed him to the men's room, and tried to hook up."

"What a jerk! You got to get rid of that guy."

"I'm not up for talking about it now, Ruth. How much you need?"

"Mel, you can't let him mess with you like this."

"I know, but I don't want to talk about that now. How much?"

"Three hundred euros should do. I'll square up later."

"I'll wire it today."

"Thanks, Mel, and I'm sorry, really sorry for not being there for you when it all went down."

"You have your own stuff, Ruth. We all do."

"My bad."

"It's cool."

"If you need anything, call me. And if you ever decide to hire someone to rough up that guy, hit me up. Remember my ex who used to work security at clubs? Pretty sure he knows someone who could handle it."

"I'll mull it over." I chuckle.

"Serious, Mel."

"Can we drop the Claudio talk, though?"

"Fair enough, but you know I got your back."

"Thanks, Ruth. Catch you later."

I hang up, gripping the phone. I'd rather forget that night, but that memory lingers. I shut my eyes and I'm back at the bar. When he sat down next to me, Imagine Dragons' 'Radioactive' was playing. I used to love that song. I can't stand it since then. Gives me chills every time.

"Look who I found outside!"

My aunt walks in, Carlos trailing behind, flashing his usual smile. I'm happy to see him, so much that I just go in for a hug. At first, he's a bit frozen, not sure what to do, but then he leans in, returning the hug. It feels like safety, like that hug could magically wipe away all my problems. I feel a tear coming on, so I step back before I get all teary. Carlos looks a bit awkward. I probably made him feel weird, poor guy.

"Sorry."

"Sorry for what?"

"For hugging you. Blame my aunt; she's turning me into a serial hugger."

"No need to say sorry. Hugs are welcome anytime."

We're both a bit unsure, the conversation tapering off until my aunt returns.

"Where are you headed today?"

"To the Fogo Lagoon."

"You'll love it, Mel. The lagoon's stunning," my aunt chimes in.

Carlos takes the coffee my aunt offers, and we chat about the island's sights. His presence is a relief; it stops my mind from racing.

After breakfast, I clean up the kitchen, and my aunt sneaks homemade cookies into my backpack. As we step out onto the street, I find out Carlos borrowed his grandfather's van again. He's genuinely sweet, and I mean it. I'm tempted to hug him once more, but I resist. Don't want to weird him out. We say goodbye to my aunt and hit the road.

No blaring horns, no traffic tantrums—just endless greenery. And a few cows, naturally.

Numb[6] by Linkin Park comes on the radio, and I begin humming softly.

I'm tired of being what you want me to be

Feeling so faithless, lost under the surface

Carlos joins in, and I gather some courage to sing louder.

Don't know what you're expecting of me

Put under the pressure of walking in your shoes...

---

6 "Numb" by Linkin Park, from the album Meteora, written by Linkin Park.

We both belt out the lyrics, giving it our all inside the van.

Every step that I take is another mistake to you

The windows are wide open, and I'm pretty sure the cows can hear us, but they don't seem too bothered, and I couldn't care less.

All I want to do

Is be more like me

And be less like you!

We keep singing at the top of our lungs. When the song finishes, we both burst into laughter.

"That's a sad song; we probably shouldn't be laughing."

"I could've written those lyrics."

"Why?"

"It's like my life story. I've always tried to please others, especially my father."

"Is that why you studied Law?"

"How did you guess?"

"When you spoke about your job, you didn't sound too thrilled."

"Well, enthusiasm isn't something I've felt in a while."

"Maybe you should switch careers."

"It's not that easy. I thought I was on the right track, had my life all mapped out, everything under control, but I don't."

"Sometimes we're lost, not knowing where to go, and then life surprises us, and we find our way when we least expect it."

As Coldplay's "Fix You" starts playing on the radio, Carlos switches the station.

"I like that song," I protest.

"I do too, but enough sad songs."

He keeps searching until a Bon Jovi track comes on. He begins singing, and I join in.

It's my life

It's now or never![7]

We spend the rest of the journey belting out rock songs, laughter filling the van. It's the kind of joy I haven't experienced in ages. Carlos sings just as terribly as I do, but it doesn't matter. What matters is that I feel alive, I feel more like myself; it's as if the carefree girl I once was has returned on this trip.

---

7 "It's My Life" by Bon Jovi, from the album Crush, written by Jon Bon Jovi, Richie Sambora, and Max Martin.

❊ ❊ ❊

I settle on a bench, taking in the stunning scenery while Carlos gets his photography gear ready. It's mind-boggling how an island barely over sixty kilometers long and fifteen wide can boast such natural beauty. This lagoon is the highest spot on São Miguel Island, perched at the summit of the grand Fogo volcano, Carlos tells me.

I pull out the drawing kit and begin sketching a bird I spotted yesterday.

"Is that a finch?"

"I don't know its name. Just saw it yesterday."

"Looks like a finch to me."

"Then it must be a finch."

Carlos starts snapping shots of the lagoon while I continue sketching the bird and then the lagoon itself. I focus on the pencil strokes, trying to shut out everything else. But it's hard, really hard. Some thoughts just won't quit, sneaking in when I wish they wouldn't. I think about Claudio and how much I despise him. I want to forget him, I want to erase him from my mind, so I try to think about Rodrigo and how much I love him. I miss him so much it physically hurts.

After a while, Carlos comes up to me and asks, "Ready to head down?"

I pack up my stuff, and we start descending on one of the trails. Carlos points out several native plant species like the Azorean cedar or the laurel.

"You'd make a great tour guide."

"I doubt it. Not my thing."

"Just so you know, you're quite good at it. You can even make the Azorean cedar sound interesting."

"Look up there, a buzzard!"

A buzzard effortlessly glides above the lagoon, way up in the sky, scanning the grounds for its next meal. It's a natural predator, much like Claudio. But there's a key difference: this predator hunts to survive, while Claudio does it purely to stroke his ego.

We continue our descent, the trail becoming steeper. Carlos opts to pack his gear into his bag and sets it down on the ground.

"I'll manage without the bag for now. The terrain's too steep."

"If you prefer, we can stop here."

"No, let's finish the descent."

I set down my backpack next to his and he holds out his hand to help me. I grab his hand but slip, losing my balance.

"Mel!"

Carlos tries to catch me, but we both stumble and end up rolling down the slope. The cedars and shrubs scratch my legs and arms. We eventually come to a halt when the ground levels out. We both lie on our backs, sprawled on the ground, surrounded by a cloud of dust.

He props himself up on one elbow and plucks a piece of grass from my hair.

"Are you alright?"

I nod. I'm pretty sure I'll ache all over tomorrow, but I start laughing. He joins in, and we're there, on the ground, laughing like a pair of lunatics.

"This feels liberating," I say.

"Rolling down the slope?"

"Yeah, tumbling down and getting all scratched up. Here in the Azores, I can leave behind Counsel Melissa."

He whistles.

"So, you're Counsel Melissa in Lisbon?"

"Counsel Melissa Lacerda de Brito, daughter of Judge Lacerda de Brito, specialized lawyer handling the divorces of the rich and famous."

"Does that mean I need to start calling you Counsel Melissa?" he teases.

"No way. Over here in the Azores, I'm just Mel, Gabi's niece, who enjoys rolling down hills."

"And drawing," he points out.

"And sipping on Kima," I add.

"I knew it!" he triumphs. "I knew you couldn't resist the taste of the best soda in the world."

"Okay, I confess. I like Kima. It's good, very good. But sorry to burst your bubble, claiming it's the best soda in the world is a stretch."

"So, what's the best soda in the world then? And don't say Coca-Cola."

"I wasn't going to say Coca-Cola."

"Then?"

"7-up."

"Seriously?!"

"Yeah, why the surprise?"

"I don't know. I always consider 7-up as the substitute for Coca-Cola. When there's no Coca-Cola, you settle for a 7-up."

"You're mistaken. When there's no Coca-Cola, you ask for Pepsi. Those who drink 7-up genuinely want to drink it."

"You should write a thesis on that."

"Maybe."

He chuckles.

"I'm glad you left the equipment up the hill."

"Yeah, by now, it'd be all smashed."

"This way, only you got a bit banged up."

"This is nothing, just a few scratches. And you, are you okay?"

"I'll survive."

"I hope you won't tell your aunt I mistreated you."

"Of course not," I prop myself up on an elbow, looking at him. "Thanks for putting up with me."

"It's my pleasure."

"Really? You don't mind having me tagging along?"

"Nope. I enjoy your company."

"Do you always have work?"

"I take whatever jobs come up, sell photos to magazines and websites, and sometimes shoot weddings when there's less work."

"What a pair we make: you handle weddings, and I handle divorces."

"Let me tell you a secret," he whispers, "I hate weddings."

"And I hate divorces!" We both burst out laughing. When we stop, I take a better look at him. "Your t-shirt is all dirty." He's wearing a tee with Garfield chomping down on a whole pizza.

"That's what washing machines are for. Garfield will look good as new after a wash."

I flick the dust off Garfield with my fingertips.

"You must be wondering why I came to São Miguel."

"Why would I be surprised you visited the most beautiful island in the world?"

"I didn't come for tourism."

"For a divorce case?"

"No. I've been facing some issues in Lisbon," I sigh.

"Is there anything I can do to help?"

"No, well, you're already helping. Being here in nature is good for me. I need to be occupied, so I don't spend my days overthinking. I needed to escape Lisbon."

"A few years back, I attended university in Lisbon."

"Really?!"

"Why the surprised? Did you think I'd never left the island?"

"No, it's not that. I just couldn't picture you studying in Lisbon."

"I went to study Computer Engineering, but I didn't even finish the first year. I didn't fancy the course, nor the city's chaos."

"I never saw you as the Computer Engineering type."

"That's because I'm not. I quickly called it quits."

"Lisbon's got its charms, but lately, I'm exhausted from the constant hustle between the office and the courts."

"I didn't expect you to be a lawyer either. When your aunt mentioned you, I pictured an artist."

"I dreamt of going to Paris to study Arts, but my father wasn't on board. So, here I am, on track to follow the family legacy. Now, they expect me to prep for Judicial Studies Center exams to be a judge, just like my father."

"Whoa! I've never met a Judge before."

"I'm not a judge yet, and frankly, I'm unsure if I even want to pursue it."

"I don't know much about it, but I bet there's more to it than handling divorces."

"Could be, but honestly, I'm not sold on the whole judge gig. Being a photographer seems more fascinating."

"I can't say if it's more exciting, but it's my thing."

"And what about your free time? You've got any hobbies?"

"Sometimes I go on motorcycle tours with friends, and I also dive now and then. Speaking of which, how about a dive tomorrow? We can try to spot some whales?"

A shiver runs down my spine.

"A dive?"

"Yes, have you ever given it a shot?"

"Nah." I mull over making an excuse, then decide to let it out. "I'd love to learn to dive, but I'm terrified."

Carlos gives me a smirk instead of teasing.

"Lots of folks feel that way, you're not alone."

"I'd like to try, I love the sea, but bravery isn't my strong suit."

"Then, we'll start with the pool. I know a guy who teaches diving. Intro sessions happen in a pool. Only later, when folks feel confident, they venture into open waters."

"I'm not sure…"

"No pressure if you're not into it. But if you're up for it, I think you should give it a try. We're all a bit afraid of the unknown."

"Yeah, true…"

"I'll chat with my friend, we'll set up a pool session, okay? And if you don't like it, no problem, no need to continue."

I don't know if it's the meds influence or a knock to the head from the fall, but despite feeling anxious about diving into the sea, instead of an outright no, I agree to think about it. Maybe it's time to step beyond my comfort zone and face my fears.

Chapter 14

When I arrive home, I find a note from my aunt on the table.

"I had to step out. You're having dinner with Mr. Manuel. Love you!"

My aunt must be kidding, surely. The last thing I want is dinner with the old man. Carlos and Mr. Manuel are polar opposites. What a brilliant idea from my aunt! I crumple the note and toss it into the trash.

Scanning my phone, but no messages from Rodrigo. Today, I've checked my phone countless times, hoping for a message that never appears. I feel a bit deflated. Rodrigo hasn't reached out, and now I'm stuck facing dinner with the island's grumpiest fellow. What else could go wrong? Could Nurse Eva be right? Is Rodrigo with someone else in Dubai? Is he tired of me?

In the shower, I brainstorm an escape plan. What if I claim I'm feeling sick (which isn't entirely false)? Or maybe a headache? No, that might not cut it. He'd probably argue that a headache isn't a good enough excuse to skip a meal. How am I going to get out of this dinner?

As soon as I step out of the shower, ding! A message alert. I sprint to the bed to grab my phone.

Hey there, angel! Missing you big time.

I practically bounce on the bed, eager to text him back.

Miss you too! What happened? You vanished.

Lost my phone in South Africa.

South Africa?! You usually don't fly there.

Yeah, work had me jet-setting. Stepped out for dinner in Cape Town, and poof—phone gone.

OMG!

They flashed a gun, I begged for my phone to talk to my girl, but no luck.

Are you okay?

Yeah, just a scare. Then the hassle of getting a new phone in that third-world place.

Thank goodness you're okay. I don't know what I'd do if something happened to you.

Don't worry, angel. I can take care of myself. What's up with you?

I'm hesitant to tell him I've been hanging out with Carlos, afraid he might get jealous. So, I type:

Just stepped out of the shower.

Thinking about that body of yours gets me horny.

I flash a smile.

Come over, and I'll take care of that.

He's quick to take things up a notch.

Send me a pic in lingerie. Or better yet, naked.

So, when are you swinging by?

Pic first.

I ditch the towel and opt for a black lace set. After snapping a selfie, I hit send.

That's better.

Now, tell me, when are you coming to visit me?

I'm not sure yet.

I'm disappointed. What if he bails on visiting?

Really wish you'd come. Missing you tons.

Don't worry, I'll make it. Just not sure when yet. Can't stand being away from you any longer.

Love you!

Love you too! Gotta run. I have a flight to catch.

Our chat was too short. I miss him terribly, and I hate how demanding his pilot job is. Sure, it's sexy, but the crazy schedule kills it. Sometimes I wish he had a normal job back in Lisbon.

Bam!

Someone's pounding on the door.

"I'm coming!"

Bam bam!

Another round of knocking.

"Just a moment!"

Great, now I've got dinner plans with the grumpy neighbor while wearing some killer black lace lingerie. I opt to layer leggings and an oversized t-shirt on top. I need to keep it low-key, no hints of sensuality here. I don't want to shock the old man. He already thinks I'm too young for alcohol. If he saw me dressed like this, I'd probably get a whole lecture.

There's another round of knocking, so I hurry to the door before he breaks it down.

"Why'd you take so long?!"

"Good afternoon."

"What were you up to that took ages to open the door?"

I prepare to give an excuse, flashing my best fake smile, but end up blurting out instead:

"Don't worry, I wasn't drinking vodka or anything. Just getting dressed."

Why did I say that? Why couldn't I keep my mouth shut?!

He looks even grumpier than usual, and I brace myself for a lecture. What if he decides to rat me out? What if he tells my aunt about the vodka bottle?!

"You've got a sense of humor," he grumbles.

For a moment, I expect a scolding, but he turns and signals for me to follow. I tag along while pulling a face. Childish, I know, but this old man gets under my skin. I'd pick dinner with his grandson any day! What an epic night this is going to be!

He leads me to the back of the house, and it starts feeling a bit weird. Why the backyard? Then I catch a whiff of smoke. What's going on? Maybe I should turn back. What's he up to?! We reach the backyard, and I realize the scent is from a charcoal grill he's firing up.

"I'm grilling a snapper I caught this morning."

I take a deep breath. Just a fish, after all. But why do I keep conjuring up crazy stories in my head?

The old man pulls a massive fish from a tray and tosses it on the grill. Plastic chairs and a table are set. He motions for me to take a seat.

"You've never had fish this fresh! Caught it this morning."

"How'd you catch fish in the morning? Didn't you open the grocery store today?"

He smirks.

"Headed out to sea at five a.m., back by eight. You youngsters don't know what hard work is."

I'm feeling rather peeved here. Who's he to suggest I don't know the meaning of hard work?!

"I'm up at six a.m. during the week to hit the gym, and then I'm at work from nine till around ten or eleven at night."

He glances at me unimpressed.

"Desk work isn't the same, kid. There's nothing like the sea. It can be your best buddy one moment and your worst enemy the next." He adjusts the coals with tongs. "Back when I was a fisherman, it was Sunday to Sunday hustling to feed the family. Nights out for the catch, back late the next day. My wife holding the fort, hoping I'd come back."

"Seems like you always made it back."

He looks down, eyes fixed on the fish.

"I made it, but not everyone did," he murmurs without lifting his gaze.

I gulp, feeling like a fool. Why did I say that?!

"Once, during a whale hunt, a sperm whale slammed into our boat, sent us all into the sea."

"OMG! What happened?!"

"There were twelve of us. Only two returned."

His story hits me hard, like a gut punch. Suddenly, I feel small, really small. I've never faced a tragedy like that. My problems seem tiny compared to such a disaster. I fumble for words, but what do you even say to someone who lost most of their crew at sea?

"Must've been rough," I manage to say.

"Supposed to be the part where I act tough, an old salty sea dog, weathering it all."

A rock amidst a storm, taking a beating from rain and wind.

"You didn't tough it out?"

"Nah, kid, I didn't. Turned to the bottle."

I gulp. He signals for me to hand over a water bottle from the table, throws a few drops on the coals to douse a flame.

"Was on my way to becoming a full-blown alcoholic. It was that or meet my end at sea. I'd show up sloshed to the boat every day. Had to fish me out of the water twice."

"And how did you quit drinking?"

"One day I walked in, and my wife said to me, 'Manuel, it's either your family or the bottle.'"

"You chose your family?"

He grabs the tongs, readjusting the coals.

"I chose life, kid. I chose life."

We both fall silent as the coals finish grilling the snapper. I hope he doesn't think I'm an alcoholic or heading that way. I toy with explaining myself but end up biting my tongue. Best not to delve more into the vodka topic. I don't have a problem with alcohol; I only drink occasionally. Sometimes, when I'm anxious, a drink seems tempting, that's all. Like right now. If I had some Smirnoff, I'd have a sip just to unwind. Just one sip. Just to relax.

"Pass me that platter."

I hand him the platter. He removes the fish from the grill, placing it on the platter, then disappears inside.

"Need a hand?"

"Nope! You're my guest today."

I watch him fetch some old-looking ceramic plates and glasses. Next come a hefty island cheese, bread, and, of course, two Kima sodas.

"Let's dig in!" He says, and I sense it's better not to ask about calorie counts, especially as I already know the answer. I pop some pills from my pocket and wash them down with a sip of Kima. In a flash, he cuts hefty chunks of cheese and bread onto my plate with a massive blade. Mrs. Maria must have learned a thing or two about serving from him. I don't protest because I've learned it's just not worth it. I taste the cheese and am blown away. Why does all the food on this island taste so good?!

"This cheese's amazing," I say, trying to shift gears.

"It's made with milk from the cows right here in S. Miguel. Bought it from Zé das Vacas, the grocery store supplier." He skillfully carves another slice of cheese with the blade. "We had two cows before. My wife used to make cheese and sell it at the market."

"What happened to your wife?"

"She's gone."

"Couldn't handle your bad temper?"

"She passed away."

Today, I just can't seem to get anything right!

"I'm sorry, I had no clue. I'm so sorry."

"Me too, kid, me too."

"What happened?" I notice a shadow in his eyes and regret asking. "Sorry, it's none of my business. You don't have to answer."

"It's okay. Keeping things bottled up," he gestures to his heart with the knife, "isn't good. It was throat cancer. It was hard to witness."

I'm at a loss for words. What do you even say to someone who watched their partner consumed by cancer? Compared to what this man's endured, my issues seem ridiculous.

"And the fish, how is it?"

"It's fantastic."

"This old man still knows his way around grilling fish." He slices another piece of bread with the blade. "Once, we reeled in a 350-pound swordfish. It was early morning, July 1976. It was me, Manuel Pato, Zé das Almas..."

He launches into the story, and I realize it's a cheerful tale, one of camaraderie, and it starts to lift my spirits.

"When we got to the island two days later, they brought a scale, and we weighed the fish: 350 pounds and 200 grams! It was the biggest swordfish ever caught in these waters!"

"No way!"

"It's the honest truth! Made it to the papers and all!"

"He spends the rest of dinner sharing fishing stories, and I relish them because they're all cheerful tales. Stories of colossal fish, fearless men, and dolphins that come to the rescue. Once we finish, he insists on clearing the table — he's not an invalid — and then heads back inside.

"Hey, we're missing dessert!" he hollers from inside.

A few minutes later he comes with a pack of Smarties in hand, and I burst into laughter. I'm laughing so hard that tears stream down my face.

"You were expecting me to whip up a pudding or a cake?!"

He passes me a cloth handkerchief he pulled from his pocket. I dab my eyes with it.

"It was you who slipped the Smarties into my shopping bag the other day, wasn't it?"

"Who else would it have been?"

"But why?!"

"Your aunt might've mentioned that the last time she saw you, you were munching on Smarties."

That's when I realize the old man in front of me, despite his grumbling, has a tender heart. Beneath that tough exterior, he's a softie. Carlos takes after him. I stand up and give him a hug.

"Thank you."

He shrugs me off.

"Enough of this mushy stuff."

"Why, can't an old sea wolf give hugs?"

He chuckles, for first time since we met, and I notice the same dimples as Carlos, amidst the wrinkles. He opens the pack, offers me a candy, and then takes one himself. He pops it in his mouth, and promptly spits it out.

"Bad idea. Too sweet for me."

I laugh.

He pulls out a metal box from his pocket, and I realize it's rolling tobacco. Then he starts rolling a cigarette.

"Your grandson is a great guy."

"He's a fine lad. All my grandkids are."

"How many grandkids do you have?"

"Three girls and three boys. Carlos and three girls are from my daughter. The other boys are from my son."

"That must be nice, having a big family."

"Your aunt mentioned you're an only child."

"Yeah, and I don't have any cousins either. Both my parents are only children."

"Is that why you feel alone?"

"I don't know, maybe. How do you know?"

"Your aunt hinted that things weren't quite right in your head."

I nervously chuckle. "Did she tell you about my panic attacks?"

"Something along those lines. That you had a breakdown and ended up in the Azores."

"Yeah, that's pretty much it."

"Life takes its twists, kid. You'll see, everything will fall into place."

"Is that why she asked you to cook dinner for me tonight, so I wouldn't lose it again?"

Or so I wouldn't go buy vodka. I wonder if he told her about the vodka bottle.

"I reckon so, and because I'm a friendly neighbor."

He gives me a teasing look.

"Well, I'm glad I didn't lose it with you."

He laughs, and there they are – those dimples on his wrinkled cheeks. They're not as cute as Carlos's, but they're still rather funny.

"You know, maybe having a small family isn't so bad. Big families have their drawbacks too. When your aunt's wife's sisters come over for vacation, it's chaos. They're always squabbling."

"My aunt's wife?!"

He gets flustered and scratches his head.

"Jasmine, I mean, Jasmine's sisters."

"No, I heard it right. You said my aunt's wife."

"Oh, I've said too much."

"Jasmine is my aunt's wife?!"

He puts the cigarette in his mouth and lights it with a match before taking a drag.

"They're one of those modern couples."

He creates a perfect circle with the smoke, the ring lingering in the air briefly before dispersing into fragments.

"I still find it strange. To me, a couple should be a man and a woman, not two men or two women. It feels unnatural."

"Why would my aunt keep that from me?"

"I don't know, kid. You're from Lisbon, so maybe you're more used to it. There must be plenty of those couples there."

"But why wouldn't she tell me?"

"I don't know, kid. Really don't know."

I'm getting the urge to ask if he's got any drinks tucked away at home, but I bet he doesn't. For someone who battled alcoholism, having booze around is likely a no-go. He probably senses my unease because he offers me a cigarette. I take it. He rolls one more and passes it over, lighting it with a match. I inhale deeply, trying to steady myself.

Why didn't my aunt tell me? Why keep it from me? I can't wrap my head around it. Is she worried I wouldn't accept it? Maybe that's why she was pushed away from the family. I picture the shock on my grandparents' faces, especially my grandfather, when they heard the news. And my father's reaction? Probably not great either. I take another drag. It's hard to decide which stings more: realizing how closed-minded my father and grandparents were, or understanding that my aunt questioned my acceptance. I'd just started to put trust in her. I wonder if all those hugs and kisses were genuine.

Chapter 15

Yesterday, when I finally got back home, I looked for something to drink in the kitchen. But guess what? My aunt's stash is seriously lacking in the alcohol department. All I found was tea, coffee, and Kima. I went for the Kima, hoping to have a chat with her later. But the moment I heard the van, I chickened out. I turned off the lights and went to my room. I didn't get any sleep. Then morning hit, and I totally missed my usual run. I've checked my phone, but there are no messages from Rodrigo. I'm so antsy to know when he's showing up. I really need to see him.

Then my aunt barges in, "Good morning, darling!" I try to plaster on a smile. "How was dinner? Did Mr. Manuel treat you well?" she asks, opening the curtains.

"Yeah, it was good. He grilled fish."

And he hinted about your secret, which you're keeping from me.

"I'm glad you liked it. Mr. Manuel can be a bit grumpy, but he's a nice guy."

"I know. I had fun listening to his fishing stories."

'I'm glad you enjoyed the dinner,' she says, planting a kiss on my forehead. Honestly, I could do without the kisses. What I really need is for her to spill the details on why she didn't mention that Jasmine's her wife. What if I just straight-up asked her about it? I take a deep breath, trying to muster the nerve. But before I can say a word, she's already making her exit out of the room.

"Get ready, I'll make breakfast."

I sluggishly get up, procrastinating on getting ready because I'm just not up for facing her at the table.

As I enter the kitchen, I glance at her and start wondering if she's more like my father than I ever realized. He can be so mechanical sometimes, utterly devoid of emotions. Is she putting on a facade too? Come on, Mel, just ask her! I try to speak, but the words won't come out. Then, a knock on the door saves me. Thank goodness, it's Carlos.

"Hey there! Where are we headed today?" I jump up with excitement.

"Aren't you going to finish up your breakfast, darling?"

"We've got to seize the day! Where are we off to?"

"You seem pretty eager today!"

If only they knew.

"So?"

"I was thinking of hitting up Ponta da Ferraria."

I have no clue what that is, but as long as it gets me out of this house, it sounds awesome.

"What's that?"

"It's a beach. Besides having a stunning view, it's got a famous natural pool with hot geothermal water."

"Hot water in the ocean?!"

"Yep. Don't forget your bikini."

"I'll grab it right away."

I dash to my room and throw on a bikini. I take a quick glance at myself in the mirror before getting dressed. I think I might've gained a pound or two. I need to watch what I eat. I can't afford to pack on any more weight! Rodrigo isn't into heavier people.

I hustle back to the living room.

"I'm all set!"

I grab my backpack and bid my aunt goodbye.

"Is everything alright, Mel?"

I think she caught on that something's up, but right now, I just want to hit the road and clear my head.

"Everything's awesome, Aunt. I love these outings with Carlos," and I mean it. "And I can't wait to dip into those warm beach waters."

"Be careful out there. Look after my niece, Carlos! That beach can have strong currents."

"Don't worry, Gabi."

I swing open the front door and practically pull Carlos by the arm.

❀ ❀ ❀

"This place is stunning!"

The beach itself is small, almost entirely covered in black rock, but the cliffs embracing the beach, the ocean, the rocks—everything is just breathtaking. We scout for a patch of sand and set down our things.

"Can you snap a picture of me?" I ask.

Carlos grabs my phone without a complaint. I guess he's realized it's not worth the argument. I strip down to my bikini and strike a few poses on a rock while he takes several shots. He hands back my phone, and I settle on the sand, choosing a picture to send to Rodrigo. I opt for one where I'm facing the sea with my back turned. My butt looks pretty good. You can't even tell I've gained a bit of weight. I hit send and type:

Look what you're missing. When are you coming?

Carlos sets up his camera gear while I pull out my sketchbook. It hits me that we've fallen into a routine, even though it wasn't planned. He takes photos, and I sketch. Funny how, when I first met him, I thought we had zero in common. I figured we'd struggle to find anything to talk about, and I'd be bored senseless. Turns out, it's the complete opposite. With each passing day, I feel closer to him. He's become a good friend.

I settle down and start drawing a seagull perched on a rock. I spend a good couple of hours at this. Every now and then (okay, more like every five minutes), I check my phone to see if Rodrigo has replied. So far, zilch. He must be flying.

"Do you want to take a dip?" Carlos stows away his photography gear.

"Yeah, let's do it. I want to check if the water's as warm as you claim."

There's this natural pool formed by the rocks. Carlos starts undressing, and I can't help but notice he could lose about four or five pounds. Not that he's overweight, but he's got a bit of a belly. And chest hair. Rodrigo doesn't have chest hair—or much body hair, really—and he's not a fan of mine either. That's why I endure those Brazilian waxes, which I absolutely despise.

Carlos takes a run and jumps in. When he resurfaces, he gestures for me to join. I dip my toe in the water and am surprised by its temperature.

"So, what's the verdict?"

"It's really warm!" I feel like I've discovered a hidden treasure.

"Come on!"

I take a few steps back, then sprint and dive in headfirst. No jolt of cold, just a comforting sensation. As I surface, Carlos seizes the chance to splash me.

"So, you want to play?" I splash back.

We're splashing water at each other, but Carlos gets the upper hand, thoroughly drenching me. I let out a childish squeal and start swimming away from him, ignoring his calls. Swimming feels incredibly freeing. The warmth of the water envelops me like a comforting embrace, reminiscent of being cradled in the womb. Obviously, I can't recall my time in my mother's belly, but I imagine it might've felt something like this—safe and snug.

Inside your mother's womb, you're sheltered, and your parents adore you unconditionally, even without laying eyes on you. But once you step out into the world, your journey truly begins. It's a challenging place out there; often, your first breaths come with tears as you face the harshness outside. Over time, you forget that you're inherently perfect and entirely enough. Yet, here, immersed in these warm, embracing waters from the depths of the earth, I feel complete, I feel enough.

I swim a bit more, then suddenly a wave splashes over my face, breaking my peaceful moment. I notice the sea has turned a bit rough, but I've had my fair share of swimming lessons. Carlos's calls echo faintly as I approach the rocks that line the natural pool. I feel a forceful current pulling me towards them. Panic surges within me; my heart races. Another wave crashes over me, and I find myself submerged, feeling dizzy and strangely paralyzed. I can't possibly be having a panic attack out here in the middle of the sea! Get it together, Melissa! This is absurd! You're a good swimmer; you'll make it back to shore. But another wave drags me closer to the rocks, and I realize it's not my imagination. The rocks are right there, and I'm about to crash into them! I thrash in the water, trying desperately to steer clear, but it's futile against the powerful current. Another wave pulls me under, and I swallow water. My heart races even faster. Suddenly, a hand grabs me, pulling me up. Someone's behind me, their body pressed against mine.

"Mel, are you okay?"

"Carlos!" It's all I can manage to say.

He slowly steers us away from the rocks. The sea is still choppy; he struggles but steadily swims us closer to the beach.

When I realize the danger has passed, I relax against his body. We finally reach shallower waters, and he releases his grip on me. I turn around, wrapping my arms around his neck.

"Are you alright?"

I nod, but he seems unsure, probably because I'm shaking. As we step out of the water, he lifts me up, carrying me to the towel.

"I'm fine, Carlos."

"You nearly drowned."

"I'm heavy. You'll strain your back."

"You're light as a feather."

He carefully sets me down on the towel.

"Are you feeling cold?"

I shake my head. He doesn't seem convinced and hands me his Garfield T-shirt to wear. I put it on, but I keep trembling. He lies down next to me on the towel.

"Is it okay if I...?" he starts.

I nod, and he leans against me, putting his arm around me. We lay there in silence until my trembling finally subsides.

"I'm a fool, I started panicking."

"You're not. That area is pretty dicey because of the currents. That's why I was warning you not to head over there."

"And I really should've listened."

"Yeah, you should've."

"If it weren't for you, I don't even want to think about what might've happened."

I turn to face him and plant a kiss on his cheek.

"Thanks, Super-Carlos, for rescuing me."

He blushes, flopping onto his back, and that's when I notice he's panting.

"I need to get into better shape," he says, trying to catch his breath.

"I did warn you I'm not lightweight."

"I'm just out of shape."

"Besides diving, have you done any other sports?"

"Does walking count?"

"I don't think so."

"And lifting beer bottles?"

"Doesn't really count either. You should try CrossFit. I hit those classes Monday to Friday in Lisbon. There've got to be gyms here in Ponta Delgada; you should give it a shot. Diving into CrossFit would enhance your superpowers even more."

He chuckles.

"If you give a diving class a whirl, I'll tackle CrossFit," he says, turning to face me.

"Deal."

"Seriously? I won't let you forget, Mel."

"Yes, it's a deal. I'll dive in, and you'll CrossFit it up."

We're both sprawled on the beach towel, facing each other. So close that I can hear his heavy breathing. He laughs, and those adorable dimples show. I laugh along. We're so close.

My phone buzzes, and I turn around until I can reach my backpack and fish out the phone. It's a message from Rodrigo!

You're driving me crazy, angel.

I smile.

That's the plan.

I'm trying to swap shifts to come over. I can't stay away from you any longer!

Carlos says something to me, but I'm not really paying attention. Then he taps my arm and says, "You're covered in sand."

ANXIOUS GIRL 125

That's when I realize I've rolled out of the towel in my eagerness to grab the phone from the backpack.

"It's alright."

"You seem awfully cheerful for someone who almost drowned a few minutes ago."

"My boyfriend is coming to see me!"

Chapter 16

When I arrive home, I see my aunt and Jasmine sitting at the table, sipping on tea.

"Good afternoon, darling."

"Hi."

Jasmine smiles but stays silent. She's got her fiery red hair tied up in a ponytail, sporting a white shirt paired with bell-bottom jeans. Quite retro.

"How was your day?" my aunt asks.

"It was great. We hung out at the sea pool."

I'd better leave out the part where I almost drowned; without Carlos, she might not have a niece right now.

"I'm glad you're having fun."

"Yeah, Carlos is a great companion."

"He's a good guy."

My aunt gazes at me, seemingly wanting to say more but holding back.

"Well, I'm off to shower and change."

"Hold on," Jasmine interrupts.

My aunt glares at her.

"What is it, Gabi?! Might as well get this over with."

I'm not sure if I'm ready for whatever *this* is, but maybe Jasmine's got a point.

"Sit down, darling."

I drop my backpack in a corner and take a seat at the table.

"Would you like some tea?"

"Come on, Gabi, why don't you just spill it all out?!"

My aunt ignores her, repeating the question about tea. My grandma used to think tea was the cure for everything. I shake my head. I don't want tea. I just want the truth.

"Will you tell her, or you want me to tell her? The kid needs to know," Jasmine's getting under my skin. I'm no kid. How does my aunt put up with her?

"You must know that Jasmine and I..." My aunt hesitates.

"It's okay, aunt. "I already know everything. Mr. Manuel let it slip at dinner."

"Have you talked to your father?"

"No, why would I?"

"Listen, kiddo, what exactly do you know?"

I take a deep breath.

"I know you two are a couple," I turn to my aunt, "and I don't get why you kept it from me. Did you think I wouldn't be cool with it?"

"No, it's not that."

"Wouldn't it be better to just lay it all out?!" Jasmine seems like she's about to blow a fuse. Opposites sure do attract. My aunt's getting fidgety. Jasmine's a volcano about to erupt.

"Calm down, Jasmine. Let me handle this my way."

But what else is there to unravel? This conversation's becoming a puzzle I can't solve.

"Were you banished from the family because of your sexual orientation?"

My aunt takes a deep breath, locking eyes with me. Jasmine releases a heavy sigh. I half-expect her to storm out.

"Kind of."

What sort of response is that? It's a simple yes or no question.

"Kind of?! What's that supposed to mean?"

My aunt's growing tense, and now I'm starting to feel the anxiety spike. This must be something serious. But what exactly did my aunt do?

"I'll tell you all," she begins, spooning more sugar into her cup. "Many years ago, before you were born, I was engaged to a man," she pauses, gathering her courage. "He was a good man, educated, honest, hard-working. He came from the North and had moved to Lisbon, working in the Lisbon Court of Appeal after being appointed a judge. We met at a dinner hosted by some friends of your grandparents."

Yeah, my grandfather must've been set on her marrying a judge.

"It was a family-approved engagement," she continues. "Your grandfather was ecstatic. Meanwhile, your dad was seeing this irreverent artist. She was a painter and had been studying in France. Needless to say, your grandfather wasn't thrilled."

My father dating an artist?! He must have been a very different person back then, hooking up with rebellious artists. That doesn't fit my image of him.

"Rodolfo and I were engaged, and your dad's girlfriend offered to help plan my wedding. Your grandparents weren't pleased, obviously, but your dad fought for her acceptance."

My father was head over heels for a rebellious artist?! When did that happen?! I think my aunt's deviating from the story. She's stalling.

"Your dad's girlfriend and I became close, spending a lot of time together. And at one point, I started questioning my own marriage. I liked Rodolfo, but I wasn't in love with him. He didn't give me butterflies, didn't make me smile whenever I saw him, didn't make me want to spend every moment with him. But she did."

"She?"

"Yes, she."

"My dad's girlfriend?" I ask, bracing for the answer.

My aunt takes a deep breath and swallows hard.

"Yes."

It's like a bomb just went off. My father dating an artist. My father madly in love with this woman. My father heartbroken because his girlfriend left him for his sister. How did he manage to keep all that from me for so long?!

"What happened?!" Now, I need to know everything. "Don't leave anything out."

"What do you think happened?" Jasmine asks, rolling her eyes.

"Jasmine, for God's sake."

"Okay, okay, I'll zip it."

"I called off the engagement, then we told your dad."

"You should've seen his face," Jasmine says.

That's when it hits me.

"You're the artist my dad fell for."

"Jasmine Santos," she says, offering her hand with a mischievous grin.

"Jasmine, this is no time for jokes."

Jasmine's still grinning, a teasing glint in her eye. I stare at her, bewildered. My father left for my aunt. My aunt! It's like a scene from a soap opera. Suddenly, I burst into laughter. Jasmine joins in, and we can't seem to stop. My aunt's shaking her head, shooting us a disapproving glare, but we keep laughing. How did this even happen? In what universe did this unfold? I try to imagine my father before all this. Who was he back then? Then the laughter fades. Being dumped for someone else is brutal—I've been there. But being left for his sister? That must've cut deep. His life must've turned upside down overnight.

After we stop laughing, my aunt looks mortified. But Jasmine? She's unbothered, still audacious. She pulls out a cigarette and stands up.

"You shouldn't smoke," my aunt scolds.

"I think I deserve a smoke today. I mean, it's not every day you tell your ex-fiancé's daughter that you traded her dad for her aunt. That's the gist, right? Did I nail it?" she quips sarcastically.

"My aunt remains silent as Jasmine leaves, settling onto the wicker sofa on the porch with a cigarette."

Coming closer, my aunt grabs my hands. "I'm sorry, Mel. I should've told you, but I was terrified of how you'd react."

"It's okay, Aunt Gabi. If that hadn't happened, Dad wouldn't have married Mom."

"And you wouldn't be here. I never looked at it that way. I hope you won't be mad at me. I couldn't help it; I couldn't avoid falling in love."

"If you two are still together after all this time, it must've been true love."

"Yeah, we're still putting up with each other thirty years later."

"I'm in love too."

"With your boyfriend?"

"Yeah. We're heading towards marriage."

"You are engaged? Congratulations!"

I let out a sigh. "Technically we're not engaged yet," I reply vaguely. "He keeps mentioning proposing, but he's waiting to change to European flights. Did I mention he's a pilot?"

"And you're tired of waiting?"

I almost quip, "How did you guess?" but just nod. I decide to keep my plan of coaxing him to the Azores for a proposal to myself.

"Does Rodrigo make you happy?"

"Does Jasmine do that for you?"

My aunt smiles.

"Yes, Jasmine makes me happy. Most of the time she drives me crazy, but I still love her. It might sound cliché, but we've got each other's backs. Look, Mel, I know you didn't ask for advice, but here's one: talk to this Rodrigo. Have a serious chat with him. Communication's key for a relationship. Passion fades, but if you've got that understanding and connection, things can last."

"I'll have that conversation when we're together next."

As my aunt heads off to start dinner, I step out onto the porch. I should be helping her in the kitchen, but I've got this itch to chat with Jasmine about that father I never knew. Taking a seat beside her, I ask, "I could use a smoke."

She hands me a cigarette, lighting it up for me. "What was my dad like?"

"In bed?" she teases.

"Stop it! I mean, as a person?"

"Relax, just kidding," she chuckles, taking a drag. "He was a young, serious lawyer most of the time, but he had moments of occasional craziness. He smoked, rocked bell-bottoms, and even hit up some rock concerts with me."

I try to picture my father in bell-bottoms but fail. I always saw him in a suit; even at home, he always wears a shirt. I think the only time I saw him in a T-shirt was at the beach.

"And he was quite the cook... and lover."

"Don't want to hear it!" I cover my ears, and Jasmine bursts into laughter.

She suddenly turns serious. "Don't think I'm heartless. It tore me up doing that to your dad because I liked him, a lot. But he didn't set my heart on fire like your aunt did."

"I get that."

"How's he doing?"

"He's good, I guess. Doing what he loves—locking up the bad guys."

"Do you enjoy locking up bad guys too?"

"Me?" I shake my head. "I deal with divorces."

"Not exactly jumping with enthusiasm."

"This wasn't exactly my dream when I chose law."

"So why law school?"

"My father and grandfather both studied Law. It felt like the natural course. My father wanted me to follow the family legacy."

"He wanted?! And you, Mel, what did you want?"

"I wanted to go to Paris for art."

"Why didn't you?"

"Not that straightforward, Jasmine."

"Of course it is. It's your life. No need for explanations or approvals."

I sink into the yellow cushions, thinking about her words. Jasmine doesn't get it. It's not that easy. I don't want to be a struggling artist relying on my parents. At least, being a lawyer guarantees a paycheck each month.

"It's not that simple."

Jasmine kicks up her legs, resting her feet on the side table.

"Life's never easy, but it's yours to shape. You can change it if you want."

Chapter 17

Having learned the whole story, I wake up earlier than my aunt and Jasmine to prepare breakfast for them. Now that I understand everything, my aunt is back in my good graces.

She strolls into the kitchen wearing a big smile, then pulls me into a hug.

"I've already set breakfast."

"Mel, darling, you didn't have to."

"You seem different."

"Do I?"

"Yeah, there's something about you."

"I feel lighter, like a burden's been lifted. Keeping that secret was tearing me apart. Now that I've shared it with you, I feel like I should have done it before."

"With a little help from Mr. Manuel."

"Yes, with a little help from him."

"Aren't we having breakfast with Jasmine?" Now that I know, Jasmine doesn't have to stay at the Hortensias Garden anymore.

"She's resting."

"Is she okay?"

"Yeah, just a bit tired."

We start eating breakfast, and I sneak a peek at my phone. Rodrigo hasn't texted me yet. I'm dying to know when he's coming.

"Waiting for a call?"

"Nah, just scrolling through messages."

I grab the pills, holding them for a second. Despite taking them, my sleep has been awful. I'm starting to think they're useless.

"Are you skipping the pills?"

"I'm starting to believe they're pointless. They only make me feel sick and zonked out."

"Did you think about what we talked about, seeing a therapist?"

"No point starting treatment here in the Azores. I'll handle it once I'm back in Lisbon."

"Some doctors do online consultations."

There's a knock on the door. Saved by Carlos!

I head to the door and open it, and I'm surprised to see him wearing a proper shirt with buttons!

"Good morning, Super-Carlos!"

The shirt looks good on him. He looks elegant. Like a *Cappuccino*.

"Hey there."

"Is that your Clark Kent costume?"

He chuckles.

"Super-Carlos?!" my aunt questions.

"Yesterday, Carlos was my superhero."

"Don't overstate it."

"Don't be modest. He saved me from drowning." Oops, shouldn't have spilled that to my aunt.

"What happened?!"

"My fault. I shouldn't have taken her to the sea pool."

"It wasn't your fault, Carlos. I wandered toward the rocks."

"You need to be careful, Mel. Your father will kill me if anything happens to you."

"Carlos will keep me safe."

"Rest assured, Gabi, it won't happen again."

I pour Carlos a coffee.

"Where are we off to? Must be a fancy spot for you to be wearing a shirt."

"Somewhere different."

"Where exactly?"

"To a day care center."

"A day care center?!"

"Every month, I head to a different day care center to snap pics of the elderly," he says, then adds, "If you find it dull, you don't have to tag along."

"Of course, I'll go. I take my job as your assistant seriously."

Carlos finishes his coffee while I handle the dishes and straighten up the kitchen. My aunt gives him a bunch of advice before we head out. She's still worried about yesterday's incident.

We hop into the van after my aunt's last-minute advice, and Carlos tells me the trip will be short because the day center's in Ponta Delgada.

"Are they paying you to photograph the elderly?"

"Nah, they don't have a budget for that. I do this as a volunteer gig. I switch it up every month, hitting up a different Day Center. Every time I swing back, the Centers are always different. New faces and some people aren't around no more."

"They're not around anymore?"

"They passed."

I go silent, not entirely sure what to expect. I've never visited a place like that before. Will I come across elderly individuals confined to their beds, reliant on feeding tubes? And the scent... Could it be that typical hospital odor, or worse, the unmistakable smell of urine? I'm beginning to think maybe this visit wasn't such a good idea.

The ride's short. Five minutes later, Carlos is parking by this old building, walls painted white, and dark wooden shutters. He heads in, lugging a bigger bag than usual, and I trail behind. Once we're in, it's a whole different scene from what I imagined. Past the entrance, we walk into this bright room decked out with pretty photos of seniors, maybe Carlos snapped them? The tables have vibrant tablecloths and flower vases. Over on one side, there are some comfy chairs where some seniors nap or flip through a book. At the tables, ladies are into crocheting or sewing. And wow, it smells good—like vanilla.

A woman, probably in her fifties, comes up to Carlos and greets him.

"Hey, Carlos, good to see you! Our seniors are excited for the photo session."

Some of the seniors greet Carlos, while others stay focused on their stuff.

"And who's this young lady?"

"This is Mel, a friend. Mel, meet Arnaldina, the director of the Day Center."

When Carlos introduces me as a friend, I can't help but smile. It's cool that he already considers me a friend, even though we haven't known each other long. Having a friend's great, especially one who lends you a raincoat and rescues you from drowning in the sea.

"Nice to meet you."

"Are you also a photographer?"

"Sorry, not my thing."

"Mel is great at drawing."

"You draw sketch portraits of the seniors."

I gaze at her, unsure of what to say.

"That's a great idea, Arnaldina," Carlos agrees.

"Thank you for coming, Mel. The seniors will love the portraits."

And just like that I become the official portrait artist of the Center.

"A girl, who looks about my age, comes over with a big bag and gives Carlos this massive hug. I can't help but wonder if there's more than just friendship going on there."

"Mel, this is Sara. She usually helps us with hair and makeup."

Her nails, painted turquoise, remind me of Cármen.

"Wow, this is turning into a professional photoshoot!"

"Our seniors deserve the best."

Sara and I dive into the wardrobe. Some ladies brought multiple outfits to see which one looks best in the photo. They're dead serious about this, and it warms my heart. Wrinkles and gray hair aside, they still love dolling up. It's pretty cool to watch.

"Hey, Mel!"

I turn and see one of the elderly ladies waving at me. How does she know my name?

"Don't you remember me?"

Is she my aunt's neighbor? Her face seems familiar, but I can't place it.

"The other day, I mentioned my granddaughter to you at the bus stop."

The bus stop. The panic attack at the supermarket. It's coming back to me. I feel my heart racing and a tightness in my chest. I hope she doesn't tell others what happened. I don't feel like talking about it.

"Do you know Ms. Julieta?" Carlos asks.

"Yeah, I mean... " I'm at a loss for words.

"The other day, both of us were at the bus stop, and I started chatting with your friend. You know how it is with the elderly, Carlos, we like to talk."

"Ms. Julieta told me her granddaughter is an architect working in Japan."

She doesn't say more, and I feel relieved. I help her choose one of the blouses she brought. We end up selecting a dark green blouse with a floral pattern that her granddaughter sent from Japan.

"Thank you for not saying anything about what happened," I whisper when we're alone.

"I've got no business sharing other people's lives. How are you doing?"

"I'm okay."

"Your aunt seems like a good woman."

"And she is."

I notice Sara and Carlos chatting in a corner. He's saying something, and she giggles, touching his arm. What does she want from him? I start feeling uneasy, not sure why. He notices me looking at them and smiles at me. She turns around and smiles at me too. Not sure if I like this Sara.

Sara steps in to work on Ms. Julieta's hair and makeup. When Carlos finishes setting up the impromptu studio, Ms. Julieta is the first one to be photographed. As she moves away to be photographed, Sara whispers in my ear.

"You don't need to get jealous. Carlos and I are just friends."

"Jealous?! I'm not jealous."

"I saw the way you looked at him."

"You're mistaken. I have a boyfriend."

"Whatever you say. But you don't need to be jealous. Carlos and I have known each other since we were kids. His older sister and I were in the same class."

I grab my drawing materials and find a spot at one of the tables. I'm done with this conversation. I can't fathom why she believes I'm jealous of Carlos. I begin sketching Ms. Julieta, trying to push away those thoughts.

We spend the whole day at the center. I learn that Mr. Zé has Alzheimer's, some days he's okay, and others he doesn't recognize his children or grandchildren. Ms. Elvira has intestinal cancer, but you wouldn't guess it by looking at her. She's the most cheerful in the room, always humming a tune. But not everyone is in high spirits. Mr. Eduardo lost his wife recently and hasn't come to terms with her death. He didn't want photos or to be portrayed, despite Ms. Elvira's insistence. Then there's Mr. João and Ms. Alberta. Both were widowed and met at the Day Center. Now they're engaged, getting married next month. They hold hands and whisper to each other like two teenagers.

As I hand over the portraits, everyone's thankful. The ladies plant quick kisses on my cheeks, and some of the men go for handshakes, while others give me these shy little pecks on the cheek. I glance at Carlos, camera in hand, he's beaming. Seeing him so happy just rubs off on me, and I feel pretty good too.

Carlos is wrapping up the gear for us to take off, and that Sara girl heads over to talk to him. They end up chatting for a bit. I can't catch what they're talking about, but I hope she won't tell him she thinks I'm jealous. Because honestly, I'm not! Why would I be jealous of Carlos?

※ ※ ※

When I get home, my aunt hasn't arrived yet. She's probably with Jasmine at the Hortensias Garden. The phone rings, and I'm crossing my fingers hoping it's

Rodrigo. I start digging through my bag, but my phone's buried under a mountain of stuff. He's not much of a caller, prefers texts, but I'm dead certain it's him. Finally, I get my hands on it...and bummer, it's my mother.

"Hey, Mom."

"Hi, Mel. How are you?"

"I'm fine."

"Are you sure?"

"Yes."

"Are you getting along with your aunt?"

"Yeah, Mom. Aunt Gabi is a darling." I realize I'm catching my aunt's habit of calling everyone 'darling' because when she says it, it's genuine, not phony like when it comes from Cármen's mouth.

"That's great. It puts my mind at ease. Sorry I wasn't more supportive when you got out of the hospital."

"I'm an adult, Mom. I can take care of myself."

"I know, Mel, but there's no harm in asking for help. When are you coming back?"

"I don't know."

"Promise me you'll set up an appointment with that therapist once you're back in Lisbon."

"I'll take care of it when I get back."

I have no intention of booking an appointment, but I don't tell her that.

"Actually, there's something else I wanted to talk about."

I hope it's not about the Clinic stay again. Can't my parents just let me have some peace? The day was going pretty well.

"Mel, are you listening?"

"Yeah, Mom."

"I lost your sound."

"It might be the service. Sometimes there's weak signal here."

"And now, can you hear me?"

"I can hear you perfectly."

"I want to talk to you about something."

My throat tightens.

"If this is about the Arcos Clinic..."

"No, it's something else."

"Something else?"

"Yes. Your dad and I made a decision."

I want to tell her to spit it out already, but that's not how we talk in my family. In my family no one raises their voice, no one swears, and no one loses control. We're all civilized, but we rarely have honest conversations. Sometimes it feels like we're a group of strangers sharing Sunday lunches.

"Go on, Mom," I brace myself for something worse than a stay at the Arcos Clinic. Maybe an exile to a clinic in the Swiss Alps because she doesn't want the media to find out that Judge Lacerda de Brito's daughter had a nervous breakdown.

"Your father and I are getting divorced," my mother's voice barely audible.

"Sorry?!"

"We are getting divorced."

I try to make sense of what she's saying, but it doesn't add up.

"Divorced?!"

"Yes, Mel."

"Divorced?!" I sound like a broken record, but it's all I can manage to say.

"I'm sorry I haven't supported you more since you got out of the hospital, but it hasn't been easy."

"Why, Mom, why?!"

My parents weren't a happy, lovey-dovey couple, but they seemed to have a lot in common, even an obsession with their careers. I always thought they were in sync, a weird and maybe unhealthy sync, but in sync. I can't wrap my head around it.

"Your father wants a divorce."

It's like a punch in the gut.

"Dad wants a divorce?"

"Yes."

I can sense the pain in my mother's voice, and it's throwing me off completely. My father, Judge Lacerda de Brito, Mr. Morals-and-Righteousness, has a secret lover. That's the only possible reason, no doubt in my mind. Then I remember what Jasmine spilled yesterday about my father, and it hits me—I barely know him. I sink into the couch. He's got himself a lover. I wonder if it's another quirky artist with wild, with flaming red hair.

"Sorry, Mel, I've got a call from the hospital. It might be urgent. We'll talk later."

"Okay."

"Sorry for telling you like this over the phone, but I didn't want you to hear it from someone else. If you need anything, call me."

As I'm about to pop the question about whether he's got a lover, she cuts the call. I'm just sitting there, stunned, speechless, clueless about what to say or how to react. I catch the sound of the door opening, but I stay put. Next thing, my aunt strolls in, holding a bag.

"Hey, darling. Brought some fresh pineapple."

"My parents are getting divorced."

"Sorry?!"

"My parents are getting divorced."

My aunt sets down the bag and comes to sit beside me.

"He has a lover."

"A lover?! Are you sure?"

"He's the one who wanted the divorce, so I'm pretty sure he has a lover."

My father, the judge who was all about being squeaky clean, who called out his colleagues when that scandal broke about judges getting caught in some wild party with high-end escorts, turns out to be a liar and a phony. Makes you wonder if he was part of those shindigs too, huh?

"That doesn't sound like your father at all, Mel."

"You don't know him, Aunt. Heck, I don't even know him, and I've lived with him almost my whole life."

"I know it's not easy, but your parents' divorce isn't the end of the world."

"It's not the divorce, it's the lies."

The phone starts ringing, and I glance at the name on the screen. Dad.

"Aren't you going to answer?"

"I don't want to talk to him."

The phone keeps ringing, and I reject the call.

"You should answer it, darling. You should hear what he has to say."

"I don't want to talk to him."

Chapter 18

Carlos told me he'd be a bit late today because he had to drop off his little sister at school. I'm chilling on the porch sofa. My father called again last night, but I rejected the call, again. He hasn't tried today, thankfully. I hope he got the message. I'm just not ready to talk to him.

What I really wanted was to talk to Rodrigo. I sent him a text last night, but no reply. I don't know if he's up in the air or resting. I decide to call him while I wait for Carlos. I need to hear his voice. The phone rings for a bit and then heads to voicemail. I leave a message asking him to call me back.

I see Carlos rolling up on his motorcycle and stash my phone in my bag.

"Today we're heading to the Furnas Lake," Carlos says as he moves his stuff into his Grandpa's van.

"Your grandpa doesn't mind you taking his van again?"

"Nah, he's cool with it. He's at the grocery store all day."

"He's old enough to retire, isn't he?"

"Yeah, but he says stopping is like dying, so as long as he's got the strength, the store stays open."

We hop in the van, and Carlos hits the road. As we pass the grocery store, we wave to Mr. Manuel, who's, as usual, puffing away outside, chatting up some customers with glasses of wine in hand.

"Everything okay, Mel? You're too quiet."

I'm tempted to flash my most convincing fake smile and go, 'Sure, everything's fine,' but I know I can't fool Carlos. Plus, I don't want to lie to him.

"My parents are getting divorced."

"Sorry to hear that."

"Me too."

"It can't be easy."

"I wasn't expecting news like that."

I feel a tear rolling down my cheek, so I turn my head to the window. Carlos notices I'm not up for talking and doesn't push. He switches the radio to some mellow tunes, and we drive in silence until we get to the lake. We park in this big dirt lot, and we step out of the van.

I'm not exactly thrilled about checking out the Furnas. The idea of steam shooting from the ground where hot water springs out kind of freaks me out. Carlos goes on about how this place has all these hot springs, geysers, and some medicinal volcanic mud, which sounds cool for tourists, but I'm not really in the mood for it. I'm just not feeling it today.

When we finally get there, I notice a bunch of stray cats hanging around.

"They come here for the warm ground."

The cats seem to enjoy the warmth, but they're smart enough to keep their distance from the geysers. One of the cats comes up to me, starts rubbing against my leg, and then starts meowing.

Carlos pulls out a pack of cat food from the trunk and hands it to me.

"This little guy wants a treat."

I tear open the pack and pour some biscuits into my hand. I crouch down to feed the cat, and before I can even fully bend, it's already chomping down. Its whiskers tickle my hand.

"Do you think they're hungry?"

"Nah. The restaurant owners around here feed them, but they're little gluttons. Every time I come here, I bring them a treat."

The smell of the food starts drawing in more cats, and before I know it, I'm surrounded. I worry they might fight over the food, but they're not bothered. They stick around, rubbing against my legs while I dish out the packet's contents. When the food's gone, they scatter off in different directions, finding their sunny spots again.

"You said these photos you're taking are for the Azores Tourism, right?"

"Yeah, we're putting together a collection of books about the Azores, and the first one's on São Miguel. I'm in charge of the photography, and there's a biologist doing the writing. Plus, we're setting up a website."

"Was photography always your thing?"

"Nah. I stumbled into photography almost by accident."

"Accident?"

"Yeah, when I dropped out of college, I didn't have a clue what to do. Did a bunch of odd jobs. Supermarket gigs, then selling tickets for boat tours, even worked at a café. I was all over the place."

"And you weren't into photography then?"

"Nope, not at all. I never cared about photography until I stumbled upon a book by photographer Franz Lanting at the local library. Went there with my little sister, and there it was: 'Eye to Eye', on the cover a close-up of a puma."

"And that's when you decided to become a photographer?"

"Not exactly. I figured it'd be awesome to snap shots of the island's animals, so I began tagging along with my uncle on these boat tours to spot dolphins and whales, and one day, we stumbled upon a beached whale over at Terceira's shore. I took a picture of the rescue, and it got published in a local paper. My grandpa, without me knowing, submitted the photo to an international photo contest. Months later, bam, turns out I won! That's when things took a wild turn. I won twenty thousand euros and a photography course in England."

"Wow! That's lucky!"

"It wasn't luck; it was my grandpa believing in me. If he hadn't sent the photo, I'd still be doing odd jobs."

One of the cats approaches again when it sees me opening the backpack.

"I don't have anything else, kitty." I let it sniff the sketchpad and pencil. Disappointed, the cat goes back to sunbathing.

"And hey, have you ever thought about getting back into art?"

I give a little smile.

"I used to dream of being a painter or an illustrator, but my family wasn't exactly on board. Now I figure it's too late."

"It's never too late, Mel. People shake things up at forty, fifty, or way beyond. There's always a chance."

"I can't just drop everything. I've hustled hard to make a name in law."

"You could still be a lawyer and chase your artsy side in your downtime."

"Free time? That's a unicorn in the office where I work. I'm pulling twelve to fourteen-hour shifts. When I finally get home, all I want to do is crash on the couch." And maybe crack open a bottle of vodka.

"Do you like that life?"

Good question. Nope, I absolutely don't. I loathe it, like seriously, with every fiber of my being. I glance at Carlos, trying to come up with the right words, you know, the 'acceptable' ones Dr. Lacerda de Brito's daughter should say.

"Hey, you can be real with me, Mel. I'm the dude who bailed on Computer Engineering after my parents went all-in to send me off to Lisbon. I ended up back on the island clueless about life. All I knew was I couldn't stand the course and it'd slowly kill me if I stuck with it."

"My job's a bummer. And my colleagues? Well, some are alright, but there's this one guy poisoning the vibe. He makes my life a living nightmare."

"Why's he messing with you?"

"Because I'm a woman and because a woman's place isn't in the office. Apparently, women belong at home, on call to fulfill their husband's every whim and fantasy."

Carlos's eyes widen. I think he's taken aback by this unfiltered, sharp-tongued version of me.

"Did that jerk really say that to you?"

"Yeah, point-blank, and trust me, that was just the tip of the iceberg."

"What a piece of work, Mel. You don't need to tolerate that. Ever thought about taking it up officially against him?"

"I'll handle it solo. I don't want to be the squealer."

"You're not being a squealer, Mel. That guy crossed a major line."

The cat approaches again and rubs against my legs. I pet it. I feel its rough fur, probably singed from some encounter with the geysers. Then it lays there, at my feet.

"Can we talk about something else?"

"Of course. Sorry if I upset you."

"No, it felt good to vent, but I don't want to keep talking about it."

"Okay."

Carlos steps back and starts taking photos. I sit down on a park bench and begin to sketch the cat. The Furnas Cat. I notice Carlos is back in T-shirts. He's wearing the Garfield T-shirt again, the one where Garfield is chomping down on a huge slice of pizza. I prefer him in a shirt, looks slimmer that way.

"Your T-shirt matches the place today."

He takes his eye off the lens, looking like he's not getting it.

"You've got a cat on your shirt, and we're surrounded by cats."

"Oh, yeah," he chuckles. "I've been a big fan of Garfield since I was a kid."

"I've noticed you've got a collection of T-shirts with cartoon characters."

"What can I say, I have good taste."

"I wouldn't call it good taste."

"Don't tell me you don't like my T-shirts?"

"Yesterday's shirt suited you better."

"Yesterday's shirt was too tight on me. T-shirts are way more comfortable. Besides, this one's my lucky t-shirt. I was wearing it the day I found out I'd won the photography contest. Plus, Garfield and I have a lot in common."

"You both love pizza and sleeping?"

"We're both adorable, and no one can resist us." He winks at me.

I burst out laughing. I watch him walk away, camera in hand, and realize he's right. He's adorable. And fun. And caring. And a genuinely good person. If it weren't for Rodrigo, it'd be very easy to fall for him. Way too easy.

Groups of tourists are wandering around, and when the geysers shoot boiling water up, they're like, "Whoa!" Then I spot this gorgeous building in the distance. I overhear some tourists saying it's the Chapel of Our Lady of Victories, the most amazing temple around here. I figure I'll sketch it. The rest of the morning unfolds like this: Carlos captures shots as I sketch, and my furry buddy lounges lazily at my feet.

"Shall we grab lunch?"

"Yeah, sure."

"Let's see if our lunch is ready." He points to an enormous pot that two men are hoisting out of a hole in the ground.

"Are you kidding?"

"Nope. I ordered a stew for us."

We approach the men, and I peer into the hole.

"But won't it taste like sulfur? I've heard it's really sulfurous."

"No, miss," says one of the men pulling the pot out of the earth. "If it's done right, it won't taste like sulfur. I've been doing this for many years - twenty years. Not to brag, but my stew is the best."

"Let's see," I say, not entirely convinced.

The man chuckles. The pot is huge! All I can think about is that TV presenter wolfing down a massive plate of stew. The Azores might be top-notch in sustainability, but definitely not in light meals!

"You'll love it. My stew is to die for," he says confidently.

"Where are we eating it?" I ask, not spotting any place suitable.

"We're heading to that restaurant we passed on our way here. They'll serve it."

"Yes, miss. This pot can feed about twenty lunches."

We walk over to the restaurant and take our seats. Shortly after, they bring out this enormous tray with the stew. I'm still a bit skeptical. I'm afraid it'll taste like sulfur. I cautiously try a bit. Turns out, it's really good! It doesn't taste or smell of sulfur at all.

"The man was right."

"Tobias was a fisherman on the same boat as my grandpa."

"Seriously? The boat that sank?"

"Yep, he and my grandpa were the only ones who made it. Tobias lost his son in that shipwreck. Then, his wife took her own life a year later."

"God, that's awful. Losing a kid and a partner so quickly. I can't even imagine how tough that must've been."

"He couldn't handle it and started drinking. Him and my grandfather."

"Your grandfather told me."

"They went from boat mates to drinking buddies."

Listening to all this, I feel sort of pathetic. How can my problems compare to those guys who lost everything at sea, right? Maybe Cláudio's right—I'm just a scared, spoiled girl.

"Your grandpa said your grandma gave him an ultimatum."

"Yeah. I remember seeing him drunk when I was little. But hey, he managed to kick the drinking."

"What about his friend Tobias?"

"Tobias kept on drinking for a few more years. But then my grandpa pushed him into treatment."

"Your grandpa sounds like a good guy."

"Yeah, grumpy, but with a heart of gold."

"So, Tobias eventually got sober?"

"Yeah, he found love with a nurse from the clinic. They're still together."

"You'd think they'd both be retired by now."

"Nope, not my grandpa. As long as he's got energy, he won't stop. Needs something to keep him busy, so he won't fall back to his old ways."

"To keep him from hitting the bottle again?"

"Yeah, to keep those demons locked away, as he says."

"Being occupied is good, especially if it's something you enjoy. Doing what you love is a whole different vibe."

"I know we just met recently, and I'm not the best person for advice, considering what I've been through. I almost went down the wrong path..."

"The wrong path?"

"Yeah, nearly got tangled up in drug trafficking. A friend had this whole pitch. It was tempting, easy cash. I don't know where I'd be if my grandpa hadn't sent that photo to the contest. Man, when I landed in England to study photography, I was freaking out. What if it sucked like my Computer Engineering course? Or what if I hated England?"

"But it worked out, right?"

"Yeah, totally! Loved the course, loved England. New folks, new culture. Stepping out of my comfort zone brought some awesome stuff. You should think about it."

"About heading to England for a photography course?"

"Getting out of your comfort zone."

"I got it, was just kidding."

"You should start with diving."

"Diving?!"

"Don't act like you've forgotten. We agreed I'd take a CrossFit class and you'd try a diving lesson."

"You haven't done the CrossFit class yet."

"Then schedule it."

"Are you sure?"

"Yes."

"Are you stepping out of your comfort zone?"

"You can bet on it. Being stuck in a gym bouncing around is totally out of my comfort zone. And you?"

"I'm used to the gym."

"Don't play innocent. Are you going to take a diving class?"

I hesitate. Thoughts of sharks, eels, and stingrays start racing through my mind. I don't know why, but stingrays terrify me.

"So?"

I see the challenge in his eyes and can't resist the dare, despite being terrified.

"Okay, fine."

"Fine?"

"Fine, I'll take the diving class."

"Great, because I've already arranged it with my friend. We're meeting him tomorrow for the first lesson."

"Tomorrow?!"

Chapter 19

"Nervous?" Carlos asks as he pulls the van up in front of the swimming complex.

"Nope," I say, but I bet my face is telling a different story because he smiles and says, "It's okay to be a bit jittery."

I should tell him I'm as solid as a rock, that if I can handle Cláudio's harassment and my father's betrayal, I can handle anything, but I know I can't fool him.

"Actually, I'm a bit nervous."

"Everything's going to be fine. Plus, I'm here, armed with superhero skills."

I crack up. Only Carlos could get me laughing at a time like this.

We step into the building, passing a group of hyped-up teenagers talking loudly about some soccer game. Next to a shallow pool, there's a group of kids in a lesson, the instructor trying to keep them from jumping off the edge, but it's a lost cause. They're having a blast, splashing and laughing. Then we get to an area with a smaller, deeper pool. On the opposite side, three guys are chatting. Carlos heads to one of them, a tall, tanned, and muscular guy. Must be our instructor. The other two guys leave, and Carlos comes back with the tall guy.

"Mel, meet Fred."

"Hey, Mel, welcome to your first diving class! I'm going to be your instructor," he says, shaking my hand firmly while eyeing me up and down.

"Nice to meet you."

I'm debating if Fred's more like a *Cappuccino* or a *Martini*. Seems too intense for a *Cappuccino*. I notice a scar on his forehead and a smaller one on his chin. But despite the scars, he's quite good-looking. Do they pick coaches based on their good looks? Because that's what it looks like.

"Ready for this?" Fred asks.

Honestly? Nope, I'm not prepared. I'm feeling pretty scared.

"Kind of. I'm a bit nervous."

"No need to be nervous. I'll make sure everything goes smoothly," he says, giving me an intense look. "I've got a wetsuit for you. Put it on, and then I'll fill you in."

Carlos leads the way to the changing area.

I strip down and wrestle with the wetsuit. It's so snug. If Rodrigo were here, he could give me a hand with this. I wonder where he is. And why hasn't he called? Eventually, I manage to squeeze into the wetsuit and head out.

Carlos is already waiting, decked out. The suit does wonders in hiding his midsection. He almost looks elegant. When he spots me, he grins.

"Ready?"

"Not really. The suit was a struggle. I think it's a size too small."

"Nah, you'll get used to it."

"How about you? Ready?" I ask, already knowing the answer. His eyes are lit up with excitement.

"Totally psyched! It's much easier than you think," he says enthusiastically.

I hope he's right, really hope so because I'm feeling far from ready.

We make our way to the pool where Fred waits, arms crossed. His pose reminds me of Leo's at the CrossFit classes, but Leo's more laid-back. Fred's more of a *Martini* type, I'd say.

"Okay, before we dive in, let's set up a signal. If you start feeling uncomfortable or anxious, just raise your right hand, and we'll take a break."

Uncomfortable? Understatement of the century. I almost feel like raising my hand and calling it quits right now, but I don't want to let Carlos down.

"Sounds like a plan."

"Alright! Let's start with the basics. We'll talk about the diving gear," Fred says, grabbing a mask and some other thing. "Diving mask and snorkel," Okay, now I know what that is. "The diving mask helps you see underwater, and the snorkel lets you breathe on the surface without lifting your head out of the water. Got it?"

I'm thinking Fred might've been in the military. He talks all strong and sure, like he's handing out commands. And those scars, I can't help but wonder how he got them. Was it from some accident or some mission overseas? He totally looks like he might've been a marine or something.

"Here we have the regulator, which is used for..."

He starts explaining the rest of the equipment, but honestly, it's too much information for me to digest right now. I'm not exactly thrilled about putting that regulator thing in my mouth or carrying that tank on my back. It must weigh a ton.

"Mel, focus!" He gestures for me to come closer. "First, make sure the valve on top of the tank is closed," he shows me. "Then, attach the regulator to the valve, and finally, put the regulator in your mouth and bite down on the mouthpiece. Got it?"

"Yeah, I think so."

"Let's give it a try!"

I glance at Carlos, who's giving me a thumbs-up. I take a deep breath and stick the regulator in my mouth. Ugh, it tastes like rubber. I'm pretty sure I'll have this taste lingering all day.

"Take a few deep breaths to get used to it," Fred says.

I inhale and exhale a few times.

"So, how does it feel?"

I take the regulator from my mouth.

"It's kind of weird." 'Kind of' is an understatement; it's pretty gross. I definitely don't like having this thing in my mouth.

"When you're in the pool, if at any moment you feel like you're not getting enough air or if you feel uncomfortable, raise your right arm, and we'll take a break."

I look at the pool and sigh. I'm nervous just thinking about getting into it with that thing in my mouth. Why did I agree to this, why?! Fred keeps talking, but all I can think about is that this isn't going to go well. Something tells me this isn't going to go well.

"...when you finish diving, you must close the valve at the top of the bottle to stop the airflow. Any questions?"

I shake my head.

"Let's repeat everything!" Fred must have really been in the military. Now I'm one hundred percent sure.

I practice a few more times, but I still don't like the feeling of the regulator in my mouth.

"It's time to put on your flippers and head to the edge of the pool."

Carlos and I sit on a bench as we put on the flippers. Then we get up and start walking towards the pool.

"We look like two penguins," Carlos says, laughing.

I start laughing too.

"Only you to make me laugh at this moment. I still don't know how you convinced me to do this."

"You'll have a good time, I promise."

I think I'll hate it, but I don't have the guts to tell him that.

Fred hands us the tanks and helps me put mine on my back. It feels like lead.

"How many kilos does this weigh?"

"Twelve."

Then he puts the diving mask on me and the regulator in my mouth. I bite the mouthpiece like he taught me. It's gross. Really gross. I glance at Carlos and then at the pool. It's pretty deep, and the tank on my back weighs a whopping twelve kilos. I'll plummet like a rock with all this equipment! I'll end up at the pool's bottom, and there's no way they'll get me back up! I'm starting to freak out about this whole thing.

Fred's signaling for me to get into the pool, but I'm frozen. It's just a pool, right? No sharks or scary sea monsters, but I'm still feeling uneasy. Fred's trying to cheer me on. Carlos jumps in, and despite my terror, I follow right after him. I sink like a rock. Down at the pool bottom, the weight of that twelve-kilo tank triggers an instant panic in me. I want out! I try to get back to the surface, but this tank is like an anchor. What was I even thinking when I agreed to this?! Carlos takes his mouthpiece out and says something, but I can't make it out. I'm struggling to get out of the pool, but I can't. He gets closer and pulls me upwards until I can grab hold of the ladder. Then Fred helps me out of the pool. Carlos follows and helps me get rid of the tank.

I pull out my mouthpiece and sit on the pool edge, breathing heavily.

"Sorry, I'm not up for this!"

"It's alright, Mel. Take your time."

Carlos sits beside me and puts his arm around my shoulder. I lean my head against him.

"Maybe this was a dumb idea," Carlos apologizes, "I'm sorry. If you want, we can leave."

"It's not your fault, Carlos. I'm just a total scaredy-cat."

Fred chuckles.

"You're not alone, Mel. Yesterday, I had a client, a forty-year-old dude who's six-foot-something, and he was even more jumpy than you. He ended up in tears. His wife thought the diving course would help him get over his water fear, but I guess it didn't. He left without taking a dip."

"You're just saying that to make me feel better."

"No, seriously! I'm not making it up!"

"Want to call it quits and head home?" Carlos asks.

I lift my head off his shoulder and look him in the eye. I can tell he feels guilty, and I don't want him to. He's not at fault for any of this.

"I don't want to let you down."

"The only person you need to worry about not letting down is yourself, Mel. If you decide to bail, I won't be disappointed or mad." I realize he's being honest. And he's right. I know he's right. I stay there, staring at the pool for a long time, trying to untangle the mess of thoughts in my head. "Want to give it another shot?" He holds out his hand. "This time, I'll hold your hand and guide you?" I grab his hand firmly, as if he could be my savior, as if he could help me overcome my fears. Because I'm sick of being scared. And because I'm beginning to understand that next to him, I'm not as frightened.

"Yeah," It's just a pool, and Carlos is right here beside me. Nothing terrible will happen. Carlos won't let it. "I'm ready to try again."

Fred helps me with the tank and mask while Carlos puts his on. He says something, but he's got the regulator in his mouth, and I can't catch what he's saying. Then he takes my hand, signaling he wants us to jump in together. I take a deep breath and jump in tandem with him. I feel the splash of water, but this time, I'm not alone. I shut my eyes and let him lead the way. I start to get nervous and grip his hand tighter. He squeezes my hand even harder, and I open my eyes. He's grinning behind his diving mask. I breathe slowly and deeply. We stay put like that until I calm down. Then we paddle across the pool to the other side, his hand always holding mine. When we step out of the water, I'm relieved, so relieved that after we take off our masks and tanks, I give him a big hug.

"I did it!"

He wasn't expecting the hug and seems a bit awkward at first, but then hugs me back.

"You did it, Mel!"

"I did it!" My legs are trembling, and my heart's racing, but I did it!

"I'm very proud of both of you!" Fred says.

※ ※ ※

When I exit the changing room, Carlos and Fred are chatting by the pool. Carlos got ready in no time.

"I hope your girlfriend liked the first lesson."

"She's not my girlfriend," Carlos says, flustered, seeing me arrive.

"We're friends."

"Yeah, we're just friends."

"If you say so. So, when do you want to come back? Tomorrow afternoon?"

"Tomorrow?!"

"Yep. Carlos told me you'll only be on the island until the end of the month, so it's better if we have all the lessons in a row before we go into the sea."

"The sea?!"

"Yes, the sea."

It's like someone just hit the panic button in my head. The sea's got sharks, rays, creepy eels, and all sorts of scary monsters! I could get attacked by one of those beasts. Or I might just wander off and no one, not even Carlos, could come to my rescue!

"Tomorrow's cool," Carlos says, and I don't have it in me to disagree.

When we get into the van, he asks me.

"Is everything okay, Mel? You're too quiet. What's going on?"

"The sea scares me. I mean, what's inside, in the dark."

"Are you talking about sharks? It's not common to spot sharks here."

"But there could be other things..."

"Other things?"

"You're going to make fun of me."

"No, I won't."

"Monsters."

I see he's trying really hard not to burst out laughing.

"You promised not to laugh."

"And I'm not laughing."

"But you really want to."

"But I'm not laughing."

I shake my head, feeling a bit embarrassed about the whole monster thing.

"If there are monsters, I'll be your protector. Remember, I'm Super-Carlos?" I glance at him and notice he's not joking anymore; he means it. "I've got your back."

"Do you swear?"

"I swear."

My phone buzzes with a new message. I rummage through my backpack, scrambling to find the phone. It's from Rodrigo! He just sent me a selfie without a shirt, along with this caption:

I'll be there next Wednesday.

Rodrigo's coming to see me! HE'S COMING TO SEE ME! I'm so excited! I must have this silly grin on my face because Carlos asks:

"Good news?"

"Yeah, my boyfriend is coming to visit! He'll be here next week!"

Carlos smiles back, but it's a different smile. Then, he glances away and starts the car.

Chapter 20

See that sign up there saying "Perfect Body Gym" on top of that warehouse-like building?

"Best gym in Ponta Delgada," Carlos claims.

"You've been here before?" I ask.

"Nah."

"Then how do you know it's the best?"

"It's the only one in Ponta Delgada."

I glance at him and see he's trying not to crack up.

"Joker! I thought you were a gym expert or something."

"Gyms aren't my thing. Actually, it's my first time."

"Your first time?!"

"Yeah."

"So, you mean you've never stepped foot in a gym?!"

"I've been in one, but never taken a class."

I'm starting to think this will be fun. I wonder if he can keep up.

We stroll in, and this brunette with a huge grin greets us. My phone buzzes with a new text. Rodrigo. I back off, leaving Carlos chatting with the girl.

Guess where I am?

Did he decide to show early?

Here in São Miguel?

Cold.

Give me a clue.

I'm at the spot where we first met.

You're in Dubai!

Yep, I'm in Dubai, hanging out in a jewelry store.

ANXIOUS GIRL **153**

A jewelry store?

Checking out a ring that would be perfect on your finger.

My heart's racing.

Are you going to make my dream come true?

You're my dream, Mel. Love you!

Love you too. Miss you tons!

Almost there, angel.

Feels like time's crawling.

I know. Waiting's killing me too.

Going to hit up a CrossFit class now.

Then go sweat it out. Keep that body in top shape for me.

Carlos signals for me to hurry, so I stash my phone. I rush to the locker room, but I can't forget Rodrigo's messages. OMG! Will he actually get me a ring?!

Five minutes later, we're both geared up for the class.

"I got something for you," Carlos says.

"What is it?"

He holds out his hand, and when he opens it, I see a pink hair tie.

"You bought this?!" I ask, laughing.

"Don't laugh. Not me, my little sister. And I got one too." He opens his other hand, revealing a blue hair tie. "Said my gym debut was a big deal and got these."

"You told her about me?"

"Yeah, of course."

"Then tell her thanks."

"You can tell her yourself. After class, if I survive, I'll get her from school, and we'll grab a snack together," he hesitates, a bit embarrassed, "I mean, if you want to tag along."

"Definitely! I'd love to. Can't wait to meet your sister," I slide on my hair tie. "How does it look?"

"Awesome! It suits you," but I can't tell if he's serious or kidding.

I snatch the blue hair tie from his hands.

"Let's see how it looks on you," and I pop it onto his head.

He shakes his head.

"I must look ridiculous."

"Nah, you're good," though he kind of does, but I can't bring myself to say it.

"No I'm not. The things my sister ropes me into," he keeps shaking his head.

"Selfie time," I grab my phone. Carlos throws a flexing pose, arms crossed, mimicking those bodybuilding types, and we crack up. I lean in, striking a playful pose. We try for a serious face, but it's a laugh riot.

"Now, one for my sister on my phone," he hands it to me. "But no goofy poses," I snap a couple of pics and give back his phone.

"Hey, these came out great, Mel. Seems you've got a knack for photography too."

I glance at the wall clock and realize it's class time.

"Class is starting! You were trying to distract me!"

"I wasn't doing anything."

"Yeah, right."

"Maybe just a bit."

I end up grinning. I can't stay annoyed with Carlos.

We head to the studio, and I realize the girl who welcomed us is the instructor.

"Hey, I'm Vera. Nice to meet you!"

"Hey there, I'm Mel. Sorry I didn't chat earlier, was texting my boyfriend."

"You two aren't a thing?"

She points at Carlos.

"Just friends."

"And she talked you into coming for class?"

"We struck a deal. I hit CrossFit, she goes diving."

"Ah, like a challenge."

"Kind of," Carlos laughs.

"Is your girl cool with you joining a friend for class?"

Vera keeps grinning at Carlos. Is she hitting on him?

"I don't have a girlfriend."

He adjusts the hair tie, looking a bit bashful. Is he into her too?

People start filing in, and Vera takes the lead. When she cranks up the music, it's like a hammer in my ears. I forgot how loud gym music can be.

"Don't get sidetracked by Vera." I'm yelling so he can hear.

"What do you mean?!"

"She seemed into you."

He laughs but stays mum.

"Alright, guys, let's start! Time to work those bodies!"

Carlos turns to me.

"If I don't make it, give the hair tie to my sister, Mel," he readjusts it.

He's on the verge of cracking up. Let's see if he's still laughing after this class.

"Let's warm up!"

We start with jumping jacks. Carlos is beside me, but I can't catch a glimpse of his face. I wish this place had those giant mirrors so I could see the goofy faces he's pulling.

"I'm all warmed up!" he says a few minutes later.

"Let's go, guys!" Vera shouts over the blasting music.

Vera's a machine. Looks like she's breezing through this. I've probably been making weird faces this whole time. Thank goodness there's no mirror in front of us—I don't want Carlos to catch my grimaces.

After who-knows-how-many sets, we move on to squats.

"Come on, everyone! Push through! Don't give in!"

"Phew. Why did she have to say that? Just when I was about to throw in the towel."

"You can't bail! You got to finish the whole class, Carlos!"

"You guys seem all chatty," she eyeballs me and Carlos. "Probably because the workout's too easy. Let's ramp it up!"

And we're back to jumping jacks, now even faster. I'm not sure I can keep up. I try to glance at Carlos, but no luck. Should've challenged him to something else. A spa day, maybe. That'd have been a better plan. Music's still blaring, and Vera's still yelling. After what feels like endless jumping jacks, we move on to the dreaded burpees. Ugh, I hate burpees!

"Mel, is this ever going to end?"

"We've barely started."

"This class feels like it's going to last forever."

"Yeah, it's going to be a long one." Seriously long.

"Faster! Faster! Let's get those bodies toned!"

My legs, arms, abs—all begging for mercy. My entire body's screaming for a break.

"I already feel more toned," Carlos jokes.

"How do you even have breath left to talk?"

"You're talking too."

"Because you're talking to me."

"Alright, enough chit-chat!" yells Vera. "We're here to work out, not gossip."

"What a drill sergeant!"

"Shut up, Carlos. If she catches you, it's more burpees for us."

"Aren't these jumping jacks?"

"Nope."

"Looks the same to me."

Vera shoots us a disapproving look, and we zip it. We move on to push-ups, and I quickly decide I loathe push-ups even more than burpees. I sneak a peek at Carlos. He's breezing through them without a hint of struggle. Why do guys always have better arm strength? So not fair! After push-ups, we switch to lifting weights, another thing I can't stand. I grab two pairs of two-kilogram dumbbells.

"This is too light," Carlos says, swapping them for a pair of five-kilogram ones.

"Now you're just showing off."

"Nope," he says, flexing his bicep with the weight. I catch a glimpse of the muscle beneath his t-shirt.

"Yeah, you are. Is that for Vera?" I notice she's eyeing him.

"Nah, not at all."

My dumbbells might be lighter than Carlos's, but they feel like I'm lifting a ton. I've come to the conclusion that this was a terrible idea! Totally backfired on me. The rest of the class goes on with more weighted exercises. Carlos is killing it. Probably going to tease me later. Should've gone for the spa. Or a Zumba class. Yeah, Zumba! I bet Carlos would rock a Zumba class!

After a bunch of sets with dumbbells and ankle weights, the class finally wraps up.

"How did I do?" Carlos asks me.

"Pretty darn good," Vera chimes in. "For a gym newbie, you rocked it."

"Yeah, I'm not really into gyms. I prefer diving."

"If you change your mind, my door's always open. Keep it in mind."

"I'll think about it."

"Here's my card. Personal number's on there. If you want to grab coffee, hit me up," she says, giving Carlos a flirty wink.

Bold move! Carlos grins but stays quiet. We bid Vera goodbye and head to the locker area.

"You're oddly quiet," he points out.

"Didn't want to rain on Vera's parade."

"What parade?"

"Stop playing dumb. She was all over you."

He brushes off my comment and fires back.

"So, how did I do?"

"Vera already gave her pro opinion."

He stops by the locker room door.

"I don't care about hers. I want yours."

I clock his smile and realize I'm being ridiculous. Vera kind of got under my skin, for no good reason.

"You killed it, seriously."

"Do you mean it, or you're just trying to be nice?"

"Truth. Scout's honor."

"Thought I wouldn't make it through class."

"Quit kidding around."

"I'm dead serious."

"Then you masked it well. You wanted to impress Vera?"

"Nah, wanted to impress you." He gets a bit flustered, and adds, "Let's hurry, my sister's waiting." And we split for our respective locker rooms.

※ ※ ※

After we shower up and change, we swing by to pick up his sister from school. We're cruising in the van, almost reaching the school, but I just can't hold back from throwing a question at him.

"Are you planning to ask Vera out?"

Eyes fixed on the road; he takes a pause before responding.

"Doesn't seem likely."

"She's a hottie and has a toned body."

He chuckles.

"After today's workout, both of us also have toned bodies."

"You're dodging the question. Are you going to ask her out or not?"

"She's a bit too energetic and bossy for my taste."

And that ends the conversation. And I'm happy. I'm happy because she's not the right woman for him. That's all.

Carlos parks near the school, and a girl with blonde braids comes sprinting toward our van. We step out, and she jumps straight into Carlos's arms.

"Hey, big bro!"

He scoops her up, plants a quick peck on her cheek.

"Hey, little sis!"

Then gently puts her down.

"This is Mel."

"No surprises there! If she's with you, she's got to be Mel."

"Hi, Joana, nice to meet you."

"So, you're the Lisbon girl."

"I didn't know I had that rep."

"But you do," she says confidently. Carlos beams, clearly proud of his sister. I can tell from his expression that he absolutely adores her.

"Snack time?" Carlos suggests.

"Yes! Can we hit up that corner bakery?" Then she turns to me. "They serve up the best custard tarts on the island." I hesitate, unsure if I should mention my rule about skipping custard tarts (or any sweets), but I figure, hey, I'm technically on vacation. I can break my own rule.

The bakery's just a short walk away, so we decide to stroll there. Joana, she's a chatterbox! She's going on about school, her friends, swimming, the medals she's won... The girl's got a lot to say, but she's a sweetheart. We get to the bakery, and Carlos bumps into someone he knows, chatting it up by the door. Meanwhile, Joana and I head inside and take a seat.

"So, are you and my brother, like, dating?"

Kids can really cut to the chase.

"No, we're just friends."

"You two seem super close though. Always hanging out. And Carlos won't stop talking about you."

"Really?"

"Yeah, totally! Well, at least when I give him the chance to speak. You've probably figured I can talk your ear off."

I nod along.

"Teachers are constantly messaging my parents because I never shut up."

"Are your parents cool about it?"

"Dad gets a bit ticked off, but Mom says that's just my personality, and there's no changing it."

I grin. Her mom sounds like a gem. I bet Carlos got his traits from her.

"I think you and Carlos should date!"

"We can't, Joana."

"Why not?"

"Because I have a boyfriend."

"Yeah, when I asked Carlos why you're not his girlfriend, he said the same. You could totally dump your boyfriend. He must be a jerk."

"Why do you say that? Did your brother mention something?"

"No, but I just feel it. He keeps saying he'll come see you, but then he doesn't."

"He's busy with work, can't just bail like that. He's a pilot, you know. Besides, I think he might propose soon."

"How do you figure?"

"He was at a jewelry store checking out engagement rings."

"So what? I still reckon my brother would make a way better boyfriend. He's a photographer, even won an award. Plus, he's super sweet. Like, the sweetest guy ever."

"I know. Your brother's a sweetheart."

"What are you guys talking about?" Carlos chimes in.

Suddenly, I feel a bit nervous, not sure why. I guess I don't want to dive deeper into that subject in front of him.

"Nothing," Joana says, and I'm relieved.

"You guys ordered?"

"Not yet."

"Then let's order," and he flags down the waiter.

Snack time sails by with laughter and some seriously delicious custard tarts. So much for my no-custard-tart rule. I sneak a peek at my phone now and then. Is Rodrigo really getting me a ring? I'm really hoping he is.

"Why are you always glued to your phone?" Joana asks.

Caught off guard, I'm not sure what to say. I don't want to spill I'm waiting on a text from my boyfriend, so I shrug it off.

"Waiting for a message from a friend."

She seems satisfied and switches gears, diving into a tale from a swimming class. Luckily, she doesn't bring up the boyfriend topic again.

Chapter 21

I've been counting down the days until Rodrigo gets here. The days have been dragging, especially the nights. During the day, I've been hanging out with Carlos. We head out in the morning to take photos (and draw), and then we hit the pool for some diving lessons in the afternoon. Jasmine stopped crashing at the rural place, so now the three of us always have breakfast and dinner together. No need to pretend she's not living here anymore. My aunt and she spend their days at the Hortensias Garden and, later in the day, they come home together. It's cool seeing them so close. Jasmine's growing on me, even though she's not the easiest to get along with. Yesterday, she had a squabble with my aunt over cigarettes. My aunt suggested she quit, and it got her riled up, but in the end, all was good. She went to the porch for a smoke, and a bit later, my aunt joined her. When I went to sleep, they were both hugging it out. There aren't any perfect relationships, I know, but there are good ones, like theirs. Those are the ones worth fighting for. That's what I'm doing - fighting for my relationship with Rodrigo because I really think we've got something ahead.

I'm still in bed, just being lazy, when the phone rings. I bounce out of bed, super excited. Grab the phone and answer without even checking who's calling because I'm pretty sure it's Rodrigo. He's coming in tomorrow, and he probably wants to plan the pickup at the airport.

"Rodrigo!"

"It's me, Mel."

I recognize my father's voice and instantly regret picking up the phone. Thought he gave up trying to chat with me.

"Hey, Dad."

"How's it going?"

"All good."

"How are things going on in the Azores?"

"Really great, actually. Aunt Gabi and her wife are amazing."

He goes quiet for a few seconds, like he's picking his words carefully. I wonder if he's aware that I already know of his thing with Jasmine.

"I'm glad to hear that," he says.

None of us says a word for what seems like an eternity.

"The exams for the Judicial Studies Center have been set. You'll get the summons in a few days."

Exams? Seriously? That's the last thing on my mind.

"The exams are in two months. You have plenty of time to prepare."

"Uh-huh," I manage to mutter.

Then, I hear him take a big sigh.

"Your mom must have told you that we're getting a divorce."

My mother. I've totally ghosted her, and now I feel kind of bad. I should've called, but communication is the Achilles' heel of my family.

"Yeah, she mentioned it."

"We'll talk face-to-face when you're back. This isn't a subject to discuss over the phone."

"Dad, there's nothing to talk about. You're both grown-ups."

"We need to talk, Mel."

Need a lawyer for your divorce? Picture me handling that! It would be hilarious.

"We really need to talk."

What does he have to say? That the straight-laced judge is a cheating husband? That he's been lying to my mother and me for years, pretending to work late while sneaking off to meet someone else? It's all starting to make sense now. Why he was always MIA, why he was clocking in overtime. And I feel betrayed. I feel robbed of his presence, his attention. I'm dying to know—who's the other woman? His secretary? A coworker? The suspense is killing me, but I know he won't tell me over the phone.

"Alright, we'll talk when I go back."

"When are you coming back?"

"At the end of the month."

"If you need anything, give me a call."

"Aunt Gabi's taking care of me."

"I know."

We say our goodbyes quickly, and I head to the kitchen.

My aunt is making breakfast.

"Good morning, darling. Did you sleep well?"

"I was sleeping like a log until a bit ago."

"What happened?"

"Dad called. The Judicial Studies Center exams are a go."

"Is that stressing you out?"

I take a deep breath. No point hiding it.

"Yep. I'm not even sure if I still want to be a judge. And the worst? Dad, who never bothered talking to me, now wants a chat when I'm back in Lisbon. Probably wants to explain himself, say he fell head over heels for some other redhead artist."

My aunt's eyes widen.

"Sorry, Aunt Gabi, it slipped out."

"Come on, sit and have some food."

I take a seat but can't manage a bite. I can't stop thinking about my father's phone call.

"I'm discovering a father I didn't even know existed. Turns out, he dated a wild artist, went to rock gigs, and cheated on his wife. He also turned his back on his own sister, keeping me from having an aunt for over twenty years. I get it was rough for him when Jasmine left him to be with you but blocking you from seeing me wasn't fair."

"Mel, things aren't that black and white. It wasn't your dad; it was your grandfather who told me he never wanted anything to do with me again. Your grandma tried convincing him otherwise, but he wouldn't budge. And when he passed away, you were already an adult, and I hesitated to reach out for a long time. I should've had the guts to contact you earlier, but I was scared."

"Scared of what?"

"Scared you wouldn't accept me, wouldn't understand what I did to your father. I betrayed him, that's the truth."

"Just like he's betraying my mom now."

"Your father might seem stern and all, but he's a decent person. Always has been. When your grandfather kicked me out, he still tried to step in despite the pain. You should wait to hear his side. I'm pretty sure there's an explanation."

"I already know the explanation. He's hitting a midlife crisis and fell for someone twenty years younger."

"You don't know if this woman is younger."

"I bet she is. Men my father's age only swap their wives for much younger ones. I see it every day at work."

"Come on, don't dwell on it now."

"You're right, I need to stop thinking about it, but sometimes I can't control my thoughts. It's like I can't switch off. I start imagining a thousand things that could go wrong, and before I know it, I'm anxious."

"I totally understand. I have the same problem. Jasmine says we should start a club: the *Overthinkers Gang*."

"I love it!"

I laugh. It's a cute name. Only Jasmine would come up with something like that.

"Speaking of Jasmine, where is she?"

"She's still sleeping."

"Is everything okay with her?"

"She was a bit sick, but she's getting better now."

Carlos taps on the door, and that wraps up our chat.

※ ※ ※

Today marks our seventh diving lesson, and Fred just dropped the news that we're diving in open waters next week.

"Next week?!"

"You're totally ready, Mel."

"But I don't feel ready."

"Trust me, today's our seventh lesson. You're getting more and more comfortable. It's time to tackle the big, open ocean."

"The big ocean?"

"Where there are no monsters, only fish."

Fred and Carlos exchange this smirk like they've got some inside joke.

"Stop making fun of me."

"Hey, if we were diving in a lake, then maybe there'd be monsters."

"You're such a joker."

Lately, I've figured out that beneath Fred's military-style facade, he fancies himself a bit of a joker. Enjoys flirting with the ladies. Not that he needs to with that look! He must have a whole fan club. I'm still on the fence about whether he's more of a *Cappuccino* or a *Martini*. Leaning toward *Martini*, but I can't be sure.

"Alright, it's set. We're diving into the sea next week."

I let out a sigh.

"Time's running out, Mel." Carlos says.

"When are you leaving?" Fred asks.

As I count the days left, I realize they've zoomed by faster than I wanted.

"In about a week and a half."

It hits me hard. In a week and a half, I'll be back in Lisbon. Office life, Carmen's bold nail colors, break room chats, and those custard pastry meetings.

"Tomorrow, I'll fill you in on the differences when we dive in the open sea."

"I might not make it tomorrow. My boyfriend's visiting me."

Carlos steps aside to take a call.

"I didn't know you had a boyfriend. That's a shame."

"A shame?"

"I thought we could hang out. Grab dinner sometime."

Is Fred trying to hit on me?!

"So, what do you think? Dinner sometime?"

"I have a boyfriend, Fred."

"That's not a problem."

Talk about nerve.

"No?"

"Of course not. I'm all for open relationships."

"Does your girlfriend feel the same way?"

"I don't have a girlfriend."

"I thought that blond girl who shows up here sometimes was your girlfriend."

"Nah, we're just friends."

"Friends with benefits?"

He laughs, avoiding a direct answer. I've got no doubts now. Fred is definitely a *Martini*!

"So, are we set?" Carlos asks after ending his call. "Are we diving into the sea next week?"

"Yeah, absolutely!" Fred insists before moving off to chat with a couple who came for a lesson.

"You'll love it, you'll see," Carlos assures me. "The ocean is magical."

"And never-ending."

"*Loud sea, bottomless sea, endless sea. Your beauty grows when we're alone*[8]."

"That's really beautiful."

"It's from a poem by Sophia de Mello Breyner. She captured the sea's beauty in poetry like nobody else."

"She agrees with me, saying the sea is bottomless."

---

8 *Loud sea*, poem by Sophia de Mello Breyner.

"This pool does have a bottom. Want proof?" And out of the blue, he grabs me and leaps into the pool.

We start splashing and goofing around, having a blast. Fred comes over with that couple, shooting us a disapproving look.

"Maybe we should bail from the pool before Fred blows a fuse, Carlos."

"Yeah, you're probably right."

We hop out as Fred escorts the couple to the locker rooms. Sitting on the bench, we mess around trying to get our fins off. Acting like kids, but it feels freeing.

Fred approaches, and we stop our shenanigans.

"You two are really in a great mood today."

We both chuckle.

"Okay, okay, scram now, I can't deal with you two," he says, laughing too.

We move away, and as we do, I hear him say:

"There's something brewing between the two of you. Your boyfriend better watch out."

I glance at Carlos, noticing he's just as flustered as me. We're just friends, so why does it feel weird? We hit our changing rooms without a word.

I shower, change, and when I step out, Fred's teaching the couple while Carlos waits by the pool. He catches my eye and grins. I'm relieved – I thought things might get awkward between us for a moment.

"Shall we head out?"

"Yup, let's go."

We say goodbye to Fred and exit the complex. It starts to drizzle, so we sprint to the van. Carlos unlocks my door first (his grandpa's van is so old it doesn't have remote locks) and then walks around to get in on the driver's side.

"Thanks, you're a real gentleman."

"You've got to decide, am I Super-Carlos or am I a gentleman?"

"You can be both. Clark Kent is a gentleman and a superhero."

"Right. So, where's my Lois Lane?"

"I can be your Lois Lane."

Why did I say that? I shouldn't have. I glance up, and he's staring at me. I freeze, unsure how to proceed. He seems lost for words too, and we lock eyes, neither of us looking away.

Thump! Thump!

Fred's tapping the window, holding a phone. Carlos rolls it down.

"Is this yours?"

"Yeah, thanks."

I can't believe I forgot my phone.

Chapter 22

I'm lying down on this massage table covered in pink towels. And this room? It's all about pink and gold. Right in front of me, there's a golden pineapple and a pink ceramic French bulldog sitting on a white shelf. And on the left wall, there's this stunning photo of a peacock with its feathers all spread out. It looks like something Carlos might've snapped. The whole vibe here is modern and peaceful, as if the calmness of the decor is meant to numb the pain of waxing. Kayla, the Brazilian esthetician my aunt's friend recommended, is getting everything ready.

Yesterday evening, Rodrigo messaged me, saying he'd arrive today at six. So, I borrowed my aunt's van, and now I'm here in Ponta Delgada, lying on a massage table, legs apart, just waiting for the torture to begin. After this Brazilian waxing ordeal is over, I'm off to the hair salon to get my nails done and fix up my hair. I've got to look top-notch for Rodrigo.

Kayla comes over with a smile. "I'll be super quick, won't hurt a bit," she says, like I'm going to believe that. This is definitely going to hurt—a lot.

She puts on the first strip of wax, and I take a deep breath. Then, in one go, she rips it off.

"Whoa, that's intense!"

"All done," Kayla says, getting ready with another strip.

She tries to trick me, but I know the torture is just beginning. I take a deep breath and brace myself for the pain. As I'm there, legs apart, getting the entire intimate area waxed to be as smooth as a baby's bottom, I glance at the peacock on the wall, all calm and serene. Human mating should be more like that of peacocks. Women do everything to attract the male of the species. We paint our nails, our lips, wax our entire body, slather ourselves with creams that promise to rid us of cellulite, apply Botox to our lips, and silicone in our chests. Female peafowls, though, they're super chill. They just sit back, waiting for the males to woo them. It's the guys who go all out, showing off their gorgeous tails and making a racket, trying to impress the girls they fancy. I bet the female peafowls have a blast! They don't have to chase after the males. And thank goodness, no need for Brazilian waxing either.

"You're all set!" says Kayla.

I glance down and it's all red and irritated. Hopefully, it's better by tonight. I should've sorted this out earlier, but I always leave it till the last minute.

I spend the rest of the day around town—hair salon, shopping—the works. After my shopping spree, I head over to my aunt's place to get ready. I slip into a sexy red dress I snagged from a shop downtown, slide on some high heels, and do my makeup. Underneath? A matching set of red lace lingerie. Rodrigo's in for a treat.

I grab my purse and keys, about to head out when my aunt and Jasmine walk in.

"You look stunning, darling."

"Absolutely stunning," says Jasmine. "Give us a twirl."

I indulge her.

"You're the most beautiful niece I have."

"I'm your only niece," I say, laughing.

"That Rodrigo's a lucky man. I hope he deserves all this," says Jasmine.

"He deserves all of it and more."

"Sure about that?"

"Jasmine, come on, that's enough."

Jasmine grimaces but goes silent.

How did my father, always so calm and collected, fall for this explosive, outspoken woman? I still can't wrap my head around that.

"You look lovely, darling. He'll be enchanted when he sees you."

"I've got to run. I don't want to be late."

I bid them goodbye and head outside. Right next to my aunt's van is Jasmine's mud-splattered all-terrain jeep. God knows where she's been, probably off rallying in the hills.

I reach the airport fifteen minutes before the expected arrival time and text Rodrigo to let him know I'm here. I make my way to the arrivals area. There are a few people awaiting the flight from Lisbon, the only one coming in at this hour. Mostly couples, probably waiting for their kids studying on the mainland. There's also a younger girl, dolled up like I am. I bet she's also waiting for her boyfriend. I take a seat on a bench and wait.

Fifteen minutes tick by, and passengers from the Lisbon flight start pouring in. Couples likely heading for some chill time in the Azores, a bunch of youngsters, and even my neighbor's girlfriend—she's got piercings and pink hair. They're doing some serious kissing right there in the airport, and it's earned them a round of applause. Last ones stroll out, grab their bags, and leave. It's just me left. I'm betting Rodrigo's probably back there having a chat with the crew. He knows everyone, everywhere.

Half an hour slides by and nothing. I fire off a text, "Everything cool?" No reply. I decide to hit up the airport staff, ask if everyone's off, if anything went down. My worry-o-meter spikes. The ticketing agent tells me all passengers are off, no glitches in the flight. I decide to call him up. It rings and rings until voicemail finally steps in. No luck. By nine in the evening, I'm stuck wondering what's next. I shuffle back to the same staff member.

"Hey again. Sorry to bug you, but my boyfriend should've come in on that Lisbon flight."

"I already told you, no issues with the flight."

"Can you check?"

"Name?"

"Rodrigo Peres."

She checks the system, clicks that mouse like it's a race, and my nerves are ramping up.

"All passengers boarded as planned. The plane was packed."

"He's a pilot. Maybe they called him back, he had to head to Lisbon again?"

"What was his name again?"

"Rodrigo Peres."

She scans the screen.

"He's not on the passenger list."

"Not on the list? How's that possible?!"

"Maybe last-minute cancel? An emergency flight call?"

"I know I shouldn't ask, but—"

"I can't spill passenger details. GDPR stuff, could get me in trouble."

I give her this puppy-eyes look, and she lets out this deep sigh.

"Okay, fine. No reservations under Rodrigo Peres' name, never has been. The flight's been fully booked for over a week, and no one canceled."

So, no tickets in Rodrigo's name, ever?! What does that even mean?! I mumble a thanks and bolt out of the airport. I check my phone, but not a peep from him either. I hop into the van and head back towards my aunt's place. When I'm almost there, I do a U-turn. I need a drink. I really need a drink.

I drive around town until I spot a bar. It's called Osmosis, and it has this black awning with golden letters. I park the van and walk in. It's not even ten yet, and the place is almost empty, thank goodness. Buzzing conversations mixing with low country music. Country tunes in a bar in Ponta Delgada? Odd. The owner must be a die-hard fan, that's my guess. There's a couple, maybe tourists, sipping beers and nibbling on fries. Three dudes sit at a table, watching some soccer game and downing beers. It's probably not a big match, or this place would be packed. Looks like beer's the go-to drink around here. Then, there's this other guy, flying solo, around his fifties. He's seated, doesn't seem too tall. Not ugly, not a total looker either. Short, dark hair. He'd be an *Espresso*. The moment I walk in, he glances up, checking me out. Must be here looking for company. I shrug it off and grab a seat at the bar.

"Hey, what can I get you?" asks the bartender, rocking a cowboy hat. I notice, behind him, a stuffed bull's head and an old-school poster of the Ponderosa hanging on the wall.

"Vodka, please."

"You're not from around here, huh?" the bartender asks while fixing the drink.

"Nope, but I've got family here. Is it that obvious I'm not a local?"

"Well, for one, the island's tiny, and I've never seen you before. Plus, you've got a..." he pauses", "more city-like vibe". He nods at my dress.

Glancing around, I realize he's got a point. Me and my red dress definitely stand out among the other clients. Sipping my vodka, I check my phone. No new messages. My mind starts racing. Did he forget? Is he with someone else? Nah, he wouldn't do that. Or would he? Maybe he's not into me anymore and couldn't face telling me. Or something's happened to him. Probably that. What if I call one of his buddies? Nah, I don't have their numbers. Whenever we've hung out with his friends, we never exchanged contacts. I don't even know his parents or any of his family. I've got nobody to call. I consider reaching out to Ruth for a vent, but she'll probably give me a lecture. She's never been a fan of Rodrigo. More people come into the bar, and I order another drink.

Something's up, something's definitely up. Just a couple of days ago, he was gushing about how much he adores me. That doesn't just vanish overnight. Jasmine's words pop into my head, and it hits me hard. What if she's right? Truth is, this isn't the first time he's left me hanging. Downing my vodka, I start thinking that women are exceptionally good at forgiving men. We forgive them for the things they promised but didn't do, and for the things they swore they'd never do but did.

Sitting there, sipping my drink, I take a look around. An Italian couple plop down beside me, talking loudly and waving their hands. I quietly scoot to the other end of the counter. I'm not up for spending the night listening to my Italian neighbors.

When I check the time, it's already eleven-thirty, and the bar's packed. Didn't even notice it was getting busy. I order another drink. Lost count of how many, but who cares? I need to chill, I need to calm this chaotic storm in my head. Feels like a never-ending tornado swirling up there. And I need it to stop, like, right now.

The bartender brings the vodka and goes, "This one's from the dude at that table."

I glance over, and it's the *Espresso* guy, grinning when I turn his way. I face the bar again and tell the bartender, "I can pay for my own drink."

Suddenly, someone sits beside me.

"Good evening."

Guess who? The *Espresso* guy. Can't I catch a break?

"You're not from around here, are you? Never seen your face around these parts."

"Look, I'm not really up for chatting."

"Okay, no need to be snappy."

I chug the vodka and flag down the bartender for another round.

"Let me guess, love's gone sour, right?"

Since I'm not responding, he keeps going.

"I don't get how a guy can mess things up with someone as gorgeous as you."

" Me neither," I mutter to myself.

"A lady like you deserves the best."

"Yep."

I chug down the drink as the bartender brings it over and then hand him a fifty-euro bill.

"I'll cover this," I say.

"Leaving? Need a ride?" the *Espresso* asks.

"Nope."

"Sure about that? You've had a few. Cops might pull your license."

I stand up, and the room starts spinning, but it's not a panic attack this time; it's the booze. Feels like I'm in a fishbowl—sounds and lights all distant. The *Espresso* stands up too, putting his hand on my back.

"I'll drive you. Don't want you losing your license."

"I don't need a ride."

"Trust me, you do. Look at yourself."

"I'm fine." I take a step forward, grabbing onto a chair or table for support.

He holds my arm.

"Leave me alone."

I struggle to free my arm, but he keeps holding on, and I start to feel uneasy. Other folks in the bar pretend not to notice. I glance at the bartender, hoping he'll step in, but he's busy clearing glasses. One guy at a table looks like a bull. I shut my eyes hard, and when I reopen them, the bull-like man has vanished. Mixing alcohol with pills was a huge mistake.

Chapter 23

I'm not sure if I blacked out or what, but when I open my eyes, the *Espresso* is kind of propping me up with one hand. Or maybe it's the vodka playing tricks on me? I try to rub my eyes to clear my vision, but everything still looks fuzzy.

"Leave her alone," someone says from far away.

I glance towards the voice and nearly jump out of my skin. There's a girl right beside me. Am I imagining things? I rub my eyes again, but I can't tell if she's really there. Is this all in my head?

"Are you looking for trouble?" The *Espresso* turns toward the girl with an intense look, and that's when I finally get a good look at her. I know her, but I can't place her. Or maybe I'm just making everything up, and there's no one there. Am I losing it? I shouldn't have drunk so much.

"Leave her alone!" the girl insists, putting her hand on my arm.

Her touch is real, at least. Her turquoise-blue nails lightly graze my skin. Those nails... I recognize them! They belong to Cármen. I squint to get a better look at the girl. She's not Cármen, definitely not Cármen.

"Do you remember me?"

So, she's real.

"I'm Sara."

I examine her face and then her nails. Suddenly, it clicks. She's the girl from the Day Care Center. Thank goodness she's there. She's proof I'm not imagining all this.

"Don't meddle where you're not needed," the *Espresso* insists.

"I've already told you to leave her alone."

"I was just trying to offer her a ride. Your friend shouldn't be driving."

My head's spinning, like I'm on a boat. I recall nights in Venice, where my head seemed to sway on the pillow. Maybe it was from the hours on the Vaporetto's, those boats cruising Venice's lagoons. That's how I feel now. My head's swaying like I'm on a boat.

"You don't have to worry; her ride's on the way."

I plop into a chair, almost missing it, but the *Espresso* catches me. The swirling in my head makes me feel sick. Their argument's not helping.

"And you're staying quiet?" Sara asks the bartender.

"I'm fine," I say, but it's as if no one hears me. It's like I'm invisible. Maybe I am. Perhaps I'm not truly here. Do you exist if no one sees you?

"I don't get involved in customers' matters," the bartender replies.

"Why are you making such a fuss? I was just offering your friend a ride."

"I'll drive her home."

I instantly recognize the voice. I try to stand up quickly and leap into his arms, but I trip instead. Thankfully, he catches me before I end up flat on the floor.

"Super-Carlos, you came to save me!"

He holds me by the waist, but there's no smile on his face. Why's he so serious? I put my arms around his neck.

"Are you really here, or am I imagining things?"

"I'm really here, Mel."

"I had a feeling you'd rescue me."

He moves my arms from around his neck and holds my waist. Still serious. Maybe I should tell him to grab a drink to lighten the mood. I don't like seeing him so serious.

"Go away," he tells the *Espresso*.

"Hey, why the rude act?"

"If I were you, I'd listen to him. My buddy has superpowers."

No one laughs at my joke, not even Carlos. I don't get it. It wasn't the funniest, but I thought it deserved a smile at least.

"Chico, don't mess with him; he's Seven and a Half's grandson," the bartender finally chimes in, breaking his rule of not interfering.

"Who's Seven and a Half?"

"Just leave!" Carlos insists.

The guy heads for the exit, grumbling something under his breath as he goes.

"Bye!" I give him a big wave. Then I turn to my lifesaver and sling my arms back around his neck. "How'd you know I was here?"

Carlos takes my arms off his neck, and I grumble. Not much fun today, huh?

"I called him," Sara says.

"Wasn't necessary. I'm good," I assure her.

"Of course, it was," Carlos insists. "One strong coffee," he tells the waiter. "Thanks for calling, Sara."

She grins and joins another girl at a table.

"I'd kill for another vodka," I mutter, wrapping my hands around his neck again. He isn't shaking me off that easily. I can be pretty stubborn when I want to.

Carlos shoots me a disapproving look, and I burst into laughter. Boy, does he need a drink. He needs to chill. The waiter brings the coffee, and Carlos makes me chug it all down. I don't get why he's being so tough on me. Then he settles the bill, and we head out. He's holding me up because my legs are still wobbly.

"You got your aunt's van keys?"

"What van?" I ask.

He grabs my bag and starts rummaging.

I plonk myself on a park bench nearby and lean my head between my legs. Then I figure lying down and stretching out on the bench is a better idea. Just need a minute to rest, just a minute.

When I wake up, I'm still sprawled on the bench, head in Carlos's lap. I feel awful, seriously awful. I barely manage to turn to the side before I start puking.

"Are you okay?" Carlos holds my head until I finish throwing up.

I glance at the puddle of vomit on the ground. The sour smell hits me hard, and I hold my breath. Carlos helps me sit up and wipes my mouth with a tissue he took from my bag. My chin trembles, and tears threaten to spill. How embarrassing. I can't look at him.

"Are you okay?"

"Don't look at me."

He ignores my plea and grabs me by the shoulders.

"Are you alright, Mel?"

I lower my gaze. I still can't bring myself to look at him.

"I need to go to the bathroom," it's all I manage to say. Because I'm not okay. I'm terrible. I'm ashamed. I'm dirty. I'm disgusting.

We head back to the bar. He walks me to the bathroom and waits outside.

I scrub my teeth and splash my face. When I'm done, I stare at myself in the mirror. I might be a bit cleaner now, but inside, I still feel gross. Ever since that night, I've felt gross. Makeup's smudged, hair's a disaster. I'm a wreck. I stand there, looking at my reflection in the mirror. That's me, that disaster in the mirror is me. Two girls walk in, and I snap out of it.

I head over to Carlos, who's chatting with the waiter. We step out of the bar, and the cool breeze hits my face. Feels good, this fresh air. Carlos swings open the van door and signals for me to hop in. He takes the driver's seat, starts the engine, and we drive away.

"Don't take me home yet, please," I ask. "I can't face my aunt like this."

Carlos drives us to the marina and parks.

"Who's Seven and a Half?"

"That's a nickname they gave my grandpa. He apparently got into a scuffle when he was younger, supposedly took down seven guys and a dog."

"A dog?!"

"My grandpa swears it's a tall tale, but the nickname stuck, and he's still called Seven and a Half."

I chuckle. His grandpa's a real character. An Azorean Captain Ahab.

"You're probably wondering why I was at the bar," I say, gazing out at the sea.

"Fight with your boyfriend?" Carlos asks.

"Nah, he didn't even show."

"He stood you up?"

"Yup."

"What happened?"

"I don't know. He's ghosting me, not responding to my texts or picking up when I call."

Carlos stays quiet, and so do I. We just sit there, taking in the view of the sea.

"You probably you think I'm being totally ridiculous."

He leans closer, using his hand to make me look at him. Our eyes meet, and I feel a knot in my stomach. He flashes a smile, and I'm clueless why. Because I look like a mess. Dirty. Gross. I can't meet his gaze, so I look away.

"No, I don't, Mel. We all go through rough patches."

He eases back into his seat.

"Alcohol's not the fix, tough. I saw it mess my grandpa up when I was a kid."

"I'm not an alcoholic."

"I'm not saying you are, but it's easy to fall into that trap. I'm not calling you an alcoholic, but vodka isn't the answer to your issues."

"Your grandpa told you I wanted to buy vodka from the store?"

Carlos nods, and I feel tiny, fragile.

"Hey, don't take it like that. I'm not accusing you of anything, I'm just worried about you."

He leans in again, eyes locked with mine. This time, I hold his gaze. I'm searching for any disappointment in his eyes, but all I see is understanding. Understanding and something else, something I can't quite put my finger on. He's still here, despite the bar drama, despite nearly being my puke target. He's not going to leave me, and that's all I need to know.

"Alcohol helps me cope with the stress."

"Your job's not an easy one, huh?"

"During the week, I'm Counsel Melissa Lacerda de Brito, the unstoppable lawyer and daughter of Judge Lacerda de Brito. But come weekends, I'm the girl who drinks untill she passes out on the couch."

"You drink at home?" I nod. "Alone?"

"Yeah, I've been feeling pretty lonely."

He reaches for my hand.

"All my friends moved overseas. Two got married, and the other jetted off to Ibiza chasing her Body Combat instructor, who's now her ex, but she decided to stick around in Ibiza and found a new flame, or a friend with benefits, or something like that. She's had so many adventures, it's hard to keep track."

Carlos grins.

"My friend Ruth's a total thrill-seeker."

"So, you stay home and drink?"

"Yeah, when Rodrigo's not in Lisbon, I hang at home. I gave up on bars in Lisbon. I'm not keen on going solo," I pause. "I don't want to chance running into a certain someone." I glance at him. "Here in Ponta Delgada, I thought it was safe, you know, didn't even cross my mind. I was so thrown off when Rodrigo was a no-show, didn't even consider it. If you hadn't shown up, I don't know what would've happened."

"Sara would never let anything happen to you."

"I'm so glad she called you," I lean in, resting my head on his shoulder. "The moment you got here, I felt safe."

"I'd never let anything bad happen to you."

I turn to face him, our noses nearly touching.

"I know."

He plants a kiss on my forehead. I place a hand on his chest, feeling his heartbeat racing. I snuggle closer, letting out a sigh, and he pulls me into a one-armed hug. We stay like that way until my phone starts ringing.

"It's Rodrigo!"

I sit up straight and answer.

"Rodrigo, what happened?!"

"Sorry, Mel! A friend had a car crash, and I had to rush him to the hospital."

"I was so worried!"

"Sorry, angel, but my phone died at the hospital. I couldn't reach out to you."

"I thought you bailed on coming."

"Never, angel. Why'd you think that?"

"I don't know."

"I'd never do that to you. I love you."

"I love you too."

"I must go, the doctor's calling me. I'll call you later. Sorry."

"Hope your friend gets better," I say, but he has already hung up.

I feel so silly, incredibly silly.

"It's all good," I tell Carlos. "One of his friends had an accident, that's why we didn't come."

Chapter 24

I wake up to find my aunt perched at the edge of my bed.

"Good morning, darling. How are you feeling?"

I'm nursing a killer hangover, and my mouth tastes like I licked a cardboard box.

"What did Carlos tell you?"

"He brought the van and mentioned you weren't feeling well, so he went to pick you up from Ponta Delgada. Why didn't you call me? Jasmine and I could have come get you."

"I didn't want to bother you."

"Another panic attack?"

I take a deep breath. I feel like saying yeah, that's what went down, that I'm a jittery yet well-behaved girl, but I don't want to lie to my aunt.

"No."

"No?"

"Rodrigo didn't show up, and I was completely thrown off."

"He stood you up?"

"Yeah. I hung around the airport for ages trying to figure out what went sideways, but nobody had a clue. The flight landed on time, everyone disembarked. I started freaking out, picturing the worst-case scenarios. Like maybe he bailed on meeting me, or worse, something bad happened to him."

"And then, what happened?"

"I ended up at this bar and drank way too much."

My aunt stays quiet for a moment, and I try to read her expression, looking for some hint of disappointment, but all I see is concern.

"Mel, I won't criticize you, but alcohol isn't the answer to your problems. Plus, mixing alcohol with your meds? Not a great idea."

"I know."

"You're getting me worried, darling. What can I do to help?"

"You're already doing it. Right now, I just need a shower and some coffee."

My aunt leaves the room, and I drag myself to the bathroom. My head feels like it's made of bricks. I crank up the shower and step in. I stand there, letting the water wash over me, wishing it could erase every trace of last night.

When I shuffle into the kitchen, Jasmine is working at the stove.

"I'm whipping up some pancakes with flaxseed and spelt," she says.

"Jasmine loves experimenting with new recipes."

"I'm not much of a cook."

"Didn't your dad show you the ropes in the kitchen? He used to be all about cooking."

"That was ages ago. He hasn't had the time to cook for years."

"So, what's the deal between you and this Rodrigo?"

I catch my aunt shooting her a glare. Since I don't respond' she goes on:

"That Rodrigo's a liar. Bailing on you like that!"

"He said his friend had an accident, so he couldn't make it."

"And he couldn't drop you a text?"

"His phone died."

"Sounds like flimsy excuses, Mel. I see you glued to your phone all the time, waiting for his replies, huh? I know the type. He's stringing you along, and you, naive, keep falling for it."

"Jasmine!" My aunt grumbles.

"Mel needs a reality check, Gabi."

"His friend had an accident. What was he supposed to do, ditch him?"

"Mel, most guys, when they sense a vulnerability in a woman, take advantage."

"Rodrigo isn't taking advantage of me."

"Do you really believe that? He keeps promising he'll propose but never pulls the trigger. Never introduced you to his folks, never bothered to meet yours. Never even showed you his place."

"He's renovating his place."

"Don't be naive, Mel. He's stringing you along. All he wants is sex, SEX!"

"Jasmine, that's enough!" My aunt shoots her a death stare. "Let's eat."

Jasmine storms out, slamming the door, and sits on the porch, lighting a cigarette.

"Don't mind her, darling. Do you want strawberries jam with the pancakes?"

"Yeah, that'd be perfect."

Jasmine keeps shooting disapproving looks through the window, but I pretend not to notice. Grabbing a pancake, I start spreading the jam. She stubs out her cigarette and comes back inside, leaving a pill on the table.

"What's this?"

"It's for the hangover, you could probably use it."

I manage a weak smile and wash down the pill with a gulp of water.

"Oh, I forgot to mention, Carlos said he'd drop by after lunch, in case you want to go with him. He figured you could use the morning to rest," my aunt says.

Super-Carlos to the rescue again.

"Carlos is a sweetheart," I say, taking a big bite of the pancake.

"Unlike that Rodrigo," Jasmine says.

My aunt's eyes widen, and Jasmine stands up.

"I'm off to Hortensias Garden. I don't want to argue with you, Gabi, or you, Mel. Might not seem like it, but I care about you. That's why I said what I said. You're family, and I won't let some jerk take advantage of you, got it? Not happening." And she storms out.

I imagine her standing up to my father, and suddenly I feel like laughing. She's so different from him. And so different from my mother. My mother is the type of person who never loses her cool, not even when her husband asks for a divorce.

"Sweetie, Jasmine might come off harsh, but I'm worried about you too. Rodrigo hasn't been treating you well."

"Rodrigo has been my rock. He's my safe space; it's not his fault I've been feeling down."

"No?"

"No. Honestly, I'm not even sure why I'm so anxious all the time. Feels like I've got a bunch of problems swirling around, like that movie 'The Perfect Storm' with George Clooney and Mark Wahlberg. Everything's just crashing, creating chaos in my life."

My aunt sets down the dishcloth and pulls up a chair opposite me.

"First, my friends ditched Lisbon."

"And that made you feel alone?"

"Yep, totally alone. My parents and I grew apart. Sunday lunches turned into torture lately. Now I know why. Dad probably had someone else already, and Mom probably had her suspicions."

I realize I haven't spoken to her in ages. Lost count of the days.

"Mel, you haven't talked to your father yet. Things might not be as they seem."

"Aunt, Dad might be honest, but come on, he's a guy. When it comes to sex, guys don't exactly think straight. Some men think women exist just for their pleasure. I've learned that the hard way."

"What do you mean by that?"

I take a deep breath.

"It was something a coworker told me. He's been making my life hell in the office."

"And your boss doesn't do anything?"

"I didn't tell him. I don't want to be a snitch."

"You should report him."

"I know, but I'm afraid it would only make things worse."

"Mel, you have to promise me something."

"What?"

I'm waiting for her to ask me to report Cláudio, and I don't know if I can promise her that. But that's not what she asks me:

"Promise me you won't drink again."

"I promise, aunt."

Will I be able to keep that promise? Honestly, I don't know, but I'll try.

I bolt up when I hear my phone ringing in the bedroom. I hope it's Rodrigo. Nope, no luck, it's Ruth. Probably needs more cash.

"Hey."

"Hey, Mel, how's it going?" She sounds way more chipper today.

"Okay."

"Okay?"

"Yeah, okay."

"Well, it seems like I called at the right time." She laughs. "Come hang with me in Ibiza for a few days. São Miguel must be a snooze fest."

"I don't think that's a good idea."

"Why not?"

"Because we'd be out all night dancing and boozing, and I'm trying to quit drinking."

"Stop joking."

"I'm not joking. I'm trying to quit drinking."

"No way, seriously?"

"Yeah, dead serious."

"What's going on, Mel?"

I take a deep breath. Should I tell her?

"You can tell me, Mel."

I'm tired of pretending like everything's okay.

"The thing is, ever since that situation with Cláudio, I haven't been okay."

Silence from her end.

"Remember when I had a panic attack at that club?"

"Yeah." Her voice is barely there.

"Yeah, well, two weeks ago, I had another one, way worse. Ended up in the hospital, and my parents wanted me in some clinic."

"OMG! I had no idea, Mel. That's why you went to the Azores?"

"I said no to the clinic, but I realized I wasn't all right and needed a break. So, I came to chill for a bit in the Azores. I'm on meds and need to avoid alcohol."

This time, I'm sticking to it. No drinking for me.

Silence on the other end.

"You don't have to say anything, Ruth. I get it. Life's an endless adventure for you and dealing with other people's stuff isn't your jam. It's cool."

I hear her sigh.

"I don't know what to say."

"Don't sweat it. I don't need your pity."

"I feel terrible. I thought you were blowing things out of proportion, like..."

"Like they were rich girl problems, right?"

"You've always been the responsible one in our crew, always had a supportive family. We all thought you had it easy."

"Looks can be deceiving. I've got my own set of issues."

"I feel awful for not taking you seriously."

"Don't."

"When you told me about what happened with Cláudio, I thought it hadn't hit you that hard. And then when you had that panic attack, I figured it was just work stress."

"But it wasn't, Ruth. Cláudio's been making my work life a living hell..."

It sucks, doesn't it? The moment you realize you're just a scared little bitch.

"Come over, spend a few days with me. I'll make it up to you."

"Right now, it's better for me to stay put on this island. I've met some incredible people, and my aunt and I are hitting it off. Plus, I'm not like you, Ruth."

"But you used to be. Remember when the four of us were in college? Thursday nights, we'd party until sunrise. We loved hitting the town, having a few drinks, and mingling."

"Yeah, those were good times. After clubbing, we'd head to that pizza joint at Docas, remember? Ordering a tropical pizza and four 7-Ups. We thought after a night of vodka, 7-Up could somehow sober us up."

Ruth laughs, but there's a hint of sadness in her laugh.

"How did we end up drifting apart, Mel?"

"I think life just took us on different paths, you know?"

"Is this the end of our friendship?"

"Nah, not at all. But let's face it, we're not eighteen anymore, and our lives and goals are way different now. I still like hitting the town and dancing, but for now, I'm going to try to steer clear of alcohol. At least while I'm on meds."

"And what about dating? Are you giving that a break too?"

"Nope, quite the opposite. I'm dead set on marrying Rodrigo."

I hear her sigh.

"I'm not sure Rodrigo's the settle-down-and-have-kids type of guy."

"I'm sure he is, Ruth, and I'm going to fight for him."

"If that's what you want."

"I hope you keep having a blast in Ibiza."

"If you need anything, give me a shout. I might not be the best listener, but I've got your back, Mel."

"I know."

We say our goodbyes, and I hang up. I didn't expect Ruth to call, especially not for that conversation. It's probably the most serious one we've had since our freshman year.

A text pops in from Rodrigo, and my stomach flutters. Even after almost a year, he still gives me those butterflies.

Mel, sorry about yesterday. Trying to snag a flight to come see you later today.

I knew he wouldn't let me down. Jasmine and Ruth are going to realize they're wrong.

Chapter 25

Carlos shows up right after lunch, just as my aunt's leaving for the Hortensias Garden.

"Hey, Mel. How are you holding up?"

"Feeling better. Thanks for rescuing me, again."

He smiles, then looks down. I do the same. I feel guilty. Guilty for dragging him out in the middle of the night to rescue me. Again.

"Want to go for a drive, or not in the mood?"

"I am, but we can't go too far. Rodrigo's trying to score a flight to come see me later today."

"Ah, okay."

I sense Carlos is a bit distant, not as upbeat as usual. Is he fed up with me and my problems?

"I was a mess yesterday. Jumped to conclusions right off the bat and turns out Rodrigo had a legit reason for not showing up."

"Want to check out the tea plantation? It's just a half-hour drive," he changes subject.

"Sure, let me grab my backpack."

We hop into his grandpa's van, and Carlos hits the road. I feel kind of stupid. Carlos has been awesome to me, and all I've done is cause him hassle.

"You probably think I'm a mess after yesterday's drama."

"Absolutely not, Mel. We all hit rough patches. You're bummed because your boyfriend didn't show. It happens."

"Rodrigo's been my rock. Without him, I don't know how I'd cope. He's always encouraging me, telling me how much he loves me."

"No need to explain, Mel. We're friends, and if you need me, I'm here." He shifts his gaze from the road to me. "I mean it."

"I know."

"Now, let's focus on today's little adventure. You need to chill out."

"Yeah, I do. Tell me more about this place."

Carlos starts telling me about the Gorreana Tea Factory. Back in the late 1800s, this lady named Ermelinda, who owned the Gorreana lands, made her first batch of tea. The soil there, kind of clay-like, and the damp weather made it perfect for brewing top-notch tea. Carlos goes on about the factory's survival story over the years and how this guy Hintze brought in machinery, but honestly, I'm just stuck on one thing.

"And it all began with a woman who refused to wait for life to happen."

"Yeah, she was a go-getter who made things happen."

"I wish I could be as bold and determined."

"Mel, you're stronger than you give yourself credit for."

"Sometimes I just don't feel it, especially after yesterday. I'm still cringing."

"No need to feel embarrassed."

"Not even about, you know, puking at your feet?"

He smiles.

"Everybody's had a wild night and puked."

"Weren't you ticked off about what went down yesterday?"

He glances away from the road to look at me.

"Nah, not a bit. Can't stay mad at you."

"You're pretty chill about everything."

"You've got it wrong. I do get upset, more often than you'd think."

"Then why do you put up with me?"

He takes a deep breath and then looks away.

"Because..."

My phone rings.

"It's Rodrigo!" Finally! "Hey, Rodrigo!"

"Hey, angel. Already landed."

"Fantastic! I've been counting down the seconds!"

"Me too! Just secured a room at Marina Hotel."

"I'm en route!" I hang up and notice Carlos spinning the car around.

"You need a ride to Ponta Delgada, right?"

"Yeah, I'm sorry. I didn't think he'd arrive so soon."

"No problem."

We cruise toward the hotel in silence. I'm second-guessing my outfit, but I thought I would have time to change before Rodrigo arrived. I'm in a white tee, jeans, and sneakers. Grabbing red lipstick, I quickly slick it on at a stoplight. Excitement bubbles up. The big day's arrived. I wonder if there's a ring in store for me.

As we reach the hotel parking, I hop out of the car.

"Thanks, Carlos!"

I sprint toward the hotel entrance and shoot Rodrigo a text.

What's your room number?

I'm at the bar.

I enter the hotel and ask about the bar's location. When I spot it, I catch him chatting up a redhead waitress—she can't be more than twenty-two or twenty-three. He's got a knack for attracting attention. His eyes land on me, flashing a smile my way. I pick up speed and wrap my arms around him.

"Easy, Mel, we're in public."

I should've remembered he isn't into public displays of affection, but I couldn't help myself. I pull away and slide onto the stool beside him.

"How was your trip?"

"Good," he says, finishing his Martini.

Then he signals the waitress for another.

"I'll pass on this one."

"Not in the mood?"

"It's too early for me."

"Understood. Ready to head to the room?"

He asks the waitress to add it to the room tab, and we head to the elevator.

"That guy who dropped you off, who's he?"

"That's Carlos."

"And who's this Carlos?"

"He's a friend of my aunt's." Best not to mention my recent island adventures with Carlos.

"Just a friend?"

"Absolutely. You know I'm all about you." I plant a kiss on his lips.

※ ※ ※

We're chilling in bed, naked. Rodrigo's sparked a cigarette, something he only does after we get it on.

"Earlier, when you said you were cool with me hanging out with Carlos, did you mean it?"

"Absolutely. Why would I mind?"

"You might not dig the idea of your future fiancée exploring the island with some other guy."

He takes a drag, eyes glued to the ceiling.

"Doesn't bug me."

"I thought guys about to tie the knot would be more possessive."

"I'm not the possessive type."

"Maybe because you're not yet my fiancé." Seriously, does he catch hints? "I'd love us to label what we've got going on."

"Mel, we've talked about this. Until I switch to domestic flights, I can't commit."

"But I don't mind…"

He goes silent, puffing away.

"What time is it?"

I peek at the phone.

"Almost eight."

He jets off to the bathroom, shower cranked up. I lie there in bed, listening to the water from the shower hitting the floor. I don't know why, but it reminds me of that day in Parque Terra Nostra. I still feel guilty about Carlos getting soaked. He hardly knew me and yet lent me his raincoat.

The phone buzzes. Probably a new message. I reach for it, but it's not mine—it's Rodrigo's.

Hey, babe! When are you coming to Porto? Miss you like crazy!

A message from some Nicole. Who the hell is Nicole?!

"Why are you looking at my phone?!"

Suddenly, Rodrigo's there, wrapped in a towel.

"Thought it was mine."

"But it's not." He reaches out for it. "Go shower; we've got dinner plans."

I head to the bathroom, then turn back.

"Who's Nicole?"

"A friend."

"Just a friend?"

"Snooping now? Shower up and quit snooping around!"

I step into the shower, water running, but seriously, who's this Nicole? Her message was way too personal. It felt like I could've written it myself. I try to shake it off, but I can't. There's this knot in my stomach. Leaning against the tiles, water pouring over me, I'm trying hard not to break down. Once I step out of the bathroom, he's nowhere to be seen.

I get dressed, rush down to the front desk, and ask the receptionist.

"Did you see my boyfriend?"

"He headed to the bar."

I head to the bar. There he is, chatting with a blonde, grinning like there's no tomorrow. She whispers something in his ear, and he casually puts his hand on her waist. Seriously, what's going on here? I move closer, but he doesn't even notice me. I clear my throat, hoping to catch his attention.

"Mel!" Finally, he spots me and takes his hand from the blonde's waist. She's frozen. "This is Sandra, a colleague. She's a flight attendant."

The blonde gives me a smile.

"Are you a flight attendant too?"

"No."

"Mel's a friend from Lisbon."

Wait, what? A friend?! Did I hear that right?! A FRIEND?!

"Want to grab dinner? Catch you later, Sandra," he says, guiding me to a table in the restaurant.

I'm stunned, trying hard to keep it together. He's glued to his phone, not even looking at me. I'm on the edge of a breakdown. The waiter hands me the menu. I can't even focus; my chest feels tight. A friend?! Seriously?! I can't hold back and ask him:

"Why'd you introduce me as a friend?"

He glances up from his phone, giving me a weird look.

"Huh?"

"You introduced me as a friend."

"So?"

Seriously?! Is he kidding?

"I thought I was your girlfriend."

"Friend, girlfriend, it's all the same."

"Nah, not really. You said you were going to pop the question. Friends don't get proposed to."

"I never said that."

What the hell?! Is he kidding me?

"You've mentioned that more than once in your texts."

"Don't take everything I type seriously, Mel. I was just kidding." He doesn't even lift his eyes from his phone.

"Kidding?"

"Yup."

"But you said you were going to get me a ring."

"Don't believe everything I write. It was a joke. Getting married, having kids and all that isn't my thing, at least not for now."

I take a deep breath, clenching my fists, trying not to lose it. I don't want to cry. I don't want to make a scene in this darn restaurant. So, I keep my cool and ask as calmly as I can:

"Okay then, when?"

He finally raises his eyes to look at me.

"If I'd known you'd turn this into a whole thing over nothing, I wouldn't have bothered coming to the Azores. Drama isn't my thing."

I'm not crazy! He straight up said he wanted to marry me. He told me our future kids were going to be picture-perfect. Why's is acting like this now?!

The waiter returns to take our orders.

"Have you decided?"

"Yes," Rodrigo says. "We'll have the beef steak."

"And for drinks?"

"Red wine. Could we check out the wine list?"

"Rodrigo, I'm not in the mood for wine."

He takes a break from the menu, shoots me an irritated glance.

"No wine?"

"I'm on meds, I can't drink."

"Seriously?!"

"Yes serious."

"What's the medication for?"

"It's for my anxiety."

He laughs, and I feel small, like a child being teased for being afraid of the dark.

"A glass of wine would do you better than those pills. Bring a bottle of red."

"And for the lady?"

"She'll have whatever I'm having."

"Sorry, I thought she didn't want wine."

"Mind your own business. Just bring the wine."

He picks up a call and steps out to the terrace. The knot in my stomach tightens. I feel fragile, like everything's crumbling. Who is this man?! I don't recognize him. The Rodrigo I know isn't like this. Something's not right because he's not like this. In his texts, he's all about loving me, buying me a ring, talking about weddings and kids!

The waiter comes back with the bottle and asks me, "Sure you don't want something else to drink?"

"I'll have some water, please. And sorry about my boyfriend." Maybe I should say 'my friend'? "He just got back from a trip today and he's dead tired."

The waiter smiles and heads off to get the water. Rodrigo's still outside on the terrace, glued to his phone. Tears are welling up, and I'm clenching my fists tighter. Time goes by, and he's still out there. I've never felt more alone. Could Jasmine and Ruth have been right?

Chapter 26

Rodrigo comes back twenty minutes later and signals the waiter to bring the food.

"Is everything okay?"

"All good. What's with the water?"

"It's for the pills."

He grabs the wine bottle and pours for me first, then for himself. He downs his glass in one go, while I just wet my lips. I haven't forgotten what I promised my aunt.

The food's here, and we start eating. Not much chatter. When he turns to flag down the waiter, I take the chance to dump my wine into a vase nearby. Not worth getting him more riled up.

"The steak's overcooked. I asked for it rare," he tells the waiter coming over.

"Do you want me to ask the kitchen to prepare you another?"

"Not worth it. I'm not up for more waiting."

"Anything else?"

"No, you can go."

Rodrigo shakes his head.

"Can you believe this? Awful service!"

I just smile, and he refills our glasses.

"Thought you were going Sober Sally for a sec there."

I glance at him and realize this might be the first time I'm with him and not even a bit tipsy or outright drunk. Our relationship has always been drenched in booze. Maybe that's why I'm finally seeing him for who he really is.

"That Nicole who messaged you, she's also your friend?"

"Yeah, Mel, she's my friend. Why are you asking?"

I'm wondering if he mentioned proposing to her too. I'm tempted to ask him, but honestly, I'm not sure I really want to know.

"Oh, nothing much."

"What's there to do for fun in this middle-of-nowhere place? Any decent bars or clubs around here?"

I only know that one bar from the other night, but I don't think it's a good idea to go there, especially since Rodrigo prefers fancier spots.

"I'm not sure, I've been laying low."

"You haven't been out with that Carlos guy at night?"

"No, I haven't." I reach across the table, trying to touch his hand.

He pulls back and grabs his phone. It's like a punch in the gut. While I'm trying to process everything, he takes care of the bill and asks about nearby bars. Turns out, there's a gin bar close by. We leave the hotel, and he gets another call. It's Paulo, one of his buddies. Can't stand that guy. He's yapping away with Paulo on the phone until we get to the bar. Then he hangs up, and we walk in. It's Thursday night, and the bar is packed. Every table's taken, so we squeeze in at the counter. The music's blasting, and Rodrigo's shouting in my ear.

"What's your poison? Gin and tonic?"

"Just orange juice."

"You kidding me?! Cut the crap, Mel. Don't play Sober Sally. I know you like to toss a few back and have a blast."

That comment sets off alarm bells in my head. My chest tightens, and I start feeling lightheaded. Rodrigo signals the waiter for two gins. A gorgeous girl brushes past and bumps into me. The gins arrive, and Rodrigo passes me a glass. My hands are shaking, so I carefully set the glass on the counter, afraid I might drop it.

"You don't drink?! What's going on, Mel? You're not your usual self."

"I'm not feeling great, Rodrigo."

"Just grab a drink, it'll cheer you up."

That suggestion only spikes my anxiety and discomfort. Two guys squeeze in next to us at the counter, and I'm wedged between them and Rodrigo.

"Please, Rodrigo, I'm really not feeling okay."

"And what do you want me to do about it? Don't tell me I came all the way to the Azores to hang out with you, and now you're going to ruin the night!"

Then the blonde hostess shows up and starts talking to him, and suddenly I'm invisible. Glancing around, I'm surrounded by a crowd, yet I've never felt more alone.

"I need to step outside. I'm not feeling well," I tell him. He looks at me but doesn't say a word. Then he turns back to the blonde and keeps talking.

Once I hit the street, my body starts shaking, and I realize I'm having another panic attack. I drag myself to the sidewalk and plop down on a garden bench a bit away from the bar. I sit there and wait, hoping he'll come after me, but time goes by, and he doesn't come.

As I look at the bare space on my ring finger, it hits me—it was all just a mirage. I curl up on the bench, not because of the cold breeze, but because it was all a mirage. The ideal guy, the engagement ring, the entire wedding plan—nothing but a creation of my imagination. I crafted a dream, the dream of a flawless life. I was going to tie the knot and start a family. I was going to prove to Carmen and everyone at work that I had it all together. I was going to show Claudio that he meant nothing to me. No hate, anger, or fear—just plain indifference. I was going to show my friends that my life was picture-perfect too. I had this grand wedding all mapped out at Jeronimo's Monastery, you know? Imagined it making headlines everywhere: 'Judge Lacerda de Brito's Daughter Says 'I Do' at Jerónimos Monastery.' Arriving in a lavish carriage pulled by two magnificent white horses. Walking down the aisle with my father, seeing his beaming pride. That was my ultimate desire. To make my father proud. Then I look down at my naked finger and bam! Reality check. I'm thrown for a loop, clueless about what to do next.

People are casually walking down the street. Some wander into the bar, others chat away outside. But no one seems to notice this wreck of a person having a full-blown panic attack on the garden bench. They're all in their own little bubbles. Rodrigo's a no-show, and I've got to get out of here. I fish my phone out of my bag, and I notice it's about to die. I call the only person I can think of before it croaks. It's like two in the morning, definitely not the best time to ring someone up, but I'm running out of options. A sleepy voice answers.

"Mel?"

"Carlos, can you please come pick me up?"

Chapter 27

I see the beat-up old van park across the street. I try to stand up, but I'm glued to the bench. Feels like I'm in a movie, just watching the scene unfold in front of me, not part of it. Carlos hops out of the van, sporting shorts and flip-flops, making me even more embarrassed. I dragged him out in the dead of night, again, to come rescue me. Why does he keep putting up with me? Why? He crosses the street and takes a seat next to me on the bench. It's windy, his hair's all over the place. My hair's probably a disaster too.

"How are you doing?" His voice, smooth with a touch of Azorean accent he usually manages to hide, sounds distant, like I'm still stuck watching some dramatic movie where the hero saves the day. Except, in this movie, I'm the one in need. And boy, am I in need right now. Will these panic attacks ever leave me alone?! I'm just so sick of feeling like this. So sick and tired.

"I'll get through this." My voice wobbles, words coming out in bits. "I'll be fine." I'm trying hard to believe it myself. I'm trying to believe that everything's okay. But it's not. I'm far from okay.

"You're shivering!" He grabs my hand. "Let's get in the van. It's freezing out here."

"The shakes aren't from the cold; I had a panic attack."

I try to stand, but my legs won't cooperate. It's like they're glued to the ground. Carlos doesn't say a word. Next thing I know, he's lifting me up, carrying me like I'm a feather. Surprising strength there. I guess you don't need to hit the gym every day to handle fifty-eight kilos effortlessly. Well, with all the food I've been gobbling up lately, I'm probably packing on extra pounds. He takes me to the van, sets me down, and swings the door open. I'm leaning against it but feeling stiff as a board. I'm wiped out, drained, and a bit queasy. He helps me into the van, straps me in like I'm a kid, and I feel tiny, fragile, like I might snap any second.

Quit faking it, Mel. I know you like to toss a few back and have a blast.

Carlos slides into the driver's seat and starts the engine.

"Take me to your place, please."

He shoots me a weird look, clearly worried and probably freaked out about the panic attack. It's interesting how most people distance themselves or pretend they didn't hear when you mention mental health stuff, as if it's contagious or something. Well, newsflash - mental health issues aren't contagious. Carlos doesn't seem to think so either. He doesn't ignore me or kick me out of the van. Instead, he asks, 'Are you sure you want to come over?' I nod, closing my eyes. I'm so tired, seriously tired.

When I open my eyes again, I'm sprawled out on a couch. Can't say I recognize the house, but I do recognize some of the photos on the wall. There's this huge snap of the Seven Cities Lake framed by vibrant hydrangeas, another of the Fogo Lagoon at sunset, and then this epic one of a fishing boat and a whale looking like it's about to crash into the boat. I'm at Carlos's place. I glance around. The living room's neat, and there's a hint of lavender in the air. I try to get up to check out the photos close-up, but I'm still feeling weak. I flop back onto the sofa's turquoise cushions and shut my eyes.

Carlos sits beside me, and I peek them open.

"How're you holding up?"

"Did I just faint?"

"You managed to reach the elevator but passed out afterward. Here, drink this hot chocolate. It should help."

I take the mug and sip it slowly. Gradually, I start feeling a bit better. Then it hits me. Rodrigo! He ditched me on the street while I was having a panic attack, busy charming that blonde hostess at the bar. What a jerk move! How could I have misjudged him so badly? How could I have been so clueless?! He seemed flawless. Almost too perfect. I should've seen through it. But I didn't. Or maybe I did and just didn't want to admit it? Everyone warned me. Literally everyone. Even Ruth. But I chose to ignore it all. My head's spinning, and I'm struggling for air. Carlos puts an arm around me.

"Take it easy, Mel. Deep breaths. In and out. Slowly."

I notice the Azorean accent in his voice again, and it makes me smile even though I feel like a mess. Feels like I've shattered into a zillion pieces, but his voice is oddly calming. Carlos is my chill pill. I lean into him a bit more. No idea how long we sat there, but eventually, I start to calm down, feeling my body relax.

"Thanks, Super-Carlos."

"Looks like you're getting back on track."

"Never realized you had an Azorean accent."

"It only pops up when I'm nervous."

"Sorry for hitting you up this late. I didn't want to bother my aunt, and I didn't know who else to call."

" You didn't bother me; I was just worried."

"Thanks for not freaking out." I glance around, a bit lost for words. What do you say to someone who rescued you from a panic attack in the dead of night? "Nice color combo in the decor. Didn't picture you with those turquoise-blue cushions."

He chuckles.

"My mom and older sister handled the décor."

"I kind of guessed that interior decorating wasn't really your thing."

I glance around and spot a framed photo of me on a shelf.

"That photo..."

He scratches his head, looking a bit awkward.

"You took that on the day I got nauseous from those winding roads."

"Yeah."

The photo looks great. I'm sitting on a log surrounded by colorful butterflies. One rests on my shoulder.

"The picture's gorgeous, but I look like a ghost. You promised to delete all the pics where I look like a ghost."

"You look great. You're beautiful" He brushes my forehead, tucking away a strand of hair. "What's going on, Mel? Do you want to talk about it?"

I'm not sure if I want to talk. I'm not sure if I want to admit I'm a fool and Rodrigo was playing me. I lay my head on his chest.

"I don't know if I'm up for talking."

"You don't have to if you don't want."

"Everything went to hell."

As soon as I say it, a tear rolls down my cheek.

"That Rodrigo guy again?"

"Yeah, I thought I'd persuade him to pop the question. I thought my life was about to flip. Engagement, marriage, cute kids."

Carlos hugs me tighter but stays quiet.

"Go ahead, you can call me pathetic."

"You're not pathetic, Mel. You're in love, and love can blind us."

"The worst part is, I don't even know if I am in love."

"You're not?"

"I don't know. Today was the first time I hung out with Rodrigo sober, and he seemed different."

"Different how?"

"We've been dating for about a year, meeting up a couple of times a month when he's got layovers in Lisbon. Kind of turned into a long-distance thing. But, like, he never opened up about himself, about his family. And when we were together..." I pause, "when we were together, it was all about drinks and sex. That's it." Carlos twirls a strand of my hair, not saying a word. "In the heap of texts we swapped, he'd go on about loving me, wanting to get married, start a family. He even mentioned buying me a ring. But then, in person, he acted like it was all a joke. Today, when I brought it up, he brushed it off, laughed it off."

"And you took it pretty rough."

"And I realized I'd built this image in my head that had nothing to do with reality. The Rodrigo I thought I knew was this perfect guy head over heels for me. But the real Rodrigo? Just a jerk with no heart."

"At least now you've seen his true colors."

"And you know what the worst part is? I'm so dumb that when I told him I wasn't feeling well and needed to leave the bar, I waited over an hour for him on the street. I'm so dumb."

He lifts my face, locking eyes with me. I must look like a mess, mascara smudged and hair all over the place.

"That guy isn't worth your time, Mel."

How did I fall for him so hard?! Seriously?! I spent a year daydreaming about a guy who's not even real. My chin starts trembling, and I just can't hold back anymore. Tears start flowing.

"Don't cry, Mel. Not for someone who isn't worth a second of your tears."

But I can't stop. I know he's not worth it, but I can't stop. He's probably cozying up to the blonde by now. And here I am, crying over him like a fool. Ugh, I'm such a fool!

"Oh, Mel."

I'm wiping away my tears with the back of my hand, trying to get a grip. Rodrigo isn't worth my tears. Not at all.

"That Rodrigo doesn't deserve you."

Carlos is still talking with that Azorean touch in his accent, and I can't help but laugh while tears keep rolling down my face. His accent's kind of funny. Scratch that, it's downright sexy.

"You're a special woman and you deserve way better."

I'm using my t-shirt sleeve to wipe off the mess, leaving smudges of mascara on it. I probably look even more of a mess now, but I couldn't care less. I'm looking him dead in the eyes. Smudged face and all, I can tell Carlos doesn't give a damn either.

"Don't cry."

I shoot him a smile, and he throws one right back. Those dimples on his face? Adorable. For some unknown reason, I lean in and plant a light kiss on his lips. He doesn't budge. I hear him gulp hard. I lean in again, giving him another light peck. This time, he kisses me back, but then stops.

"Why did you stop?"

He looks away.

"I can't do this."

"Why?"

I'm getting anxious, feeling all worked up. I want him to kiss me again.

"I can't take advantage of your vulnerability, Mel."

"I was the one who kissed you."

"Tomorrow you'll regret it, and I'll feel like a total jerk."

"I won't regret it."

He leans in, and just when I think he's going for my lips, he plants a kiss on my forehead.

"I love you, Mel, but I can't do this."

I take a deep breath, snuggling back into his chest. I'm really want him to kiss me.

"Carlos?"

"Yeah?"

"I'm a grown-up, I'm not drunk. If anything, I'm the one taking advantage of you."

I raise my head, locking eyes with him. I realize he's as into this as I am. His pupils are dilated, his hands a bit sweaty. I scoot in closer and kiss him again. It starts tender, but it escalates into this deep, almost possessive kiss. I hadn't seen this side of Carlos, and boy, am I into it. He pulls me onto his lap, and there's no mistaking his arousal against my thighs. Suddenly, he stops and grips my shoulders.

"Mel, we can't do this."

"Why not?"

"Right now, you need a friend, not a lover."

"Don't you find me attractive? Don't you like me?"

He swallows hard, pupils still dilated.

"Of course, I do. A lot. Too much. And that's why I can't do this."

"Why?"

"Because, when it happens, I want to be sure you really want it. I want to make sure you won't regret it in the morning."

"I want to be with you, Carlos, isn't that enough?"

"Mel, please, this isn't a good idea. You're not okay." He gently shifts me off his lap onto the couch.

"I'm a complete wreck, aren't I?"

He doesn't say a word but plants a gentle kiss on my forehead. I start tearing up again.

Chapter 28

I wake up to a ringing phone. Eyes half-open, I realize I'm still crashed out on Carlos's couch. He took off my shoes and covered me with a blanket. The phone keeps ringing right there beside me. Carlos shuffles out, looking a bit disheveled, wearing shorts.

"Let me check who's calling." He motions for me to grab the phone from the side table. "I don't usually get calls this early."

I reluctantly pass him the phone without checking who it is.

"It's your aunt. She's probably freaking out about you."

I'm clueless why she'd be calling. I was supposed to have spent the night at the hotel with Rodrigo. Carlos waits a few beats before picking up, rubbing his eyes.

"Hey, Gabi. What?!" Suddenly, his tone changes. I can hear my aunt's voice on the line, but I can't make out what's happening. "No worries. We're heading there now."

"What's happening?!"

"We need to go." He's calm, but I can tell he's trying not to stress me out. "Your aunt and Jasmine were in a car accident. They're at the hospital."

※ ※ ※

Carlos pulls up near the ER entrance. There's this ambulance just arrived, and two paramedics are hauling a stretcher out. A middle-aged man lies on it, looking terrified. I can't help but think of the bald and mulatto who took me to the hospital. Was I that scared-looking when I arrived? Carlos motions for me to follow, but the last thing I want to do is step back into a hospital. The moment we walk in, that smell hits me, and it's like I'm right back in that hospital bed. I try to brush it off and keep up with Carlos, but it's too much. Way too familiar.

We get to this jam-packed waiting room. There're these little kids making a racket, playing on the floor. One woman, standing off to the side, is crying. I look around, but I can't spot my aunt or Jasmine. Some bearded guy gets up when they call his name, and that's when I see my aunt, sitting alone in a corner. No sight of Jasmine anywhere.

"Aunt Gabi, what happened?!"

My aunt's got scratches on her face and a gash on her forehead, but she seems alright.

"Mel, I didn't want to stress you out. I didn't know you were with Carlos. I called him because I didn't know how to get us back home."

"What happened?"

"We got in an accident heading to the Hortensias Garden. The paramedics brought us here."

"Is Jasmine okay?"

"Her arm's really hurting. She went for an X-ray to check if it's broken."

The door to the medical rooms swings open, and an assistant rolls in a bald woman on a wheelchair.

"Why's she here?" the woman asks, pointing at me.

That's when I recognize the voice.

"Jasmine?!"

She shrugs and shakes her head.

"Digging the George Costanza look?"

"What's happening?!"

Jasmine points to her head.

"Breast cancer. Well, the cancer didn't make me bald. The chemo did."

"Chemo?! Why didn't anyone tell me?!"

"We didn't want to worry you, darling. You've got your own stuff going on."

"You knew about this?" I turn to Carlos.

He nods.

"Sorry to break up the family gathering, but I've got to take her for more tests."

"What about the X-ray?"

"We've got to wait for the results. Should have them in about half an hour. Now, if you'll excuse me, I'll take her for the tests."

I grab the only open seat next to my aunt. The room's packed, and Carlos says he'll wait outside.

"You should've told me."

"I didn't want to stress you out, Mel. You've got enough on your plate. Why were you hanging out with Carlos? Shouldn't you have been with Rodrigo at the hotel?"

"Yeah, I was supposed to be."

"What happened?"

"Things didn't go well between us."

Ping! A message. Is it from Rodrigo? Did he realize he messed up and wants to patch things up? That's got to be it. I bet he finally realized he acted like a jerk. But when I check the sender's name, I freeze. It's not from Rodrigo, it's from Cláudio. He sent a pic with a caption:

Check out where I was last night.

What does he want?! And where the heck is that place?! I zoom in on the photo and my stomach drops. I know that spot. It's the bar where we hung out that night. I can hardly breathe. Why's he messaging me now?! Why won't he just leave me alone?! I get up and look around.

"Where you headed, darling?"

"Where's the bathroom?"

My aunt points down a corridor to the left, and I walk away quickly. I need to get out of there! I need him to leave me alone! I find the bathroom and almost bump into a woman coming out.

"Watch it!"

"Sorry."

"Next time, watch where you're going."

She seems like she wants to get into a fight, but I'm not in the mood. I hurry into an empty stall and shut the door. I'm trying to take deep breaths, but it's hard. The place reeks of pee, and there's toilet paper on the floor. Seriously, why can't people aim for the giant hole in the toilet and toss the paper in the bin? I wipe down the toilet seat and sit, resting my head against the wall. Then, I hear another message coming in.

Recognize the place or were you too wasted to remember?

Won't he just leave me alone?! What does he want?!

LEAVE ME ALONE!

Just reminiscing about the good times.

LEAVE ME ALONE!

When are you coming back? Miss you.

What a jerk! I block his number. No more messages. I lean my head against my knees, huddled up. I feel so fragile, like I could shatter any minute. But it wasn't always like this. There was a time, even after that happened, I didn't feel this way, I wasn't this fragile. I felt furious, enraged. But as time went on, I swallowed that anger, buried it deep inside. I convinced myself it was all my fault, that I was overreacting.

"Is everything okay?" My aunt's knocking on the door. "Open up, Mel!"

I open the door but stay put.

"What's going on? Was it a message from Rodrigo?"

"No. It was from a coworker."

"An ex, huh?"

I let out a bitter laugh. "No."

"That guy you've been having issues with at work?"

I don't answer. I don't want to answer. I can sense the question on the tip of my aunt's tongue. She's no fool. She knows something serious went down. "Don't ask, don't ask," I tell myself as I squeeze the phone in my hands. I just want to hurl it against the wall.

"What did he do to you, Mel?"

I want to say nothing happened, that everything's fine. But I can't say it's fine because it's not. Because things were never the same. Because I was never the same.

"It'll be good for you to get it off your chest."

"I know."

I go quiet for a bit, trying to gather the courage to piece together those memories. I can't remember everything—I was wasted, way too wasted to recall it all. But I recall the exact moment when something inside me snapped. I shut my eyes, attempting to rewind to where it all began.

"About a year back, I went with Ruth to this bar—the one in the photo." Aunt bends down, holding onto my hands. "She met some guy there and left with him. I stayed back, alone, drinking."

I'm waiting for a lecture from my aunt. Waiting for her to tell me I shouldn't drink so much, that I should be ashamed. But she doesn't say anything—just listens.

"Then this coworker, Cláudio, pops up. He was new at the office, and I barely knew him. He sidled up and started buying me drinks." My voice starts to tremble.

My aunt grips my hands tightly.

"I got pretty drunk, and he offered to drive me home. I don't know if I blacked out or just can't remember, but next thing I know, we're parked in front of his place. I remember him saying he lived there."

"Goodness, Mel!" I can hear the fear in her voice, afraid of what I might say next, but she asks anyway. "What happened next?"

"He..." I remember the taste of his mouth and cringe. "He started kissing me." Sometimes, I wake up with that taste lingering in my mouth. "His hands were all over me, touching me. I told him to stop, but he just wouldn't. I'm sure I told him to stop."

"Oh, darling, I'm really sorry."

"I remember getting out of the car, and then things got heated."

I pause, trying to piece together what happened.

"We were on the street, arguing, when a group of younger girls passed by and got involved, confronting him. It turned into this huge mess. I tried to leave, but he grabbed my arm. Then they threatened to call the cops."

"And what about him?"

"He eventually took off. The girls hailed a cab and took me home. I never crossed paths with them again." I should've asked for their contact. I should've thanked them.

"Mel, it's great those girls helped you out."

"When I got home, I felt so alone, so lost."

"Your friend Ruth should've never left you alone at the bar. What kind of friend does that?!" My aunt's tone is charged. I've never seen her like this. "Did you tell anyone?"

"I told Ruth. She thought I was blowing it out of proportion and suggested we take a vacation in Dubai."

"You didn't tell your mom?"

"No, she's always swamped with work at the hospital, and I didn't want to stress her out."

"Did that Claudio try anything else?"

"No, but he's always playing these messed-up mind games with me. I think he can't handle being turned down."

"You should've reported him, Mel."

I gulp hard.

"I felt too embarrassed."

Aunt Gabi pulls me into a hug, and I start sobbing.

"No need to feel ashamed, Mel."

Logic tells me she's right, but shame still consumes me. I'm ashamed because I drank too much. I'm ashamed because I was wasted, completely out of it. If the news of Judge Lacerda de Brito's daughter getting smashed made it to the papers, I shudder to think of my father's reaction. I sit there, crying my eyes out for what feels like forever, and the more I cry, the more it feels like I'm drowning. My aunt sticks with me until I've got no more tears left. When I finally stop, she grabs my shoulders, and looks me in the eye.

"You're not in this alone, darling. Anytime you need to talk, I'm here. And we'll figure out a way to get rid of that scoundrel once and for all. I won't let him bother you again."

Chapter 29

I wake up with a pounding headache and my phone glued to my hand. No clue what time it is. I've checked my phone—guess what? It's eleven, and no new messages. I'm so, but so stupid! Still holding out for Rodrigo to say sorry after all that drama. Will I ever learn?

I bolt out of bed and head straight for a shower. Yesterday we spent the entire day at the hospital, so I need to scrub that smell off me. While the water's hitting me, I start to think. I don't want to, but my brain kicks in. Rodrigo's on my mind. And that jerk Claudio too. What am I going to do now?! Soon enough, I'll be back to my miserable life at the office. I'll have to look at his face every single day. EVERY. SINGLE. DAY! I'll have to keep up with Carmen's comments and my colleagues' jokes. Nothing's going to change. Nothing! And that scares me. It terrifies me. I can't keep dwelling on it. I must stop. I step out of the shower and get dressed.

I hit the kitchen, and there's Jasmine, trying to butter her toast left-handed. Her right arm's in a cast, but besides that, she's good. She's still recovering from cancer, so they ran all these tests just to be sure it was only her arm. Thank goodness she's back to rocking that red wig. It hurts to see her without hair. It seriously hurts.

"Good morning. Let me take care of that."

I try prying the knife from her hand.

"I'm not helpless!"

She keeps trying to spread the butter on the toast but only manages to send it flying off the plate onto the floor.

"Damn it!"

I crouch down, snatch the toast, and chuck it in the bin. Jasmine makes a face but doesn't say anything. I plop down next to her, grab another slice of toast, and spread butter on it. She's clearly peeved but keeps quiet.

"Where's my aunt?"

"She went to the Hortensias Garden. Some English guests arrived this morning."

After dishing out her breakfast, I take my pills and grab two pineapple slices.

"What were you up to with Carlos last night? Weren't you supposed to be having a steamy night with that Rodrigo guy?"

I have to bite my tongue to stop from rolling my eyes. Jasmine's straight talk gets under my skin. I should've known she'd pick up that something went wrong. I play dumb, but she won't let it slide.

"Come on, spill it, Mel! What did that jerk do to you? And wipe that look off your face because even without meeting him, I'm pretty sure he's a jerk."

I sigh. No point hiding anything from her. She's relentless. I've known her long enough to get that.

"Everything seemed fine until dinner, and then…"

"Out with it, Mel," she insists between bites.

"When I went to meet him at the restaurant, he was there chatting up some coworker and introduced me as a friend."

"Friend?! But aren't you two a couple?!"

"Yeah, that's what I thought too."

"That guy's got some nerve."

"When I asked him about it, he goes, 'I don't like labels.' Then I asked, 'Is it normal to introduce your future wife as a friend?' And he's all, 'Just kidding, I'm not ready for the whole marriage and kids deal.'"

"I had a feeling he was playing you."

I let out a sigh.

"And you, got yourself drunk again?"

I make a face.

"No, no drinks for me."

"You bounced, right? Tell me you left that jerk solo."

I wish I've had the guts to do that.

"No, I didn't leave," I confess. "We had dinner, but he got ticked off with our conversation, and then…" I take a deep breath. Here comes a lecture, a mighty long one. "Then we hit a bar. It was packed, crazy loud, music blaring, and I…"

"And you?"

"And I started having a panic attack."

Jasmine sets down her half-eaten toast, and I notice her expression shift. She isn't mad now. She's worried. She feels sorry for me. I can see it in her eyes. And I feel like I'm crumbling, like I'm about to cry, again. And I don't want to cry. I'm done with crying!

"So, what went down after that?"

My throat feels tight, tears threatening to spill. I clench my fists hard.

"I told him I wasn't feeling great and needed some air."

"What did he say?"

"Said I was wrecking his night."

"What a jerk! Then what?"

"I left the bar and waited outside, hoping he'd follow."

"Let me guess, he ghosted you, right?"

I nod, feeling like if I keep talking, I'll lose it and will start crying.

"And you rang up Carlos to rescue you." Jasmine sighs, sidling closer. Suddenly, her arms are around me, attempting a hug despite her cast. "Oh, Mel, I knew that Rodrigo guy was bad news."

"I'm not surprised he got upset. He came all the way to the Azores for me, and I messed it up." My voice is barely a whisper.

Her eyes widen.

"You didn't mess up anything! He's the one who screwed it all! Don't defend him. If he really cared, he wouldn't leave you stranded in the street having a panic attack. Forget him, Mel! You've got to let him go. He's not worth it!"

I lower my gaze. I know she's right, but I can't shake off this feeling that I messed it all up. Messed things up with him and then wrecked it with Carlos. Carlos! How am I going to face him after what happened?!

"That Rodrigo isn't your guy, kiddo. He didn't have your back when you needed him. Total jerk!"

"I know." And I do know, but deep down, I'm still waiting for him to knock on my door any minute. Still waiting for that apology. Because I can't believe my perfect plan fell apart. Just can't.

"You don't need someone like that sticking around."

"You and my aunt, though, you make a pretty great pair," I say, trying to change the subject.

"But hey, it's not all sunshine and rainbows, Mel. No such thing as perfect relationships. We're all different, with different habits and quirks."

"You and my aunt seem to be in sync."

"Sometimes," she chuckles. "Other days, I wonder why I'm even here in the Azores."

I'm taken aback. I didn't expect her to say that.

"But I thought you liked being here in the Azores?"

"I do, but I had other plans for my life."

"Other plans?" Is she about to spill that she's thinking of splitting up with my aunt too? No, that can't be!

She grabs a cigarette from the pack on the table and asks me to light it.

"You're lighting up in here?"

"Your aunt's not around. Plus, I think a broken arm earns me a smoke in the kitchen."

I spark up her cigarette.

"I was living with your aunt for a few years when I got an invite from an American gallery for a year-long artistic residency in New York."

"No kidding? New York?"

"New York. The Big Apple. It was a dream come true, a nod to my artistry. Your aunt tagged along. I adored the city, the buzz, the noise, the lights—everything about it."

"I've been there too, but just for vacations with my parents. It's a vibrant city."

"Man, I loved it, but your aunt? She hated it."

"What happened?"

"Eight months later, we came back."

"You gave up your dream for my aunt?"

"Yeah."

"Don't you ever regret it?"

"I think about it most days, how life would've been if I stuck around. Wouldn't have been a breeze though; making it as an artist isn't easy anywhere. But then I wonder what life would be like if your aunt had married her fiancé."

"So, no regrets?"

"Nah, not really. If I did, I wouldn't be here. Was it a piece of cake? Heck no, and it still isn't. Life is a series of choices; we have to live with what we pick. Sometimes we make the wrong decision, sometimes the right one. That's life, you know."

"Are you happy?"

"Nobody's happy 24/7. Life's a rollercoaster of ups and downs, wins and losses. Let's just say I've had more highs than lows."

"Thought you and my aunt were tight."

"We are, mostly. Sometimes we butt heads. Plus, the whole deal of sharing a house with someone's no cakewalk. Your aunt's peeved because I shed hair in the tub and leave the toilet seat up, like guys do. Sometimes I do it just to rile her up. I like messing with her," she chuckles. "And I get ticked because she's all about planning everything. Even when we hit the city, she's got a list in hand of places to hit and stuff to buy. I hate lists. I like to go without a plan, on an adventure, and that drives your aunt nuts."

"I'd go bonkers too. I'm all about planning everything."

"Yeah, you guys should be honorary members of the Overthinkers Gang. You should get a badge or something for that. I'm not a planner at all. Your aunt knows I need my space now and then. Sometimes I wake up, pack my bags, catch the first flight to nowhere, and explore the world. When I come back, your aunt's there with a smile, waiting for me. Nobody else could handle my moods and quirks like she does."

"World traveler, huh?"

"Yeah. But don't get me wrong, I'm not out there on these trips cheating on your aunt. I travel to visit museums or meet artists all over the globe. That's my thing when I'm out and about. Sometimes, I drag her along. We're a team."

The phone rings, and I get this knot in my stomach. Is it Rodrigo? Jasmine seems to read my mind because she says:

"If it's him, don't answer."

I glance at the caller ID.

"It's Carlos."

Seeing it's him doesn't make me feel any better. After last night, I'm clueless about what to say. Jasmine heads off to finish her smoke in the bedroom. My aunt's going to flip about the room smelling like smoke.

"Hey, Mel."

His voice is flat, too neutral.

"Hey."

"How are you doing?"

"Okay. And you?"

"Fine."

Silence. Neither of us talks for what seems like an eternity.

"Today's the day to drop off those photos of the elderly at the Day Care Center. Not sure if you want to tag along?"

I take a deep breath.

"Are you upset with me?"

"No, not at all. Are you upset with me?"

"No."

And I mean it, even after the pathetic scene I made last night, even after he said it wasn't a good idea for us to hook up.

"So, you want to come?"

"Sure, if you want."

"Absolutely, Mel," he pauses, then adds, "What happened yesterday doesn't change a thing. I still want us to be friends."

Friends. He wants to stick to being friends. I'm not sure what to make of that. I don't know if I was expecting him to declare his love or something, but that's not what he said. He just wants to be friends. Carlos wants to keep being my friend.

"I also want to keep being your friend," and I truly do. I've lost Rodrigo; I can't lose him too.

"Good to know."

"Will you take much longer?"

"I'm outside."

"You're here?" I swing open the front door.

He's standing in front of his grandpa's house. We both stand there, awkwardly staring at each other. Neither of us says a word.

"Hey, Carlos! Where are you guys headed today?" Jasmine shouts from the bedroom window.

"We're hitting up the Day Care Center," he says, flashing me a shy smile.

"Just need to grab my backpack," then I add, "hang on a sec, Super-Carlos."

He chuckles, those dimples showing, and as I glance at him, I realize why I kissed him. I know exactly why I kissed him. And I know it's going to be okay. We'll figure things out.

The ride to the Day Care Center is easygoing, like nothing's happened. Carlos tunes in to an '80s music station on the old radio, and we share thoughts about a Bon Jovi song. It's a quick trip, and before long, we're parking right in front of the Day Care Center.

As we step in, the elderly welcome us with kisses and hugs. Ms. Julieta's there, so is Ms. Elvira, Mr. Zé, and the lovebird duo, Mr. João and Ms. Alberta. Checking out the place, I'm left speechless. My drawings of the seniors are hanging on one wall like they're masterpieces in a gallery. It gets to me, and I don't know why, but I'm fighting back tears.

"Have you seen your portraits up on the wall?" Ms. Julieta asks.

I nod, tongue-tied.

"They're amazing!" Ms. Alberta says, laughing. "João and I want you to paint us on our wedding day!"

"Amazing, simply amazing!" Ms. Elvira chimes in.

"Hey, that's because I had some great models," I chuckle.

They all burst out laughing.

"Alright, enough about my art. Let's check out Carlos' photos?"

Carlos starts passing around the photos. It's a lively scene; the seniors are thrilled, and I'm not surprised. t's my first time seeing the photos, and wow, those photos are stunning. No wonder Carlos won an award. He's an amazing photographer.

We're invited for lunch by the Director, so we eat at the Center. Some of the seniors retell their stories from the other day, but Carlos and I play along like it's all new. Ms. Alberta and Mr. João ask Carlos to photograph their upcoming wedding, and he agrees. Ms. Julieta tells me her granddaughter's visiting in a couple of weeks, and it makes me happy for her.

I sit there, watching Carlos chat with the seniors. His dimples when he laughs, even that bit of a belly—it's kind of cute. How he engages with the elderly, sharing laughs over their tales. No wonder they adore him. He's a solid guy. He'll make some lucky girl really happy. And seeing him like that, so joyful, it makes me want to be that girl. Makes me want it a lot.

Chapter 30

When we pull onto my aunt's street, I notice a top-of-the-line Mercedes parked in front of the house. Leaning against the car is the last person I expected to see there: Rodrigo. I'm not sure I'm ready to talk to him. Honestly, I'm not even sure if I want to hear his apologies because I'm pretty certain that's why he's hanging around.

Carlos parks right next to the Mercedes.

"Is that..."

"Yeah, that's Rodrigo."

"Do you want me to stick around?"

"Thanks, but I've got this."

I step out of the van, and Carlos takes off.

"Nice ride," Rodrigo says, teasingly.

"How'd you find my aunt's place?"

"I checked the messages you sent and remembered you mentioned your aunt's rustic retreat was called Hortensias Garden. This island isn't huge. I asked around at the café across from the hotel, and they pointed me to your aunt's address."

"What are you doing here? I thought you had left."

"I've been trying to reach you all day, but your phone's been off."

"I've been busy."

"So, are you hanging out with that guy who dropped you off?"

"Are you getting a little jealous now?"

He laughs.

"Nah, not at all."

"Then why did you come?"

I'm expecting an apology, hoping he'd admit regret for acting like a jerk, but instead, he says:

"My flight isn't until eleven tonight. I thought we could hang out."

And have sex. He doesn't say it, but I'm pretty sure that's why he's here. Not a single word about what went down yesterday. Jasmine was right.

"I can't, I'm tied up."

"Come on, Mel, quit playing hard to get." He moves closer.

"Rodrigo..."

"What's up with you?" He steps in, grabbing me around the waist. "You used to be so much fun."

Used to be so wasted, that's what he should say.

"You let me leave the bar alone last night."

"You're ticked about that? You're a grown-up and wanted to leave. I wasn't going to stop you."

"But you could've gone with me."

"You didn't ask. If you had, I would've."

"I wasn't feeling well."

"You didn't tell me that."

Did he not catch that? The music was blasting. Maybe he didn't, and I blew it out of proportion.

"You know I care about you, Mel."

"But not enough to pop the question."

"Let's not get into that now, Mel. Someday, we'll discuss it when I'm only jet-setting around Europe."

"Are you serious?"

"Absolutely. I adore you."

I look into his blue eyes and hesitate. I hesitate because that was my dream for so long. I hesitate because I can't believe it was all an illusion.

"Adore her?! Doesn't look like it!" Jasmine appears at the doorstep.

Rodrigo lets go of me and spins around to see who's talking.

"You must be Rodrigo."

He looks at her but says nothing. Seems like he's stunned by the lady with the fire-red hair and the loud voice.

"Okay, Rodrigo, I'm only saying this once: leave Mel alone!"

"Excuse me?!"

"You heard me loud and clear!"

"Mel's a big girl, she can make her own choices."

"Don't get smart, young man. I'm old enough to be your mom."

"Who's this crazy woman, Mel?!"

"Crazy?! Did I hear that right?! You just called me crazy?!"

"Jasmine, please, calm down," Aunt Gabi, who came outside too, pleads.

"Calm down?! How can I calm down?! This jerk left Mel stranded in the street having a panic attack at night, while he was knocking back drinks at the bar, and now he's got the nerve to show up here trying to deceive her again?!"

"I didn't come here to deceive anyone!" Rodrigo raises his voice too.

"Yeah, you did, you jerk!"

"Who are you calling a jerk, you crazy woman?!"

"I'll show you crazy!" Jasmine lunges at Rodrigo, grabbing his hair with her good arm. He tries to wiggle free, but she's got a tight grip.

"Let her go!" my aunt pleads, getting in to break them up.

"Stop! Stop!" I shout, but it's like no one's hearing me.

Rodrigo tries to pull away and ends up with Jasmine's wig in his hand.

"You jerk!" Jasminee shouts. "Give me back my hair!"

He looks at the wig, then at her, and bursts into laughter. Jasmine snatches the wig from his hand.

Suddenly, there's a gunshot. My heart races. What in the world was that?!

"Hey," Mr. Manuel pipes up suddenly, pointing a rifle at Rodrigo, "you're going to hit the road, and you're going to do it now!" He presses the rifle against Rodrigo's chest. "I won't ask twice."

Rodrigo looks at me, then at Mr. Manuel, and back at me again, his face incredulous.

"Mel?"

I feel a knot in my stomach. What should I do?! Should I tell Mr. Manuel to lay off Rodrigo, or should I tell Rodrigo to leave me alone?! My head feels like it's about to explode. Mr. Manuel keeps his rifle aimed at Rodrigo, who raises his arms, frozen with panic.

"Angel, are you seriously going to let these people treat me like this?" His voice turns soft, almost pleading.

I glance at him, recognizing the Rodrigo I met in Dubai—the charming guy who swept me off my feet. But this isn't the Rodrigo from last night, nor the Rodrigo from the past few weeks. Because I haven't forgotten everything that went down. I remember how I felt when he stood me up at the airport, leaving me waiting for hours. I remember him staying at the bar, knocking back drinks, as I stumbled into the street alone in the dead of night while having a panic attack. I remember feeling incredibly lonely, even when he was right there. And suddenly, it's like a veil has been lifted, and I see things clearly. Because now, I finally see the truth. In this relationship, I've always been alone. I gather my courage and blurt out:

"Go away."

I can see surprise in his eyes. He didn't see that coming. I bet he thought I'd apologize, maybe even beg.

"Are you sure?"

I take a deep breath. Ruth was right, Rodrigo isn't a *Cappuccino*—heck, he's not even a *Martini*.

"Yes."

He makes a face. Then he laughs, but it's a kind of nervous laugh. Next, he backs up toward his car, eyeing the rifle. Another shot goes off, nearly deafening me. For a second, I'm scared Mr. Manuel shot him. Then I hear the old guy laughing. More laughs coming from the porch. Even my aunt and Jasmine are cracking up. What's so funny?! I glance over at the Mercedes and see Rodrigo sprawled in a puddle next to the car. He gets up, his once-white shirt now all muddy, face speckled with dirt. Then he looks at Mr. Manuel, terror written all over his face.

"Go away! Next time, I won't miss!"

Rodrigo tries to get into the car but, with the rush, trips and ends up falling into the front seat. Mr. Manuel fires another shot into the air. I can't help it—I start laughing too. Rodrigo's expression is priceless. Eventually, he manages to sit behind the wheel and floors it. The tires slip on the grass verge, but the Mercedes gains traction and speeds off, leaving in a hurry. The four of us keep laughing, seems like forever.

When we finally stop, it hits me—it's over. There's no turning back. It's over. And now, what am I going to do?

Chapter 31

I sink into the couch, feeling clueless. There's less than a week left until I head back to Lisbon, and my plan just went down the drain. What on earth do I do now?!

"Mel, darling, are you okay?" my aunt settles beside me on the couch.

"I'm not sure."

That's the honest truth. I'm not sure. I don't have a backup plan.

"You'll be fine," Jasmine chimes in. "You just kicked that jerk to the curb for good. Did you see his face when he yanked my wig?!" She cracks up. "Looked like he'd seen a ghost."

"I think he went into shock."

"And when he fell flat on his face in that puddle?!" Jasmine keeps going. "You got to admit, Mel, that was priceless."

"Yeah, Jasmine, it was pretty hilarious."

"His face! Poor guy! His Burberrys shirt all messed up."

"Calvin Klein."

"What?"

"The shirt was Calvin Klein. Rodrigo only wears Calvin Klein shirts."

Jasminee keeps laughing.

"What a clown, Mel. He's good-looking, but man, he's a jerk."

I glance at my aunt, and she's not amused.

"Sorry for all this craziness on your doorstep."

"No need to apologize. That Rodrigo crossed the line. He shouldn't have called Jasmine crazy."

"Jerk! Manuel should've popped a shot at him. In the butt. Yeah, a shot in the butt. That's what he deserved. Spend a few months needing a silicone cushion or whatever to sit."

"Jasmine, come on, don't exaggerate. Nothing justifies violence."

"But seriously, wouldn't it have been kind of funny if Manuel shot him in the butt?"

My aunt shakes her head and then signals Jasminee to give us some space. She must want to chat with me.

"Well, I think I'm going to take a nap. Pain meds always knock me out," she yawns. "Catch you later."

My aunt sits beside me and takes my hand.

"Are you doing okay, darling?"

"I think so."

"I get why you fell for him, Mel. He's good-looking, but his attitude sucks. He treated you all wrong. Fed you false hope for months. Left you alone on the street in the middle of a panic attack while he partied at the bar like it was all good. You don't need someone like that around."

"I know, but..."

"Do you still love him?"

"It's not that." And now what? I'm stuck without a backup plan. Rodrigo was my whole game plan. "I don't know what to do."

"Mel, you're grown, and I don't want to meddle in your life, but I think you should forget about him. When relationships start, that honeymoon phase flies by."

I let out a sigh.

"And after that phase, what's left? Companionship, bonding, and if you're lucky, some fiery moments that remind you why you picked that person. And if they're the right one, they'll stand by you through the good and the bad times."

"Or in those moments when you're having a panic attack and you've got to hit the streets in the dead of night." Rodrigo wasn't there, but Carlos was. Super-Carlos saved me. Again.

"Yes, at those times. That's when you realize that person's got your back, that they really care about you. You know, me and Jasmine, we've been through some real tough stuff too."

"Yeah, she shared a bit with me."

"Those initial years were brutal. I'd never even considered being into women, I was engaged to a great guy. Giving it all up and getting pushed away from the family by your grandfather was very hard."

"I can't even imagine how tough it must've been."

"My whole life just vanished in a flash. No more father, mother, or brother. Your grandma tried to understand, but we only met sneakily because of your grandpa. I started doubting my choice. Wanted to turn back time. Went to your grandfather, and he kicked me out, again. Felt like I was free-falling. I plunged into a deep depression. I didn't eat, I didn't sleep."

"How did you pull through?"

"With Jasmine's support. She had faith in us, even when I didn't."

I feel like tearing up again, thinking about what my aunt went through, all those years I could've had an aunt, and didn't. My grandfather wrecked his daughter's life with his narrow-mindedness.

"Months later, Jasmine convinced me to join her, and things started looking up, bit by bit. It took ages. I had to make peace with the fact that my father would never forgive me."

"That must've been so rough."

"Yeah, it was, but no regrets. Jasmine was the silver lining. Sure, she drives me bonkers sometimes, but I adore her. When she got diagnosed with breast cancer, it shattered me."

"Is she going to be okay?"

"Yeah, I think so. She finished her treatments last week. We got to keep an eye out, though, because you know how cancers are—they can sneak back."

I slide in beside my aunt and give her a tight hug. I'm being selfish, caught up in my own heartache while Jasmine's battling through cancer recovery.

"It's all going to work out. She's going to be okay. Sorry for barging into your lives like this."

"That's nonsense, darling. One of the best things after meeting Jasmine was when you called saying you wanted to visit. You're part of our family too, Mel, and I love you."

"Aww, I love you too, Aunt Gabi." I'm starting to really like this free-spirited aunt of mine.

"Are you feeling any better now?"

"I'm feeling kind of lost. I'm not sure what I'm going to do. Might sound silly, but I was dead set on convincing Rodrigo to propose, thinking that would solve all my problems." Saying it aloud makes me realize how silly and naive I've been.

"Life throws us curveballs sometimes. We must learn to deal with the surprises."

"I'm not really keen on going back to Lisbon, back to the office."

"Because of that coworker?"

"Not just because of him. It's everything. I'm tired of that life, always rushing from work to home and vice versa. I can't stand my job."

"You should report that colleague of yours."

"I don't want the whole office to know."

"He shouldn't get away with it. Did you ever thought he might pull the same thing on other women?"

My aunt's making sense, but I don't think I'm ready to make my story public.

"No need to feel ashamed, Mel. He's the one to blame, not you."

"True, but I'm not ready to deal with the fallout of going public."

"And you're going to keep working in the same office as nothing happened? It's not good for you."

"I don't even know if I want to head back."

"To the office?"

"To Lisbon. This time on the Azores made me realize there's more to life."

"You don't have to be stuck in a life that doesn't make you happy. So, what's on your mind?"

"I don't know. Maybe I could rent out my place and hang around here for a bit. Here I have you and Jasmine."

"And Carlos…"

"Yeah, Carlos."

"You're into him?"

"Yeah."

"We've noticed he's into you too."

"I really like him, but I'm all over the place. One minute, I'm thinking I'm falling for Carlos, and the next, I'm crying over Rodrigo."

"Maybe it's time you put yourself first, figure out what you want for your life."

"And maybe take a break from men."

My aunt chuckles.

"It wouldn't hurt, at least for a bit."

"If I stuck around, I'd need a job."

"Shouldn't be too hard. There's a shortage of lawyers around the island."

"Seriously? That's good to know, but I've got a career in Lisbon, I've worked my tail off to get to where I am. Plus, there's that course at the Judicial Studies Center for the judge gig."

"Are you dead set on becoming a judge? Is that what you really want?"

"I'm not sure."

Feels like my head's about to burst. I always did what everyone expected. Now I'm stuck. No clue what to do. No clue what's the right move. Maybe I should ditch the pity party and head back to Lisbon. Back to the grind. Study for those exams. Become a judge. Like my father. Like my grandfather. But the thought alone freaks me out.

"What do you think I should do?"

"Mel, that's a call only you can make. I just want you to be happy."

"I want that too, but I'm scared I'll let people down."

"People?"

"My father. I'm scared he'll be disappointed. What will he think?"

"What your father thinks doesn't matter, Mel. What other people think doesn't matter. It's about not disappointing yourself. Life is yours, and you've got to figure out what you want to do with it. You're the one living it; no one else can do that for you. So, do what makes you happy."

As if it were that simple. As if I could spend the rest of my life hanging around the island with Carlos. Because right now, that's all I want. That's what makes me happy.

"Think about what I said. If you set up a practice here, clients wouldn't be hard to come by."

I could do that. I could ditch everything in Lisbon and move to the Azores. Living costs are way cheaper here. Maybe I could rent a house and an office space. Start my own business. But do I still want to pursue law? And if I stick around, what will happen? Will Carlos and I be together?

Chapter 32

I tossed and turned all night, couldn't catch a wink. After the whole thing with Rodrigo, I'm at a loss. I'm not in the mood to head back to Lisbon. Just thinking about going back to the office and diving into divorce cases ties my stomach in knots.

I get out of bed and head to the kitchen. I need a coffee. My aunt and Jasmine are already out, so I grab breakfast alone, lost in my thoughts. I spot a pack of Smarties on the counter and snag it. I'm craving something sweet. I take one and savor it with my coffee. Coffee and chocolate, the perfect combo. Carlos had to take his sister to some tournament on another island today, so he's out. I'm debating whether to join my aunt at the Hortensias Garden or just chill at home when I hear the key turning in the lock. My aunt probably is checking up on me.

"Mel, you're up. Awesome!"

"Hey, Aunt Gabi."

"You've got a visitor."

I furrow my brow. Last time I had a visitor, it didn't end well. Is it Rodrigo?! What if he's here to apologize?! What do I do?! I glance at my aunt's smile and realize it can't be him. If it were him, she wouldn't be so cheery. It has to be Carlos, it's got to be him. Maybe the tournament got called off. I stand up, all excited. As she steps aside, in walks the last person I ever expected to see there.

"Dad?!"

I'm in shock. What's my father doing here?! And why's he rocking jeans and a tee? Is this some new 'trying-be-young' style for his new girlfriend? I bet that's it. All he's missing is dying his hair to cover those grays. Guys, especially middle-aged ones, are just something' else. They think a fresh look, or a new haircut will magically turn back time. Pathetic, just pathetic.

"Hey, Mel, came to see how you're doing."

"Aren't you working?"

"I took a few days off."

It's smack in the middle of the week, and I know he's got a bunch of high-stakes trials lined up. He never takes time off now, never!

"To spend time with her?

That must be it. He's taken his fling on some lovey-dovey escape to the Azores, no doubt. But why'd they pick this place? I just hope she doesn't tag along. I don't want to meet her.

My father looks uncomfortable. I guess he's not digging this unfiltered version of his daughter.

"What are you talking about?"

"Mom told me everything."

"Everything?"

"About the other woman."

"What other woman, Mel?"

I can't believe he's going to act like nothing's up.

"Your mistress, who could it be?"

He looks at me, then at my aunt, and shakes his head.

"What are you talking about?! I don't have a mistress, Mel."

"Mom said you asked for a divorce."

"Yeah, but…"

My eyes widen. This can't be. I can't believe it.

"It's a man? Are you gay?!"

My father shakes his head and gives a little smile.

"Come on, Mel. What did your mom tell you?" His tone shows real confusion. "I don't have a lover, male or female."

"No?!"

But then why? Why would he ask for a divorce? I'm even more lost now.

"Your mom's the one having an affair with a colleague."

"Mom?!"

"Your mom's involved with someone else," he says.

I meet his gaze and sense the honesty in his words. I'm speechless. Emotions swirl within me. My mother has a lover. A lover! I'm in shock. How did this happen?!

"Sit down, let's talk it out." He sits on the couch, motions for me to sit beside him.

"You two need to talk," my aunt says and heads inside.

My mind first goes to the tennis coach. But my mother doesn't do tennis. So, it must be the personal trainer! Wait, no, she doesn't have one either. She's all about yoga, but her instructor is a woman.

"Who's he?"

My father either doesn't catch on or pretends not to. He's sitting there, staring at the wall, acting like he's clueless about what to say. This is the first time I've seen him unsure, like he's holding back.

"Why'd you think it was me with a lover?"

I let out a sigh.

I don't know, maybe because you were never around.

"Why, Mel?"

"You were always working, never had time for us." He hangs his head and lets out a sigh. "Courts, cases, always more important than us. I started to think maybe you had no cases, just a secret lover."

He starts to say something, but then goes quiet. We both go silent. I grab another candy and let it melt in my mouth. My father looks at me and smiles, but it's a sad smile.

"You probably don't remember, but I used to bring you a pack of Smarties whenever I had to stay late at the court, or whenever I was away for work, always brought you some."

"I remember."

"You do?"

"Yes."

He runs a hand through his graying hair; it really needs a trim. Or maybe not. Adds a bit of a messy look, which suits him. Makes him seem more human.

"Sorry, sweetie. I should've been around more."

Yeah, you definitely should've.

"I miss those old times."

"Me too, Mel, me too."

I pass him a candy, and he takes it. We sit there, in silence, as the chocolate melts in our mouths. It's weird sharing a pack of Smarties with my father, like really weird.

"From now on, I'd like things to be different. I'd like to spend more time with you," he adds after a while.

"Why did you come, then? Was it Aunt Gabi who rang you?"

"No, it was Jasmine."

"Jasmine?!"

"You've probably heard about our drama."

"Yeah, they filled me in."

"First, it was Jasmine who left me for your aunt, and now your mom, who left me for her assistant. I never saw that coming."

"Augusto?!"

"Yeah."

"He's barely older than me!"

What was she thinking?! Augusto must be in his thirties. Could practically be my brother.

"I don't blame her, Mel. I've been an absent husband for way too long. Work became my everything, I forgot about the family."

I'm speechless. This talk with my father, it's a new one for us. I've never heard him apologize before. To anyone.

"Jasmine called to give me a piece of her mind for not looking out for you."

I swallow hard.

"I know what went down with—"

"I'm over it, Dad!" I cut in. "Rodrigo's old news."

"She didn't call me about Rodrigo, Mel."

"No?"

I don't know if I want to hear what he's about to say, but he spills it anyway.

"She called me about Cláudio."

My stomach knots up, pulse racing. I don't want to discuss my issues with Cláudio with my father. Why did she tell him?! Why couldn't she just keep quiet?! He was the last person I wanted to talk about this with.

"It'll be okay, sweetie." He reaches for my hand. Instinct says to pull away – I'm not used to my father touching me, but he doesn't let go.

"What did you do, Dad?!" I just hope he didn't do anything. "Did you talk to Azevedo?!"

He intertwines his fingers with mine.

"No, Mel, I didn't. I wanted to, but Jasmine forbade me."

"Good, I'm glad you didn't. I'm an adult, I can handle my own issues." I'm trying to convince both him and me that it's true. I'm trying to play tough, but I'm close to tears.

"I know, Mel, but I'm your dad, I won't allow any jerk to harass you."

I squeeze my dad's hand tight. I don't want to cry.

"You really didn't talk to Azevedo?"

"Nope, hopped on a plane to come talk to you."

"Thank goodness."

"You've must report him, Mel. If you let me, I'll handle everything."

He's right. I know he's right. I know I can't let Cláudio keep affecting me like this, but just the thought of everyone in the office knowing, it makes me so anxious.

"Mel, we can't let this guy keep harassing you or do the same to other women. I'm your dad, and I won't let him bother you anymore."

"What do you mean by that?"

"I won't let him hurt you."

"What did you do?"

"I didn't do anything, but I sure wanted to. Before coming here, last night, I stood outside his apartment."

"What happened?!"

"Nothing happened. I didn't do anything to him, but I wanted to, really wanted to, Mel. I wanted to grab him by the collar and punch him in the face."

I look at my dad, and for the first time, I see the man who used to wear bell-bottoms and go to rock concerts with Jasmine. That man would've punched Cláudio without hesitation. And that man is my dad.

"I'm filing a complaint against him. It's time to end this. It's time to stop being afraid."

"Will you let me handle everything?"

I nod.

"That jerk won't dare bother you again, Mel. I won't allow it." And I know it's true. Now I know my dad won't let anyone harm me.

I rest my head on his shoulder and relax. My dad hugs me. It's a bit clumsy, but it's a hug. I return the hug and bury my face in his chest. I've missed this hug so much. I've missed this dad so much.

※ ※ ※

We're all sitting down for dinner, the gang's all here—me, Dad, Aunt Gabi, and Jasmine—and it's kind of weird but nice. We're a family, a weird family, but still a family.

"What about Madalena?" Jasmine asks.

Aunt Gabi shoots her a disapproving look as she steps away to grab a dish, but Jasmine's not letting go.

"And Madalena?"

"She's gone away for a few days."

"With her new guy?"

"Yeah, go ahead and tease. She jetted off to Barcelona with this new guy who could practically be her son. Happy now?"

"A younger dude, huh? Smart move. He probably doesn't even need Viagra yet."

Dad grimaces but doesn't say a word.

"Don't get all upset, Nandinho."

"Nandinho?"

"That's what I used to call your dad. A pet name."

"What did he call you?"

"Can't spill the beans," she says with a sneaky grin.

Aunt Gabi comes back with a dish, and Jasmine switches topics fast.

"What's up with that politician's trial? You think he's guilty?"

"You know I can't comment on cases."

"The dude looks sketchy, though."

Dad shakes his head.

"You haven't changed a bit."

"Unlike you. You got a bit chunky and all gray-haired."

"Jasmine!"

"It's okay, Gabi, I'm used to your wife's bluntness. She's right, though. I need to shed a few pounds."

"You could try CrossFit."

"That might be a bit too intense for my age, Mel. I was thinking of taking up golf."

"That's for old folks," Jasmine says.

"I'm not getting any younger. Besides, I prefer the outdoors over being cooped up in a gym."

"I didn't know you liked the outdoors."

"There's a lot you don't know about me, Mel."

"I know you used to smoke, wore bell-bottoms..." He chuckles. "...and went to rock concerts."

After dinner, my aunt and Jasmine tidy up the kitchen, and my dad and I head to the porch.

"I've got a flight tomorrow at nine. I didn't want to leave just yet, but the day after, I have a hearing," he says, lighting up a cigar he pulled from his shirt pocket.

"Cigars?"

"I used to sneak one now and then away from your mom's sight. Now that I'm a nearly divorced man, there's no need to hide my vices."

I laugh.

"Got any other vices I should know about?"

"None. Well, except one. Good food. Your mom was always on some diet and wouldn't let me eat what I wanted. I miss indulging in all that greasy goodness."

We both burst into laughter.

"I wish you could stay a few more days."

"Me too, Mel, but I can't postpone the trial."

"I understand, Dad."

"You know, I've been thinking about taking a sabbatical. Traveling. You and I could go on a vacation together…"

"I'd love that, Dad. And you could meet someone new…"

"I'm not even thinking about that. I'm still wrapping my head around the whole thing with Mom."

"Do you think there's no turning back?"

"We haven't been happy for many years. Discovering her affair that Friday just sped up the process."

"That Friday?!"

"Yes, the day you were hospitalized. They called from the hospital because they couldn't reach your mom. She wasn't at work and wasn't picking up. So, I went home to check on her."

"That's when you caught her with Augusto?"

He nods.

"I think you should take that sabbatical. Seriously, Dad, take a trip or something."

"Tomorrow I'll ask Judith to organize my schedule. I'm going to wrap up my current cases and then put in for a sabbatical. It's set."

"You know, I thought Judith was your mistress."

"Judith?!"

"It's a classic, Dad. Most of my clients have affairs with their secretaries. Or their kids' babysitters."

" You have an overactive imagination."

"I know."

"And what about you, ready to head back to the office?"

I take a deep breath.

"I don't know. I could stay here, you know. Seems like they're short on lawyers on the island."

I'm half expecting him to talk me out of it, but he just says:

"Whatever you decide, I'm behind you, Mel."

"You're okay with me sticking around?!"

"I just want you to be happy and not repeat my mistakes." He pauses, taking another puff of the cigar. " Is it because of this Carlos guy? Jasmine said he seems a decent guy."

"And he is. He's a photographer."

"I know."

"And you don't mind?"

"Of course not. I have a soft spot for artists too."

We both crack up laughing.

"I haven't made up my mind yet, Dad."

Chapter 33

Today's the day, and I'm super nervous—like, really nervous. We're on the boat with Fred and a bunch of his students. Everyone's hyped up. For most of these folks, it's their first dive out in the open sea. There's this middle-aged couple snapping pics non-stop since they hopped on board. They probably want to show off to friends, you know, prove they've still got it, even if they're not spring chickens anymore. I glance at the sea. Left, right or port, starboard—Carlos explained it to me—it's just endless waves. The island vanished like it got swallowed up by the ocean. Not a speck of land in sight, and that freaks me out. Fred signals us to suit up. Reluctantly, I get up and try to wriggle into the wetsuit. Carlos lends a hand.

"Are you okay?" His smile shows he's just as pumped as the rest. He's got this sparkle in his eyes. I could plaster on my fakest grin, tell him I'm all good, just as stoked as he is, but what's the use? I can't fool him. Never could.

"I'm scared out of my mind."

"It's okay. I'm a bit scared too."

"You're just saying that to make me feel better."

"Nah, seriously. Even though I've dived a zillion times, I still get that little flip in my gut."

"I don't have a flip. I've got a whole black hole!"

He helps me slip on the fins.

"Don't worry. Once we're down there, we'll be so amazed by everything that the fear will disappear."

"Down there..." I glance at the water—it's deep, dark, like a pitch-black night. I can't see a thing underwater. Who knows what's swimming below? Carlos catches my drift and says:

"Relax. We're the only 'monsters' down there. At least, that's what the fish think. Some flee when they see us, but others, the curious ones, come closer."

The group starts diving in one by one. Backward diving freaks me out. I prefer seeing where I'm headed. Carlos helps me gear up, adjusting the tank and checking my mask and mouthpiece. The older couple is the last to go. He jumps first, and she follows suit. Then it's our turn. I gulp. I edge closer to the drop-off and peek down. This was a terrible idea! Carlos moves closer and dives in. I catch a glimpse of his grin before he hits the water.

"Your turn," Fred nudges me.

"Wait."

"It's now or never, Mel."

I take out the mouthpiece.

"Hold on. I just need a sec."

"It's either jump and face it or let fear win."

I spot Carlos resurfacing, signaling for me to dive. I fix my mask, take a deep breath, and put the mouthpiece back in. I turn around and get ready. Eyes shut tight. Totally freaked out.

I don't want to remember, but I do. I remember the music playing at the bar, I remember the taste of his mouth, I remember his voice in my ear...

It sucks, doesn't it? The moment you realize you're just a scared little bitch.

The fear? It's not out there in the ocean; it's right here, inside my head. I can almost touch it. And it's been here for so long that it's like an old friend, as if it had always been a part of me. But it wasn't always here. There was a time when I wasn't afraid. There was a time when I was happy. There was a time when I waited eagerly for Dad to come home, to give me a goodnight kiss and a pack of Smarties. There was a time when I woke up every day excited to go to school. And later, to go to college. There was a time when office work made me happy. There was a time when I wasn't this anxious, bitter person. I was just a cheerful, happy girl. I want that girl back! I will get that girl back!

Screw you, Claudio!

I let myself fall. I feel the impact as my body hits the water. I keep my eyes shut as I descend into the dark waters. Suddenly, a hand grabs mine. Even before I open my eyes, I know it's him. It's my Super-Carlos. He holds my hand and guides me. We pass by curious fish, then go deeper. And you know what? Carlos was right. The sea floor isn't as far away as I thought. I spot some colorful little fish, and I immediately recognize the Queen Triggerfish. They're just doing their fishy things, as if having a bunch of humans around is totally normal. Carlos was right: it's a magical world. I don't know how long we spent down there, minutes, or maybe hours, but when Carlos signals for us to surface, I'm kind of sorry to leave that enchanting world behind.

When we pop up, I see the other divers have already surfaced and are totally hyped about something. I glance in their direction and... wow! I'm left speechless. Right there in front of us is this sea monster, but a cool one, not scary at all. I recognize the whale from the pic Carlos has at his place. It's a sperm whale, and boy, it's huge! I take off my diving goggles for a better view. Suddenly, the sperm whale takes a dive, creating these huge waves that reach us. We barely catch a glimpse of its body and then its tail disappears into the deep sea. Just like that, it's gone. We take out our mouthpieces, and start laughing and chatting away, like a bunch of kids.

We hop back onto the boat, take off our gear, and I grab a seat on a bench, staring out at the sea.

"I'm really proud of you," Carlos says.

I look at him and smile.

"I'm proud of me too."

I shift my gaze back to the sea and realize it's not as dark or scary as before.

❊ ❊ ❊

When we get back to the island, Carlos drives me to my aunt's place, and we hang out in the van for a bit, just talking.

"Did you enjoy it?"

"Absolutely! The sea, the fish, and that mammoth-sized sperm whale..."

"Probably a male, given its size."

"Huge."

"Yeah, those males can clock in at twenty meters..."

He starts talking about sperm whales and the time he snaped that winning photo. He's wearing his favorite Garfield-eating-pizza tee. While I'm watching him, I can't shake the thought that our trips, our talks, it's all going to end. And I don't want it to end. I can't deal with the idea that it might all be over. He's sharing insights about sperm whales' love lives, but I'm not really focused; I'm feeling down because in three days, I'll head back to Lisbon, and I'll miss seeing him every day. So, I cut in while he's talking because I don't want to talk about whales. I want to talk about us.

"If you ask me to stay, I will."

He takes a deep breath, cracks a smile, but it's different this time. I can't quite figure out what's going on in his head. Maybe I should've just kept quiet. But I've stayed quiet for so long. I've held in so much.

"I'd totally love for you to stick, Mel..." He avoids eye contact, and my stomach starts tying itself in knots.

"But..." I smell a 'but' coming.

"But I can't ask you to stay, it's not right."

"Why?!"

He looks up, meets my eyes.

"It's time for you to do what you want and not what others want you to do."

"You don't want me to stay?"

My voice shakes a little.

He takes a deep breath and holds my hand.

"Of course, I do, Mel. But I can't ask you that. I care too much about you to make that call. That's got to be your decision."

"What if I decide to stay?"

"If you decide to, I'll be thrilled."

Neither of us says anything else. Silence hangs heavily between us as our goodbye lingers in the air. I stand there watching him drive away in his grandpa's old van, and it's hard, very hard. It's hard because I remember these past few weeks. It's hard because I remember when he saved me from drowning, when we rolled down the lagoon slope, when we had limpets for lunch and drank Kima. And I remember him photographing the elderly while I drew them. I remember when he rescued me from that guy in that bar. I remember the way he looks at me, how he smiles, the dimples on his face, the T-shirts with comic book characters. Us diving together, laughing together, me crying on his shoulder. The touch of his lips on mine. His hands on my skin. I think about every minute, hour, and day we spent together, and it's so hard. I stand there, in front of my aunt's house, long after the van vanished down the street, long after I stopped seeing him. I stand there, hoping he'll turn back and ask me to stay.

Chapter 34

"Goodbye, darling. I'm going to miss you so much," Aunt Gabi squeezes me tight. I'll really miss these hugs. I'll miss her a lot.

"You take care, kiddo," Jasmine says, giving me a hug.

Now that I've gotten to know her better, I get why Dad fell for her. Jasmine's a free spirit, doing her thing without caring what others think. Sometimes I wish I could take on the world like her, no apologies for being herself.

"It's not goodbye, it's 'see you soon'. I'll swing by whenever I can, and I hope you'll come visit too."

"Absolutely," my aunt says, tears welling up. "Our house is your home too. Now that we've reconnected, I won't let life tear us apart."

"I've got something for you."

I open my suitcase, shooting a wink at Jasmine, and pull out a tee I had made with *Overthinkers Gang* printed on it. The letters are decked out with flowers I drew.

"Oh, Mel, thank you!" my aunt chuckles.

"Do you like it?"

"I love it. I'll wear it every day. That way, every morning when I wake up, I'll think of you," she says, a tear trickling down her cheek.

"If you start crying, I'll start too."

"Everything's going to be okay," my aunt starts to tear up, and I can't hold back anymore. Both of us start crying, clinging onto each other.

"What a couple of crybabies I've got here! Are you trying to make me cry too?" Jasmine says, pulling us both into a hug. "Gabi, let the girl go, or she'll miss the flight."

"You're right," she releases me. "If you ever need me, just call, and I'll be there. You know you can count on me. You can count on us," she corrects.

I nod because words won't come. I'm just overwhelmed. A mix of happiness and sadness floods over me. Sadness for leaving the Azores and the amazing people

I've met, yet happiness for finding the courage to make a decision. I'm not sure if it's the right one, but it's my decision.

They climb into the pickup truck, which doesn't seem as ugly to me now; instead, it looks charming and picturesque. I stand there waving until the van disappears. I dab my eyes with a tissue and head into the airport. Just like the day I arrived, it's still quiet. The airport remains tiny, with maybe a few dozen people inside. I drag my suitcase behind me, scanning for an empty seat. Settling on a bench, I wait for my flight's gate announcement.

While I wait, memories of my time on the island flood my mind. The first impression of my aunt. Her delicious food. Her warm hugs. Her advice. Jasmine's wild spirit. Her lectures. The surprise Smarties from Mr. Manuel tucked into my shopping bag. The fish he proudly caught. Ms. Julieta, sitting next to me at the bus stop. Sara, my savior from the bar incident. Rodrigo. Rodrigo, who deserted me during a panic attack. Rodrigo tumbling outside my aunt's house. My father's unexpected visit. My father and I sharing a pack of Smarties. My father's comforting hug. And Carlos, my Super-Carlos. Carlos and I rolling down the lagoon's slope. Carlos and I savoring a stew in Furnas. Carlos and I diving into the sea together. Carlos and I kissing.

A young couple, wrapped up in each other, sits on a bench nearby. They're clearly in the throes of new love. He pulls her onto his lap, and they dive into a kiss. Soft chuckles ripple from the other passengers on nearby benches, but they're oblivious or simply don't care. Their attention is wholly absorbed in each other, like they're trying to eat one another, because that's what it looks, like they want to devour one another.

The thought of sending a message to Carlos crosses my mind. My phone buzzes with a new message. Even before checking the sender, I know it's not from Rodrigo—I blocked his number. Retrieving my phone from my bag, I confirm it's from Carlos. It's almost as if he knew I was thinking of him.

Hope you have a safe trip, Mel. I'm going to miss you.

I'm going to miss you too.

For a second, I think about typing in all caps, REALLY GOING TO MISS YOU A LOT, but it seems unnecessary. I know he knows.

I'm wearing the Garfield t-shirt.

Last night, when we said goodbye, he gave me his favorite t-shirt, the one with Garfield eating pizza. It's a bit loose on me, but I don't mind. It still smells like him, and that's comforting.

I'm sure you and Garfield will be good pals. Have a safe trip!

Suddenly, I get this urge to bolt out of the airport and head straight to him. I want to leap into his arms. I want to hug and kiss him. There's this split-second where I think I'll get up, dash out of the airport, and go find him. I imagine him waiting for me at the airport entrance. But I stay seated. And I know he's not out there. Because deep down I know he's right. Because deep down I know I'm not ready for a new relationship.

Dr. Vera, my therapist, said I need to stop second-guessing all my choices. It took me forever to even admit I needed help—like, seriously forever. It's tough to own up to needing help, especially when you've been pretending everything's alright for so long. I had my first appointment in Ponta Delgada, and it was okay. Well, truth be told, I was kind of scared. Dr. Vera isn't the type of therapist you picture, all sweet and soothing, telling you everything's going to be fine. Nope, she straight-up told me she wasn't there to babysit me. She said we're going mess up my head a bit more and then start organizing it all neatly into drawers. Since I'm leaving the island, we agreed to do the next sessions online.

The couple's still going at it with the kissing. Some passengers are staring, but they're totally zoned into each other. I'm staring too, unable to look away. I'm still staring when a speaker announces: "Passengers for flight 651 to Lisbon, please board at gate 19."

Finally, the couple stops smooching. He plants a kiss on her forehead and insists on lugging both their huge suitcases. What a gentleman. Just like Carlos. A tear slides down my cheek. I've made peace with my decision, but part of me still hopes he'll stroll into the airport to come get me.

Once the announcement for the flight to Lisbon rings out, people start shuffling toward the boarding gate. Anxiety starts creeping in. My head feels kind of woozy, and my breathing picks up speed. I stand up and look for the nearest restroom. I need to hurry. I can't afford to miss this flight.

I splash water on my face, then stare hard at my reflection in the mirror. I see a glimpse of myself, lounging on the couch, binge-watching trashy TV, chugging vodka, and devouring pizza slices. I remember that night at the bar in Ponta Delgada, getting wasted. I remember throwing up outside the bar while Carlos held my head. I remember begging for Rodrigo's love. I remember sitting on the bench outside that bar, while having a panic attack, waiting for Carlos to come to my rescue. I never want to feel like that again! I'll never let myself feel like that again!

The voice on the speaker announces another flight: "Passengers for flight 796 to Paris, please board at gate 25."

I glance at the ticket and notice a slight tremor in my hand. I'm scared. I'm truly scared that I might've made the wrong decision. This is the first time I've made a big decision just for myself. This is the first time I don't care about what others think. I look at my reflection in the mirror. Here I am, with all my flaws and imperfections, with all my fears and anxieties. I think about the men in my life. I think about Rodrigo, who turned from Prince to Frog. I think about my dad, who, despite everything, showed support for my choice. I think about Carlos and how much I'll miss him.

"Passengers for flight 796 to Paris, please board at gate 25," the speaker repeats.

I feel the anxiety swirling in the pit of my stomach and take a deep breath. It's time. I grab my suitcase and leave the restroom. I quicken my pace towards gate 25. I'm anxious, but it's a good kind of anxious. I can't wait to start my new life. I don't know if I made the right choice, but it's my choice.

I choose life.

I choose me.

THE END

Author's Note

As I sit down to write these words, I'm overwhelmed with gratitude and emotion. First and foremost, I want to express my heartfelt thanks to each one of you who embarked on this journey with Mel in "Anxious Girl."

To every reader who laughed, cried, and empathized with Mel's highs and lows, thank you for allowing her story to touch your hearts. Your support, your feedback, and your connection with these characters mean more than words can express.

And to my fantastic team—beta readers, ARC readers, reviewers, designers, and everyone who poured their heart and soul into this book—thank you! Your dedication and expertise have been invaluable in shaping this story.

For everyone who walked alongside Mel on her rollercoaster journey, remember this: in life's whirlwind of chaos and endless choices never forget to put yourself first. Choose life. Choose yourself. Because your story matters just as much.

Thank you for being an essential part of this unforgettable journey!

Rosa

PS: I'd like to ask one last thing from you. Help keep Mel's story alive by sharing your thoughts using *#anxiousgirlbook* on social media and leaving a review on Amazon. Your voice matters immensely!

BONUS EPILOGUE

Are you eager for more of Melissa and Carlos's story? Subscribe to my Newsletter at rosasilvawrites.com to unlock an exclusive BONUS EPILOGUE and explore the next chapter of their journey!